THE TRAP
and
A DANCE IN THE SUN

DAN JACOBSON was born in Johannesburg and grew up in Kimberley, South Africa. Since the mid-1950s he has made his home in London. He has revisited South Africa several times and has also served various terms as a visiting professor at different American universities. He now lectures in English literature at University College, London.

Dan Jacobson has published his short stories in a wide range of periodicals on both sides of the Atlantic. His books include *The Price of Diamonds*, *Inklings* (short stories), *No Further West* (travel), *The Beginners*, *The Rape of Tamar*, *The Wonder-Worker*, *The Confessions of Josef Baisz*, and *Her Story*.

DAN JACOBSON

The Trap

AND

A Dance in the Sun

—◆—

WITH A NEW PREFACE BY THE AUTHOR

OXFORD UNIVERSITY PRESS
1988

TO MICHAEL AND LIEBE JACOBSON

Oxford University Press, Walton Street, Oxford OX2 6DP
Oxford New York Toronto
Delhi Bombay Calcutta Madras Karachi
Petaling Jaya Singapore Hong Kong Tokyo
Nairobi Dar es Salaam Cape Town
Melbourne Auckland
and associated companies in
Beirut Berlin Ibadan Nicosia

Oxford is a trade mark of Oxford University Press

© *Dan Jacobson 1955, 1956*
Preface © *Dan Jacobson 1988*

The Trap *first published 1955 by Weidenfeld and Nicolson*
A Dance in the Sun *first published 1956 by Weidenfeld and Nicolson*
This edition first published 1980 by Secker and Warburg
First issued, with Dan Jacobson's new preface, as an
Oxford University Press paperback 1988

British Library Cataloguing in Publication Data
Jacobson, Dan
The trap; and, A dance in the sun.
—Twentieth-century classics).
I. Title. II. Series
823'.914 [F] PR6060.A3
ISBN 0–19–282107–5

Printed in Great Britain by
The Guernsey Press Co. Ltd.
Guernsey, Channel Islands

Preface to the Oxford Paperbacks Edition

The Trap was completed in 1953, and was published two years later in England and the United States. It is the only one of my novels or novellas with a South African setting which was written wholly in that country. It was not, however, the first attempt I had made at a piece of longish fiction. Soon after leaving university in Johannesburg I had settled temporarily in London, and while living there had tried to write – indeed, had completed, after a fashion – a novel in four parts. Before that I had produced just one or two short stories and a few poems, none of which had seemed worth keeping. Once the excitement of writing them had passed, they appeared to express only the ambition which had provoked that excitement: nothing else.

Much the same was to be true of that London novel. Yet in working on it I had at least experienced a few instructive surprises. The chief of these was that if I was going to be a writer of fiction – a remote enough prospect, it seemed – I would have to resign myself to being one of a different kind from anything I had imagined beforehand. I would have liked my writing to be sophisticated, talkative, urban, jaded, wry, wise, weary, tremulous. What had actually come out was obsessed with the forlorn and undescribed landscapes of the veld around my home town, Kimberley; it dealt with people who were solitary and inarticulate, sometimes fiercely so; it was much preoccupied with expressing physical sensations of all kinds – especially, perhaps, mutually resistant or contradictory ones.

Well, all this had somehow to be digested. The first step in doing so was to acknowledge that the novel which had taught me these very lessons was itself no good. Soon after finishing it, for reasons quite unconnected with my writing I left London and returned to Johannesburg, where I began working as a journalist. The most strenuous part of my job was translating editorials and other political matter from Afrikaans newspapers and journals into English; once the craft had been mastered, I found I had time on my hands. So I began writing again. On this occasion I confined myself initially to short stories. Several of these were to be published in various magazines over the next few years. At the time, however, I made no effort to find an outlet for any of them, but embarked instead on the writing of *The Trap*.

Once again I found myself trying to find words for the sad, bleached landscape of the Northern Cape, and for some of the lives it gave shape to. In doing so I made use of people, of a farm, and of events and incidents which had been known to me years before. Setole, the drunken Zulu plasterer and mason; Willem, the apparently humble and reliable 'boss-boy', the achetypal 'good kaffir'; van Schoor, the sun-hardened Boer farmer and his notoriously difficult wife (who in 'real life' had jointly managed, on some kind of profit-sharing basis, a farm owned by my father to the north of Kimberley) – these, and others like them, were people of whom I had seen a fair amount during my boyhood. The setting of the novel was another ranch which my father, in one of his expansive moods, had taken over; this one, with its straggling rock-encased river frontage, was about thirty miles south of town. It was there, early one morning, during a school holiday, that I had come on Setole, unconscious, badly beaten up, lying among the rocks – just as van Schoor finds him in the novel. At the time I had got little enough out of Setole about how he had come to be lying there, in that condition, and nothing at all out of Willem.

In writing *The Trap* I brought Setole together with the van Schoors, who (so far as I know) never actually met him; I placed the van Schoors on a farm that (so far as I know) they never visited; I put into Willem's mouth accusations about Setole's sexual proclivities that we had heard from other blacks; I used the fact that (after Setole had left the farm) Willem was indeed revealed to have been involved in stealing my father's sheep, in collaboration with a white, English-speaking butcher from the nearest *dorp* . . . However, what strikes me most about the book, looking back on it – especially if I think of it as a 'first' – is not that I juggled people and events as much as I did for the sake of the story, but that it is in fact so little autobiographical in nature.

Anyway, having laboriously completed a full draft of it, I came to the decision that it was quite unsatisfactory. So I simply put it aside, and went on to try to write some new stories. I also wrote – not quite at a single sitting, but in great haste, and without having the faintest idea of how the story might develop beyond the scenes I was putting down – the first three chapters of what was to become *A Dance in the Sun*. Then, precisely because I did not know what would happen next, I put that aside too. It was around this time, however, that I sent some of the earlier batch of stories I had written to an American monthly, and was delighted and astonished when two of them were accepted for publication. Filled with the glow of this success I looked around in the material I already had for another item that could be plausibly offered for publication. There was that draft of *The Trap*. Had I been wrong about it? Would it do?

No, it would not. But I could see what might make a difference to it. It could be cut: not just here and there, gingerly; but radically, wholesale, with no regard for the labour I had put into the passages I was now excising. The task actually gave me pleasure of a not wholly perverse kind; a pleasure that was to be experienced on many occasions subsequently. First of all, I was sure that the cut-down version of the tale was better than the original, and that was in itself a pleasure. It was not that my idea of the characters and the plot had changed, in abstract terms; rather that in the sparer, tighter story which began to emerge, the people seemed to have become inextricable from the events they had to enact or endure. Secondly, the actual process of cutting the work in such a thoroughgoing manner taught me to rely on certain instinctive, quasi-physical intimations, impatiences, seekings for balance, which were novel and exciting in themselves. Paradoxical though it seems to say so, I felt myself to be more of a writer, less of a mere hopeful novice, while slicing away paragraphs, pages, and even chapters, than I had when first putting them down.

Of course, experience gained in the past seldom makes a new project easier to see through; it hardly makes the next page easier to fill. So I discovered when, back in London a couple of years later, I resumed work on what was eventually to become *A Dance in the Sun*. I reread the episodes written in such haste a couple of years previously – the journey of the narrator and his friend to Mirredal, their arrival at the house on the edge of the village, their uncomfortable dinner, the appearance of Joseph, the outcast black, with the purloined letter in his hand – and was surprised at how 'finished' they appeared to be. So I made up my mind to find out what was actually going on in and around that house. The novel essentially takes the form of the narrator and his friend making the same discoveries I was compelled to make as I wrote the book; and I should say here that in different contexts and circumstances, this strange process of searching for the resolution of a puzzle which I myself have yet to create has occupied me over and over again. For all the considerable differences between them in setting, subject matter, and mode of narration, this is how almost all my novels have been written: it is as true of the most recent one, *Her Story*, as it was of the two tales in this volume.

The fact that the new novel was in the first person did not, incidentally, mean that it was any more autobiographical than the first. I had never hitch-hiked through the Karroo; I had never accidentally found myself in a household haunted by the past as the one in the novel is; and so forth. No matter: that was how it was going to be done. And if, in visiting again some of the least populated and least amenable of South Africa's landscapes, I once more came on a handful of uneasily triumphant whites and truculently dispossessed blacks locked together in a kind of throttled domesticity, in a pattern of betrayal and self-betrayal from which not even their own acts of violence could release them – then so be it.

Certain other resemblances between the two books are obvious to me now, though I was hardly aware of them when they were written. The first is that both are concerned with the uncovering of a crime, or a series of interconnected crimes; both of them also are about the different acts of betrayal which the crimes themselves involve or subsequently enforce. In *The Trap* the initial crime is the one Willem commits against his employer; in *A Dance in the Sun* it is the crime (or what the law in South Africa then deemed to be a crime) commited by Nasie Terblanche in complicity with Joseph's sister; then there is the greater crime which Fletcher commits in order to cover up the consequences of this illicit sexual union. It is striking, however, that in both cases the ultimate 'victim' of these crimes – Setole in the one case and, in *A Dance in the Sun*, Joseph in his own right and as surrogate for his sister – elects to keep his own counsel, to take what revenge he can in his own way, certainly to make no appeal to those in authority over him.

Why should this be? Is it merely a reflection of the characters with which they have been endowed? I think not. In both cases I would suggest (speaking less as the writer of these books, which I once was, and more as the reader of them which I now am) that they act as they do because they do not feel the law which the others have broken to be in any sense 'theirs'. On the contrary. They have been wronged and they know it. But the law as an institution, and all its machinery and manifestations, appear to them as part of the entire pattern of relationships between white and black, master and servant, which has rendered them as vulnerable as they are. They are on their own, and they have to act accordingly.

All the characters in the tales, black and white alike, are banefully affected by the fissures and constrictions of the social order within which they live. Theft, murder, and assault take place everywhere, in all societies. Their shading away into other activities which are not necessarily 'unlawful' in the usual sense of the word (betrayal of trust, lying, adultery, and so forth) is also to be found everywhere. What is so corrupting here is the knowledge of all involved that there are deeds which will be condoned or even encouraged when they are committed by certain kinds of people, in certain circumstances, and which will be savagely punished when done by others. Confronted with injustices which contrive to be at once systematised and arbitrary, people are bound to rely for their self-defence on cunning, on primitive loyalties, on the manipulation of the kindness or vanity of others – all of which, of course, carry within them the potentiality of their own forms of corruption.

I have emphasised here what the two tales seem to me to have in common: it hardly needs to be said that they also differ greatly in tone and narrative mode and structure. The greatest difference, from the reader's point of view, is that in *A Dance in the Sun* a narrator stands between the reader and the events related. The characters in *The Trap* can be said to have no reflective life, as it were, outside the action; whereas in *A Dance in the Sun* the narrator and his friend insist, for most of the length of the book,

5

that *their* life, their real life, is to be found elsewhere; that they are only accidentally or trivially involved in what is going on in the Fletcher household. As things develop, however, the tables are turned on them – twice. They discover that their involvement in the events they witness is by no means as tangential as they had supposed; and when they have recovered from the shock of that discovery, they learn that the help they are now eager to offer is not wanted and that their newfound sense of responsibility is not prized nearly as much as they would wish it to be. It is for others to decide, perhaps, how 'allegorical' this aspect of the book should be taken to be. What I can say here is that the ever-deepening involvement of the two young men in the drama they have stumbled on was itself, while I was writing the story, as dramatic and unexpected an element in it as any other.

Imaginative writing is in some respects a curiously merciless business: merciless to the writer, I mean. On the one hand he wants what he has written to have a life of its own, to be answerable for itself, to speak to the reader on its own terms and for its own ends. On the other hand, the completed story or poem is bound to reveal more about his mind and sensibility than he can even know. The work will not conceal from others his need to hide himself within it; nor can he hope to surprise the reader if he has not succeeded in surprising himself.

THE TRAP

1 Setole

In the silent rush of light across the veld, van Schoor turned and looked back the way he had come. He was alone. Behind him was his house and the little lavatory – the corrugated iron roofs shone gold as they caught waveringly, like water, the sun. To his right was the river, sunk into its cleft in the land, between the banks of rock. The water, where it could be seen, was green and running swiftly. Now early in the morning, when the sun was still low and there remained the night's coolness on the rock and even in places the night's dew, the land looked as though it were reposing; peaceful, and as yet not savaged by the sun. Van Schoor stopped short and stared at the black and grey bundle from some distance away.

It looked like a heap of old clothing, something abandoned, shabby, thrown away. One unlaced shoe pointed straight to the sky. One arm lay flung outward palm up, empty.

'Setole?' van Schoor said.

He came closer, and leaned over. He saw a bubble of blood swelling and collapsing beneath the African's nostril.

'Setole?' he said again. He took the man's coat in his hand and lifted the upper part of the body from the ground. The head sagged back, exposing the neck. He let the body go back to the ground.

He remained for a few moments silently at the side of the body. Then he heard a heavy, unconscious sigh, and gently he slapped the man's face.

'Can you hear me?' he said.

There was another sigh. Van Schoor could feel the slap tingling on his fingers; though he had acted in kindness it felt strange on his hand.

Then the breathing of the man beneath him changed, and he leaned forward and listened to the louder and more irregular expulsion of breath as the injured African struggled to be released from his unconsciousness. Van Schoor watched the struggle, way beyond his reach, and then left him and ran back towards the house, a few hundred yards away. He saw the native girl sweeping the back stoep and called to her to fetch Willem, the boss-boy.

He came back more slowly, hearing his footsteps grating against the rock, and crushing the grass in his path. How quiet everything was, and peaceful – the cool veld, the indifferent broken line of the river. Only Setole was a flaw in the morning: a crack in the cup of stillness; a mark on the veld.

When he came back, Setole was awake. At any rate, one eye was open, and through it he was staring at the high morning sky. He seemed at peace then, lying on his back, as though he had just been born and was staring around him with wonder, and no suspicion. He stared at van Schoor in the same way, as the white man leaned over him and said questioningly:

'Setole?'

There was a pause before Setole answered. His eye did not waver: all it did was to focus lower, from the sky to the man, but the scrutiny he gave to each seemed the same.

'Ja, baas.'

'Are you all right, Setole?'

'All right, baas?'

'Yes. Are you all right . . .?'

Van Schoor was relieved. He said, 'You gave me quite a fright. I thought you were dead when I first saw you.'

'No, baas,' Setole said.

Van Schoor did not know what to do next. 'Do you want to sit up?' he asked.

Setole seemed to think the matter over. 'No,' he said at last, simply.

'Oh,' van Schoor gestured with his hand. 'But you can't lie here like this. Come, let me give you a hand.' He took Setole's body in his arms and propped him against a rock.

'There, that's better.'

Setole neither resisted nor agreed. Now that he was sitting up he could see more, and his incurious wondering eye went over rock and grass and the long view of the river.

'Am I on the farm?' he asked.

'Yes, you're on the farm. What did they do to you in Dors River that you came home like this?'

'They caught me,' Setole said.

'Who?' van Schoor asked.

'I can't remember,' Setole said, and from the clear directness of his gaze it might have been true. He lifted his head to the sun, and said, 'Look how low the sun is.' He seemed a man with no memories or desires: he was still counting the simple perceptions, one by one.

'It's still early,' van Schoor reminded him. He too looked at the sun, and the dark-blue line of the horizon beneath it, and the level light that shone above and through the grass and thorn trees, and on the rocks. Even on that hardened veld the morning rested with tenderness, the softness of birth. And Setole, one eye open and blood on his black skin, sat on the ground and looked about him, open to the veld, seeming almost in his patience and simple perceptiveness, a part of it.

For a moment they sat together in silence. Then van Schoor stood up. 'Can you walk to your hut?'

'Not yet,' Setole replied.

Van Schoor laughed. He said, 'As long as you're comfortable.'

'I'm comfortable,' Setole said. He too began smiling, and the thick injured lips slowly opened wider and forced the smile through his flesh; blood was suspended in his open mouth.

'God, they half-murdered you, Setole,' van Schoor said, seeing the blood.

But this time Setole did seem to remember something. He shook his head, closing his eyes. Then he opened them slowly. 'There was only one of them,' he said.

'Only one of whom?'

'There was only one man who caught me. And it wasn't at Dors River. I remember. I think I was already on the farm when he caught me.'

'Why didn't you fight him off if there was only one?' van Schoor asked.

'I was too drunk,' Setole said.

Van Schoor shrugged. 'Then it's your own fault. If you

didn't drink so much then they wouldn't be able to catch you.'

'Ja, baas,' Setole said.

'So are you going to stop drinking?'

'How can I stop drinking, baas? I've always been drinking. I don't steal and I don't chase after women, all I do is drink a little too much. What can I do, baas?'

'Stop drinking.'

'Ah, baas,' Setole said. 'It is easy for you to tell me to stop drinking. But it isn't easy for me to do it.'

'I know. When I took you from Baas Harris in Lyndhurst, he said, "Setole is a good boy, and a good plasterer as long as he stays sober. But when he's drunk, look out!"'

'Baas Harris is also a good baas,' Setole said.

'You mean any baas is a good baas who doesn't give you the sack when you come home drunk.'

'That's right, baas. Like Baas Harris said, when I'm sober, I work well, and I only get drunk on Sundays.'

'Instead of going to church!'

'Does the baas go to church on Sundays?'

'Not very often,' van Schoor laughed. 'You get clever when they give you a hiding. But you'd get even cleverer if you went to church like Willem.'

'Willem?' Setole said, as though he had never heard the name before.

'Yes, Willem. My boss-boy.'

'Oh that Willem,' Setole said. But he seemed confused. 'Willem?' he said again. He lifted his head to van Schoor and stared at him in confusion; van Schoor saw his eyes cloud and become obscure, 'Willem?'

'He's coming just now,' van Schoor said. 'I sent for him to come and help you. Willem is a good boy. He goes to church, you know.'

'Willem?'

'Yes, Willem,' van Schoor said, a little irritated by Setole's incomprehension.

'I don't like that Willem,' Setole said unexpectedly.

Van Schoor said: 'I don't listen when my boys talk about one another. I'm not interested in whether you like Willem

12

or Willem likes you. If you have a proper complaint you can make it.'

'Ja, baas.'

Van Schoor stood up. He stood for a moment above Setole. 'I'm going now to have my breakfast, and Willem will help you to your hut. If you need anything from the missus you must ask for it – there's iodine in the house. That's to clean it,' he added, seeing that Setole did not understand, 'to clean it where they hit you, so that the cuts won't go bad.'

'There was only one of them,' Setole said.

Again van Schoor laughed. 'You've told me that already. And it won't make any difference to the cuts.'

'Ja, baas.'

Van Schoor turned to go. But before he left he said to Setole, 'You must look after yourself. You're not a young man any more and if you keep on drinking and if they catch you like this every time you won't last very long. And there's my work – I don't want to be kept waiting while you get sober or get fixed up from what they did to you.'

'Ja, baas,' Setole said. 'I am getting an old man.'

'All right then, Setole.' But as he said it, putting his hat on his head, he saw Willem coming across the veld towards them, and waited for him.

When the other came, he took off his hat to van Schoor almost formally. 'Morning, baas,' he said.

'Morning, Willem,' van Schoor replied, and only then did Willem turn to look at Setole. 'What have they done with you, Setole?' he asked in surprise. Then he immediately again turned his attention to the white man. 'The baas sent for me,' he said. He held his hat in front of his chest. He was dressed in clothes almost as ragged as the blood-bespattered ones that Setole was wearing, but he carried his more bravely, and he had a proud pair of army boots on his feet. He was rather a slightly built African, lighter-skinned than Setole, with a small receding forehead. His brow was perpetually lined, it gave his face an air of responsibility, and his gravity was enhanced by the controlled movements of his body from his hips as he watched and listened to his master.

'Ja, baas,' he said, when van Schoor had finished telling how he had found Setole. He looked at Setole, without expression, as if to confirm the story. Then he asked, 'What does the baas want me to do with him?'

'To take him away.'

'Take him where, baas?'

Van Schoor jerked his head. 'Where do you think I want you to take him? I want you to take him into my house, and give him a bath, and put my clothes on him, and put him in my bed. What else should I want you to do with him?'

Willem's head dropped. They enjoyed the irony for a moment, Willem smiling faintly. Van Schoor went on: 'Take him, look after him, do what you like with him, but, Willem, don't come and ask *me* what you must do with him.'

'Ja, baas,' Willem looked up, smiling strongly. 'I understand now, baas.'

'Good.' Van Schoor turned to Setole. 'Hy, Setole,' he said, 'can you stand up?'

'I can try, baas.'

'Then try, dammit.'

'Ja, baas.' Setole stood up slowly, rising from his knees. He would have fallen if Willem had not caught him and steadied him. But not sooner was he well on his feet than he jerked away from Willem, and stood by himself, tottering slightly, but standing.

Willem shook his head. 'A drunkard is a terrible thing, baas,' he said lightly.

'As long as he does work I don't care what he is.'

'Ja, baas. That is all that matters for the baas and for the farm,' Willem smilingly agreed.

'It is the farm that matters,' van Schoor said.

'What would the farm be without the baas? The baas is the farm.'

'Then you've got a *grootbaas*,' van Schoor said, and again they laughed.

Setole did not laugh. He said, swaying slightly, 'I am a good boy. I do my work properly, and I don't worry the women, and I don't swear. I am drinking a little too much, that's all.'

'That's all!' Willem said ironically. He looked to van Schoor

14

for approval, and encouraged by the amusement on van Schoor's face, he said again: 'That's all!'

Setole chewed for a moment and then spat some saliva on the ground; he remained staring at it. Now that he was standing he looked merely wretched, a tattered and broken Zulu. He was dressed in a vest and a pair of grey trousers from some white man's suit, and a bunny jacket cast off from some white man's army. He wore canvas *takkies* on his feet, his toes poking through the ends. Van Schoor studied him. He said: 'What can you expect if you spend all your money on drink?'

Setole frowned. Then, when he spoke, his voice rang surprisingly firmly. 'At least it is my own money that I spend on drink.'

'Come on, Setole,' Willem said, jerking his body angrily. 'The baas hasn't got all day to listen to your noise.'

'When the baas is tired of me, the baas will send me away,' Setole replied.

Van Schoor stopped what seemed to be an incipient quarrel between the two men. 'Well, the baas is tired right now. The baas is going to have breakfast.' He turned away, smiling.

But Setole stopped him. 'Baas,' he said, 'baas.'

'What is it?'

'Baas, I may drink a little too much, but I have eyes to see what is happening on the farm, and ears to hear.' Tenderly, afraid of hurt, he touched his eyes and his ears with his hand. 'The baas does not know what is happening on this farm. But I also know that I don't belong on this farm, so people mustn't be frightened that I am going to say anything. I am here to do my work and then I go back to Lyndhurst. That is all.'

'What is he talking about?' van Schoor asked Willem.

'He doesn't know what he is talking about, baas, so how should I know?'

'I know what I am talking about,' Setole said.

'Go, the two of you,' van Schoor said. 'I've heard enough for one morning.'

Willem leaped to Setole's side. 'Come, Setole,' he said, placing his arm around Setole's waist and beginning to lead him away.

'Good-bye, baas,' Willem said. He looked back to van Schoor with a sort of grin on his face, expressing amusement and distaste for the job he had to do. Van Schoor watched the two of them go, Setole shambling alongside Willem.

'Bring my horse to the house, after breakfast. We must ride up to see the cattle,' he called.

'Ja, baas,' came the reply from some distance away.

In the evening of the same day Willem came before his baas again, very gravely, this time, accompanied by his son. He stood before van Schoor and his wife, as they sat on the stoep enjoying the cool of the evening, and said: 'Please, baas, may I speak to you?'

'What is it, Willem?' van Schoor asked.

Willem hesitated. He said: 'I can't speak in front of the missus, baas.'

'What have you got, Willem? Secrets?' Mrs van Schoor called out jeeringly from her corner.

Willem looked down. He made no reply, and shielding his servant from his wife, van Schoor asked:

'Can't it wait until tomorrow morning?'

'No, baas,' Willem said firmly. 'Please, baas,' he added. 'Baas must understand that I can't talk about these things in front of a woman.'

Mrs van Schoor shrank more deeply into her corner. 'Go and listen to his things,' she said to her husband, and van Schoor stood up from his chair, getting away from her. Rather wearily, he walked down the path of the garden. When he reached the fence he stopped and turned to Willem who had followed him.

'Well? No one can hear you now.'

Willem said: 'I have something to tell the baas.'

'I've heard that already.'

'Ja, baas.' Willem thought for a moment. 'Baas must understand that it isn't an easy thing for me to tell.'

'What is it, Willem?'

'I said to myself, I must tell the baas. The baas will understand.' But he did not continue. He waited, perhaps for encouragement. Half-impatiently, van Schoor took a strand of the fence and rattled it, sending it vibrating down the length of the garden. They listened to the shrill jangle dying away. Then, from the native huts, a dog yelped, yelped, yelped. That, too, died away in the darkness.

'I'm listening,' van Schoor said.

Willem twisted his body, finally coming to rest and holding one arm up as though he were taking an oath. He brought out his confession with difficulty: 'Baas, I must tell the baas the truth. It was me who beat up Setole like that last night.'

'You!' van Schoor exclaimed. He stared through the twilight, trying to make out the expression on Willem's face. But he could see nothing. The veld around them was dark, and the rocks were humped closely in still blacker masses. High in the sky, there hung a thinner darkness, the sky still held some light, as faint as a breath, and as tenuous. A yellow lick of light came from the front room of the house, and there was an orange flame far off from one of the native huts. The rest of the world was hooded in darkness. 'You?' van Schoor asked.

'Ja, baas,' Willem said humbly.

'But why?' Willem did not answer. 'What is going on here?' Repeating his question, Mrs van Schoor's voice called from the stoep, 'What's happening, Jacob?'

Van Schoor turned to her. 'In a minute,' he called through the gloom. Her question still waited. 'What is happening?' he asked again, searching for Willem's expression.

The question had been asked three times. Willem answered it abruptly: 'Dirty business!'

'What sort of dirty business? And why did you beat up Setole? What's he got to do with it?'

'Everything, baas. I beat him up because he's a dirty man.'

'How – dirty?'

'Baas,' Willem said, 'the baas knows me well. I'm not a bad Kaffir. I do my work and I do it well. Has the baas ever had to complain against me that I didn't do my work properly?'

'No, Willem.'

'And I am honest, baas. Has the baas ever missed anything that he gave me to keep?'

'No.'

'Ja, baas. And the reason, baas, the reason is that I am a Kaffir with respect. I've got respect. I'm not the sort of man who goes around without respect for anything. The baas knows that I have respect.'

'Respect' . . . van Schoor had often heard that word from Willem. It was the heart of his values. It was the core of his religion, his sobriety, his awareness of his status and his skin, and that of his master, his honesty, his faithfulness to his wife. Once there had been a difference between van Schoor and his servant over the question of a key. Before van Schoor's arrival the key to the shed behind the house had been kept by Willem, and van Schoor had simply taken over the system as he had, indeed, taken over Willem himself with the farm. But after a while he had decided to change it: he wanted the key to himself. He could still remember Willem's injured voice: 'Baas wants to treat me as if I've no respect. Does the baas believe that I am a man with no respect?' He had let Willem keep the key.

He said now: 'Yes, Willem, I know that you are a boy with respect.'

'Ja, baas. Then if I've got respect, what must I do with a man who's got no respect at all, who's filthy – a dirty man, baas? I can't say how dirty he is, baas.'

'But you must say, Willem, otherwise I know nothing.'

'Ja, baas. I know. That is why I am here. Baas, last night, Sunday night, Setole came home drunk from Dors River. I found him there . . .' his voice trailed away to indicate the distance . . . 'on the road when I was coming back from church. I helped him, baas, even though he was so drunk it made me feel sick just to look at him. I brought him here. He could never have found his way here if I hadn't helped him. I almost carried him.' Willem stopped and drew in a breath.

'Yes?'

'Now comes the part that is difficult to tell the baas. I don't even know if the baas will understand what I am saying. Baas, when we got home this man, this Setole, wanted to make dirty business with me. With *me!* Does the baas understand?'

18

There was a long silence. Van Schoor leaned against the fence, and felt the steel strand against his back, through his shirt. Willem stood with his head averted. Only the little boy was looking curiously from the one man to the other.

'Yes,' van Schoor said at last. 'I understand what you mean. I have heard of such things. But it is hard to believe, Willem.'

Willem said simply: 'Baas must believe it. It is the truth.'

They were silent again. From the stoep, van Schoor heard the sounds of his wife moving in her wicker chair, and he turned away, leaning against the fence, his back towards Willem and the house.

'Baas, when we came to the huts, it was then that Setole wanted to start this business with me. At first I didn't know what the man wanted, but he wouldn't leave me alone. He followed me and called out to me and tried to take hold of me.' Willem shook his head violently. 'I never knew of such a dirty business before in my whole life, I didn't understand it, I didn't know what was going on. But when I did understand what he wanted I hit him. I hit him again and again. What else could I do, baas? I was so angry. He ran from me and I chased him and caught him and hit him again. Then he fell over and lay on the ground, and I said, "Setole, if you ever start your dirty business again I'll kill you. I'll kick you in the face, do you understand?" And I kicked him on the side to show what I meant. He lay on the ground like the dirty thing that he is. I said to him again. "Do you understand?" So he said, "Ja, Willem." "Good," I said to him, "then you know that this farm isn't a place for your dirty business." He is just a kind of a dog, baas, he isn't a man. And I walked away from him to go back to my hut. When I walked away he was still lying on the ground where I'd caught him. And the next time I saw him was when the baas called for me to come and help this morning. I did help him, baas. If the baas gives an order then I must do what the baas says. But I didn't like helping him. I can tell that to the baas now.'

They were both silent. Then van Schoor said, 'Why did you not tell me?'

He saw Willem gesture in the dark. 'Baas, I will tell you

now. I did not tell the baas, and I am not a boy who likes not to tell the truth to his baas. I hope the baas will forgive me for not telling him the truth.'

'I can't forgive you until you tell me why you did not tell me the truth.'

'I know, baas.'

Van Schoor shifted his weight from one foot to the other, and sighed, and looked around him. The night had deepened, he saw, and the sky had grown blacker, and the first stars were no longer vague, but each pricked sharply through the velvet sky. Willem waited to continue, submissive to his master's weariness. The little boy was squatting at the side of his father's leg, staring up at the two men. The whites of his eyes shone, the rest was darkness. Silently, almost experimentally, van Schoor slowly put a foot forward, caught the boy on his projecting knee, and pushed. The boy fell over on his back, 'A, nee baas!' escaping from him as he sprawled. He pulled himself back to his squatting position, teeth shining in a smile. When he had brought himself to balance, van Schoor's foot again came silently forward and again the boy fell. Neither Willem nor van Schoor said anything. This time the boy did not say anything, nor did he smile.

'Why did you not tell me?' van Schoor asked, turning back to Willem.

'I did not tell the truth to the baas, because, baas, I did not feel that this was the affair of the baas,' Willem said haltingly.

Van Schoor said: 'Everything that happens on this farm is my affair.'

'Ja, baas, I know that now.' Willem's voice dropped in admission. He said, explanatorily: 'Baas, I thought I was doing the right thing. I did not want to come to the baas with the things that happened among the Kaffirs here and which I thought the baas would never need to know about. I thought, "Why should I drag the baas into such a business? It is dirty, and the baas will hate me for coming to him with such dirty stories. You see, baas, I thought I had given Setole such a lesson that he would never dare start anything like that again as long as he is on the farm. I thought he would finish his job

20

and then go back to Lyndhurst and whatever he does there, and the farm would be finished with him. Then why should I come running to the baas with my stories?" That is what I thought, my baas.'

'But –'

'But I was wrong, baas. When it first happened I did think that I must tell the baas. I must tell the baas because he can chase Setole away, and that is all he deserves, to be chased away like a dog. That was when I was angry. I know, now, that I was right when I was angry, not afterwards. When you have such a sin on the farm nothing is clean until you have chased it away and can live clean again. It is like mud in water, a little can make a river dirty.' Willem's voice died away. He said, 'Ja, baas,' though van Schoor had made no comment, as if he were formally bringing his story to an end; it was like an amen at the end of a prayer.

But the story was not ended. Willem leaned forward and brought one hand up, cupped, an imploring gesture it seemed in the darkness. 'If only I had done it,' he said.

'What would have happened, Willem?'

Willem's hand shook backward and forward, and then his body swayed too, in grief. He said in a low voice: 'My child would not have known of the sin there is on this farm. Oh, my baas, can you believe that anyone would do such a thing to a child?'

'No,' van Schoor said. 'No!'

'Yes, my baas, yes. *This* child.' He ducked and brought the child up, holding him by the back of the neck. 'Setole came and worried him the same way that he worried me. Only this morning it happened, when we were riding to see the cattle. And I did not tell the truth to the baas!'

Faintly, van Schoor asked, 'Is this true?'

'It is true, baas. Where should the child have learned about such things if not from Setole? He hadn't known about such things until that man came to the farm. He learned when it happened.'

'What do you mean – happened?' van Schoor cried out.

'Nothing happened, baas. The child ran away before anything could happen, and this evening he asked me what did

Setole want of him, why did Setole worry him? What could I tell him, baas? I told him nothing, but I brought him with me to the baas, so that the baas could see for himself.'

'I have seen.'

'Ja, baas.'

A silence followed. Then agitatedly, Willem broke into speech again: 'Please, baas, chase that man away from the farm. He can't stay among us. We are good people here and we don't know what to do with such a man. Who will he worry next? He has already done so much damage.' He rocked the child in front of him, who now that he was an object of attention had his head deeply down. 'Please, my baas, I have come to you, my *grootbaas*. Chase that man away from the farm tonight, tomorrow morning. Don't let him stay among us any longer. I ask the baas to do it.'

There was a silence.

'I will do it, Willem,' van Schoor said.

'Ah, thank you, baas,' Willem said gratefully. 'I am glad to hear that from the baas.'

'I can't believe that such a thing could happen on my farm,' van Schoor said. He stared out to the night, towards the huts. But nothing could be seen from them: that one flame had flickered and gone out long before. He said:

'Yes, Willem, it's a bad business.'

'Ja, baas,' Willem said. He waited for a moment. 'Now I can tell the baas that if he had not said that Setole must go I would have asked the baas to let me go.'

'No, Willem,' van Schoor said, 'I wouldn't have let you go.' He shook his head. 'I can't let you go just like that.'

Willem was tremendously gratified. He put his hat on his head and took it off again, a quick, humble salutation. 'Thank you, baas, thank you.' He smiled. 'Now I will only ask the baas to let me go as far as Dors River tomorrow morning. My uncle is very sick there.'

Van Schoor smiled too. 'I think I can let you do that.'

'Thank you, baas. I will be back as soon as I can.'

'All right, Willem.' Willem was a good boy, van Schoor felt. He could be trusted. He was a good Kaffir. In a teasing voice, he said: 'So, Willem, you are a boy with respect.'

Willem caught the teasing tone, but also the affection behind it. 'Ja, baas, I am a Kaffir with respect.'

'And the *klonkie*?' Van Schoor shot out a hand and cuffed the little boy on the head. 'Has he also got respect?'

The little boy ducked away, and hid behind his father. 'I hope he will have respect when he grows up,' Willem replied gravely.

'All right, then,' van Schoor said, his voice resuming its gravity, 'I will fix it up tomorrow morning.'

'Ja, baas. Thank you, baas. Good night, baas.' He turned to the boy. 'Say good night and thank you to the baas.'

Strained and shy, the boy's voice came: 'Good night, baas. Thank you, baas.'

'Good night, *klonkie*,' van Schoor replied.

He stood at the gate and watched them go from him. How quickly the night swallowed them up! He smiled, staring after them, hearing their footfalls growing vaguer in the night. They were black enough.

The next morning, when the day had cleared from the horizon and the early summer sun fell strongly on the flat and customary veld beneath it, van Schoor emerged from the house. For a moment he stood in the sandy garden, ringed by the wire fence, and stared beyond to the kraal. They were already working on it: Piet and Sout were sitting on the wall, and Jan Blom was wheeling a barrow load of rocks towards them, very slowly. Setole could not be seen.

Jan Blom put the wheelbarrow down, and rested for a while, sitting on the rocks he had been wheeling. Piet and Sout were arguing, apparently, though the smoke from their pipes rose peacefully enough into the air. They waved their arms. Sout pointed and Piet shook his head. Sout shook his fist, vaguely, at nobody and in no particular direction, and then he put his pipe back in his mouth and leaned luxuriously over on the broad wall, hand hugging his knees. He leaned still further back until he was in imminent danger of falling, and then, like a pendulum, swung his body back. The two of them smoked, and nearer to van Schoor, Jan Blom stood half-doubled and began pushing the wheelbarrow forward. It stuck and he jerked at it violently a few times. He shouted to the other two, but they just waved at him, not even bothering to turn round. All injury, he stood with his arms akimbo and shouted at them some more. They ignored him entirely, and his voice slackened off. He jerked madly at the wheelbarrow, legs and arms flailing, and finding it obdurate, sat down again. This time he began feeling for his pipe. He also sat and smoked. He wore a cap way over his eyes, and an old vest. His trousers came to just a little way below his knees, and his boots were held together by bits of wire. But he was full of leisure, and stared at the world, holding his head back curiously in order to do so from under the brim of his cap; neck cricked, he looked like a perpetually surprised insect. And now everybody was still, Piet, Sout, and Jan Blom, even the little goat tethered near one of the native huts. There seemed to be no one else nearby, not even any women from the huts. Just the three leisurely workers, the descendants of Adam Kok's bastard tribe, stretching themselves in the sun which warmed their bodies without any difficulty through the tatters of their clothing.

Van Schoor crept silently behind Jan Blom and knocked his cap off his head. Jan Blom turned, with an attitude of defence, but seeing who was before him, dropped it rapidly and seized hold of the wheelbarrow. He jerked at it a few times.

'Baas can see for himself,' he finally panted.

Van Schoor reversed the wheelbarrow and pushed it aside of the little clump of pebbles on which it had been stuck. Jan Blom shook his head in utter amazement, and then suddenly smiled, showing both his teeth. They were quite symmetrically placed, one on either side of his upper jaw.

Van Schoor walked on with Jan Blom shoving the wheelbarrow before him, and groaning as he went. Piet and Sout had slid off the wall, and when van Schoor entered the kraal Piet was brandishing a hammer above his head and Sout was prodding unsuccessfully at the cement which Setole was carefully mixing, scooping it up in smooth liquid swathes and letting it slide again into the pool.

'Morning, baas,' Piet and Sout said in unison. They stopped working for a moment, out of respect. They then fell on their work with vast energy.

Though it was still early in the morning, Setole had already managed to cover his face with cement. The fine grey powder was in every line and wrinkle of his face, and on his forehead. He wore on his head the ripped-off bottom of a cement bag, and his hair too was powdered.

'Morning, baas,' he said. He scooped another spadeful of the mixture, and away it flowed, falling heavily into the pool. The spade went in again, circled, lifted with its load, let it fall.

'Setole!' van Schoor called abruptly.

The spade swung in its arc, hesitated, and this time the cement simply poured from it.

'Baas?' Setole said.

'Come. I want to talk to you.'

Setole paused for a moment. He walked over to the kraal wall and leaned the spade against it. The last few drops fell on the floor of dry green dung. Piet and Sout were not working: they were watching the others. Then Jan Blom came hurtling round the corner at top speed, wheelbarrow rattling and rocks bouncing. 'Lo-o-ok out!' he cried and let the wheelbarrow go, which disappointingly stopped running and fell to the ground with a jolt. 'Hell! *Donder! Bliksem!*' Jan Blom shouted. Now he was exhausted. He wiped the sweat from his brow and shook it out graphically on the ground.

'I am ready, baas,' Setole said.

'Come.'

They walked out of the kraal, watched by the three workers. Van Schoor did not look behind him. Setole took off his cement-bag hat and threw it on the ground just as he left the kraal, and their feet left the soft dung and struck once more on the rock and earth of the farm.

Van Schoor led the way. He walked towards the house, then swerved away from it. Finally he came to a stop in front of the house, but at some distance away, at the beginning of the incline the cattle used when they came down to the river to drink.

'Setole?' he said, and heard with surprise the questioning tone of his own voice. 'Setole,' he said again.

'Ja, baas.'

'Setole, you must take your things and go. I can't have you on the farm.'

'Ja, baas.' Setole's reply was so flat and unmoved that van Schoor turned, clearing his eyes of the vague view of the house on the rise, and looked straight at Setole.

He saw again that the man in front of him was simply a wretched and humble Kaffir. He looked at Setole's bruised face, with the cement upon it, and the flat fleshy nose and half-closed eye, and all the other marks of the beating Willem had given him – the peeled, indecently pink parts of the cheek where Willem's fist had landed, the scab beginning to form on the chin, and the blood that had dried and not been washed off under the ear. His clothes were worse than van Schoor had remembered them to be, all filth and rags. And he was small, though van Schoor had always thought of him as a stockily built man. He now saw him to be slight; he saw the high ridges of bone beneath the black skin where the shirt was open at the neck; and relief gave way to contempt.

'Setole, you must go,' he said. 'Today.'

'Today, baas?'

'Yes.'

Setole said nothing.

'Yes, today. You must get the hell out of the farm, and don't you dare ever come back here again. If I ever see you near my farm, if I ever see you in Dors River again, I'll flog the skin off your back, do you hear? I'll set the dogs on you.' Van Schoor shook his finger. 'I'll teach you a lesson, a proper one, not the one that Willem gave you.'

'Ja, baas.'

Van Schoor started walking away. Setole did not move. He stood as he had stood while van Schoor had been talking to him, with his hands hanging in front of his loins, his shoulders slack. He was staring towards the river when he heard van Schoor's voice, from a few yards away:

'Well, what are you waiting for?'

Setole still stared towards the river, his back to van Schoor. Suddenly he felt a hand on his shoulder. The cloth of his vest tore with a sharp rip. Van Schoor shook him by the shoulder, and his body waggled loosely, without dignity.

'Well?' van Schoor said.

'Well,' Setole replied.

The shaking doubled in violence, until van Schoor let go and Setole staggered back. He tripped and fell. The white man towered above him. 'I told you to go,' he said.

Setole stood up. He said nothing.

'Go!' van Schoor said. 'Go!'

'Ja, baas,' Setole said.

Van Schoor moved away again, but this time only a little way, watching Setole. The veld was quiet, and the heat was beginning to beat up from the ground. Setole's eyes were narrow against the sun, and van Schoor's shadow fell on the ground between the two men. Van Schoor moved; and his shadow moved, closer to Setole.

'Well?'

Setole said nothing. He did not seem obstinate; it was more as though he were too old and tired to waste his breath in a vain shouting across the desert between them. Rock lay between them; all was the rock of van Schoor's farm, pale brown, pale grey, hard, beginning to burn in the sun. Van Schoor's shadow slid silently over the rock, closer still.

'What are you waiting for, Setole?'

Setole moved unexpectedly. It was just a small inconclusive movement, a gesture of his arm.

'No,' van Schoor said. 'You must go. At once. Do you hear me?'

Setole shook his head. He looked round him once more, to the river behind, to the right where Dors River station was hidden in the long swell of the land away from the river, only the tops of the trees poking above the horizon, and close ahead, to the kraal, where the three other boys were standing on the wall looking in their direction.

'Go, damn you!' van Schoor shouted, his voice swinging up shrilly.

Setole said quietly and reasonably, 'I am going, my baas.'

'Go then,' van Schoor said. 'Go now.'

Setole moved his arms, holding them away from his body, like someone ready to go but not sure of the direction. His head moved this way and that, in quick searching jerks, strangely uncoordinated, like a bird trying to fly with a broken wing, or a fractured hand trying to grasp an object. Van Schoor stood aside: it was like a direction that he was giving. And Setole took the direction.

Head down, he dived past van Schoor, little shabby body moving in the strong sunlight, white vest, grey trousers, black skin. Then his back was to van Schoor, and he was walking towards the huts with his usual stumbling gait. Van Schoor saw a piece of his *takkies* flapping open with every step he took, flapping open and closing, opening and closing, flapping open again. 'Wait!' he shouted. 'Setole, wait for me!'

But when he got to Setole he did not know what to say, he did not know why he had called Setole. They stood and looked at each other again, van Schoor wavering a little. At last, shrinkingly, he asked, 'You haven't asked me why I am sending you away.'

'It wouldn't help if I did know.'

'No, it wouldn't help.'

'Then I must go. Does the baas know if there's a train to Lyndhurst?'

'There's a train every day.'

Setole started to move away, then stopped. 'And my pay, baas? When will the baas pay me?'

'Your pay? Of course, I forgot all about your pay. I'll pay you now if you come to the house. I can give it to you at once.'

'Ja, baas.'

'How much is it that I owe you?'

'Doesn't the baas know how much he owes me?'

Van Schoor began calculating aloud. 'Four pound eighteen,' he said at the end of his calculations. 'Is that right?'

'Ja, baas.' Setole acquiesced without calculation.

'I think I've got that in the house. I'll go now to see if I have. Come to the house when you've packed your things.'

'Pack, baas? What should I have to pack?'

'I don't know, I thought perhaps you had.... Anyway, I'll see you at the house just now.'

28

'I can come now, baas.'

'No, don't do that. I'll see you in the house in a minute. All right?' And he turned and struck towards the house. He walked through a little bush, and the thorns on its thin branches scratched at his trousers sharply, without tearing them.

And then he knew that Setole was following him. He stopped. Setole stopped too.

'Didn't I tell you?' van Schoor said angrily.

'Yes,' Setole said. 'But what was I to do? I have nothing to pack, baas.'

Van Schoor waved at Setole, ineffectively, as one waves at a dog that insists on following one. Like an untrained dog, Setole flinched slightly, but did not budge.

'I can't have you walking next to me.'

'Why not, baas? You have done nothing wrong.' Though his remark was bold, Setole himself was not. His voice was evasive, and his body diffident; he was looking down. They began walking again, side by side, in silence.

When they reached the fence that surrounded the garden, Setole asked, 'Where shall I wait?'

'Here in front,' van Schoor replied. Then he saw Willem's son coming round the corner of the house with a spade in his hand, to continue his lackadaisical labours at the garden. The boy stopped when he saw van Schoor and Setole, and watched them cautiously.

Van Schoor did not know what to do. 'Or wait at the back,' he said.

'I can wait at the back if the baas wants me to.'

Van Schoor stood unhappily between Setole and the boy. He looked from one to the other. They both looked at him, and he felt himself clumsily in the way, between them, among them.

He jerked towards the boy. 'Go away,' he said. 'You can't be here now. Go back to your hut. You can come back in the afternoon, but go away now.'

'Ja, baas,' the child replied. He was reluctant to go. He began moving away slowly, looking back all the time with round staring eyes, and van Schoor stood, waiting for him to go. He could feel the sun pressing heavily down upon him; he felt himself rooted, stuck to the hard earth and exposed to the sun.

The boy walked off slowly, climbing through the wire fence, and pausing half-way through, body straddled, to look again. But at last his back was towards them and he wandered off in the direction of the huts.

Van Schoor said, 'All right, Setole, I'll bring you your money now. You can wait here in front if you like.'

Setole squatted down, within the garden but very close to the fence, as if he did not trust to go in deeper. He looked up at van Schoor.

'Ja, baas.'

Van Schoor went into the house. He did not see anyone at all, though he heard voices from the kitchen. The house was dark and stifling after the brightness of the air outside, and he groped in the wardrobe where they kept the money, behind his wife's clothes. He took out two notes; the rest he put back. They had to have some money in the house.

He went outside again, and came towards Setole carrying the notes. 'I'll post the rest to Baas Harris in a couple of days, and you can collect the money from him in Lyndhurst,' he explained.

'Ja, baas.'

Now there was nothing more for either of them to say or do. Setole started walking away, and this time van Schoor knew that he would not follow him. He would stand where he was, stand, and watch Setole go. He would see him go to his hut, and come out carrying his few belongings, he would see him begin walking up the cart track that curved to the house so graciously from the main road through the farm. Setole would stumble away, out of sight, out of the farm, and it would be done with.

'Good-bye, baas,' Setole said.

'Good-bye, Setole.'

Setole said suddenly: 'One day I hope the baas will hear the truth of what is happening on this farm.'

'I have heard the truth,' van Schoor said.

'The baas believes that he has heard the truth. But he has not heard all the truth, and I am not going to tell him. I could also tell the baas some stories . . .'

'I have heard one story. It was enough. What stories could you tell me?'

'They are things that I have heard and I have seen. But why should I tell them to the baas? Why should I help you, baas? The baas must see for himself what is happening on the farm, otherwise he will believe anything that's told to him, and no matter who tells it. I am not going to help you, baas, because I don't want to help you.'

'I don't know what you're talking about.'

'I know, baas.'

This time there was no mistaking it – Setole was mocking his baas. Van Schoor stared steadily at Setole, and Setole looked back. Setole's eyes were weak, bloodshot, and there was a faint blue ring round each iris, a pale unlikely colour in that dark face. His eyes were like mud, the sort one finds near a river's bank, slightly iridescent. Setole's eyes were gleaming, in mockery.

'Setole, is there really anything on the farm that you know about?' van Schoor asked.

'What should the Kaffir know that the baas doesn't know?'

'It isn't like that now. I am asking you.'

'It is always like that, my baas.'

'If you know anything that's been happening on this farm, tell it to me.'

'Why should you believe me? If they told you the truth, then I am lying now. If I am telling the truth, then there are other people you must chase away from the farm and keep me on. You can't believe both of us. But I am going away, so perhaps it is better if the baas believes the story of the people who are staying. It will be more peaceful for you, baas.'

'I don't want peace. I want the truth.'

'You will learn it then. I don't think the truth of this farm will be very peaceful for you though. Good-bye, baas.' Setole was unshaken. 'Ja, baas. Good-bye, baas,' he said again. 'Baas,' he said for the last time, as though he were saying a name to remember it, and shambled away.

About an hour later, Willem asked van Schoor again if he could ride over to Dors River.

'Yes, all right,' van Schoor said. 'I told you you could last night.'

'Ja, baas, I just wanted to make sure it was all right.' Willem paused, then said, 'Thank you, baas, for chasing Setole away.'

'Yes,' van Schoor said.

'Thank you, baas. The baas is good to his Kaffirs.'

2 Maclachlan

The cat on the stoep railing suddenly stretched its body, and arched its back. It leaped lightly from the rail on to the stoep and sharpened its claws on one of the wooden supports holding up the roof over the stoep, and then sprang into the garden. It crept along the warm earth, legs moving slowly in the dust between the stalks of last season's flowers. Its tail wove to and fro. It dragged its soft belly over the bricks at the side of the path, and across the path itself, to the other side of the garden. There were no beds for flowers there, only a few small orange trees with the winter's tiny oranges rusting away out of reach. The ground between the trees was bare. The earth was dark grey in colour, and fine. The cat squirmed through the dust.

It paused, huddled itself into the ground, shoulders working in small rehearsal of its spring. It lay crouched for some time, and then jumped forward, one, two leaps, and pounced. It danced and fell daintily forward again on its prey. It played with it for a little while, then came trotting back to the stoep. It leaped up easily, and ran the length of the stoep. As it passed him, Maclachlan saw the leg and papery wing of a locust protruding from the cat's satisfied mouth.

'Skats!' he hissed, and shot out a leg. But he was too late, and the cat disappeared round the corner of the stoep. Now

Maclachlan had only the dusty, empty road to stare at, the blank railway lines on the other side.

But 'Baas', came a voice from the passage. An African stood behind the gauzed door to the house. 'Baas.'

Maclachlan struggled in the chair to look behind him. 'Why don't you stand where I can see you?' he complained, his voice constricted.

'Baas,' the servant said without moving, 'Willem of Drie-hoek wants to see you.'

Still screwed in his chair, Maclachlan said, 'Well tell him to come round and see me.'

'Ja, baas.'

Maclachlan heard the man's bare feet padding down the passage, and he turned slowly back to the normal position.

The fig tree, out of sight to the side of the house, crackled, a twig snapped. Maclachlan started. Then Willem appeared round the corner. Maclachlan straightened himself in his seat, his loose bulk around him, his head back and his light-grey eyes staring at Willem.

Willem did not seem to be daunted by Maclachlan's stare.

'Mister Maclachlan!' he said, enunciating the English words with a certain éclat.

'Yes?'

'How is it?' Willem asked, friendly.

'All right.'

'I'm glad to hear that.'

'You didn't come here simply to inquire after my health,' Maclachlan said, nervously sarcastic. 'I trust,' he added.

Willem shook his head tentatively, a little puzzled, and encouraged by this, Maclachlan said: 'What was it then that induced you to leave your native habitat and persuaded you to come and visit my own poor self?' His sarcasm exhausted itself early: he looked anxiously at Willem.

Willem's brow relaxed when Maclachlan's speech was over. He said in Afrikaans, 'You still know more English than I do.'

'I should bloody well hope so,' Maclachlan said, also speaking Afrikaans. 'Well, then, what is it? What do you want of me this time?'

'Nothing.'

Maclachlan shook his head. 'Have you gone mad? What will people say?' He stopped and jerked his head forward. He whispered furiously: 'Look there now.' A man was walking down the road, looking towards them, seeing Maclachlan on the stoep and the African in the garden before him. The man waved at Maclachlan, who waved back and watched him go out of sight. The road was empty again. 'Do you think he isn't asking himself what van Schoor's boy is doing talking to me like this? Hey?'

'I don't think he is,' Willem replied casually. His voice sounded loud after Maclachlan's whisper. 'You worry too much.'

'You're a cheeky bastard. You're a black swine. You bloody black swine!'

Willem shrugged.

'Swine!' Maclachlan said, answering the shrug. 'If you've got nothing to tell me, get the hell out of here. Do you think I like looking at your monkey face?' He screwed his own face grotesquely. 'That's what you look like.' He heaved forward in his chair, and stuck his face, still hideously contorted, towards Willem. 'Do you know that?' he cried. 'Do you think I enjoy having something like that standing in front of me every day?'

'I don't come every day.'

'Thank God for that. I'd go mad if you did. With your monkey face and your English talk –goed morning, Mistaire Maclachlan – trying to talk English! Who's ever heard of a black monkey talking English? Go back to your trees, you black baboon!' Even in his shallow frenzy of hate Maclachlan was quite pleased with that last remark. He repeated it, and scratched himself under his armpit. 'Do you want monkeynuts? Is that what you've come for? Go to Levy across the railway line, he's got bags of monkey-nuts in his shop and he'll give you some, if you don't behave like a cheeky Kaffir!'

But he could not go on. He had to lean back, stomach churning, and as the paroxysm exhausted itself his guts called out to him that it was not worth it, it was not worth it, no money was worth it.

34

'I haven't come for monkey-nuts,' Willem said. 'But you can tell your boy to cut me some bread and jam and make me some tea before I go.'

'All right, I'll tell him. But you promise you'll go when you've eaten?'

'No, I don't. I can't go away until we've had a little talk.'

'I asked you if you had anything to tell me. You said no. So what do you want of me now?'

'I have got something to tell you, but it can wait. Why are you in such a hurry, Mister Maclachlan? You don't open the shop for another half-hour.'

'I know when I open my shop.'

'Yes – and you also know where you get the meat that you sell,' Willem said, smiling. 'Don't you?'

Maclachlan started swearing again. He swore at Willem and at Willem's black skin. He ran through the usual litany of curses, but Willem seemed quite unconcerned. He was light, almost gay; his movements were freer, his brow less darkened; he was far more relaxed a person than he was on the farm. He began to whistle, standing with one hand on his hip, and the other in the pocket of his grey trousers. He was wearing his near-best clothes. His shirt was clean; formerly khaki, the colour had been scrubbed practically to extinction and was now almost as pale as white, and where it was open, his skin could be seen gleaming darkly. His hat was on the back of his head. Maclachlan thought of the eager and humble boy to whom he had first broached his scheme, and looked at the cocky Kaffir in front of him.

Willem broke off whistling abruptly. Someone was again passing down the road. They waited in silence until he too disappeared. He had not looked at them.

'I suppose I better tell what I have to tell you,' Willem said. He laughed: 'If a little visit from me makes you worry like this I don't know what you're going to do when you've heard my news.'

'Why? What do you mean?'

'Well, it's bad news.'

'What bad news?'

'I'm telling you. I have bad news.'

35

'For God's sake, what is it?'

'The worst sort of bad news.'

Maclachlan made a noise. There were no words; it was hardly a cry, just a high-pitched noise in his throat.

Willem looked at him for a moment. 'Listen to what I have to tell you.' He leaned forward, and as if hypnotised, Maclachlan did the same, over the rail of the stoep. Willem breathed it out: 'There's someone who knows about us,' and as he said it Maclachlan's head jerked back as though Willem had spat in his eye. Willem pulled his head back more slowly, and surveyed the khaki-clothed, loose-fleshed man before him, with his wavering grey eyes, and blond hair, thin on his head, growing in a stubble from his chin, curling on his arms and legs.

'Oh my God,' Maclachlan said. 'Oh my God.' His lips trembled, and he lifted one hand to cover his face. He rested like that, leaning his head on his hand. His elbow was on the armrest of the chair; the basket-work had loosened and hung from the revealed wooden bone of the chair in coils.

Eventually he lifted his head. Willem saw the tears in his eyes, sprung there involuntarily, like tears from a blow.

'What are we going to do?'

'We are going to go to jail.' Willem took off his hat and bowed his head, as though in defeat, humiliation, despair.

'No,' Maclachlan said.

'Yes,' Willem replied softly, in the tones of defeat.

'Does he know me too?'

'He knows everything.' Slowly he lifted his head. 'There is nothing he does not know.'

The tears that had hung in Maclachlan's eyes now began to trickle down either cheek. He made no noise of weeping, and his body hardly moved. 'We can't go to jail,' he implored Willem. 'I can't go to jail.'

'Ask Sergeant Prinsloo whether you can go to jail or not.'

'What'll happen to my children? I was just going to write to my sister to say that she should come and look after them because I can't manage on my own. What must I do now? I can't go to jail.'

'It is a pity about the children,' Willem said.

Maclachlan asked: 'Who is this man that knows about us?'

'It's a new Kaffir on the farm.'

'How does he know?'

'He saw us. Two nights ago, when you came.'

'Did he see me too?'

'I told you. He saw everything.'

'Have you done anything with him? Please. What have you done with him?'

'What can I do with him? Kill him?'

Maclachlan shook his head blindly. 'No, you can't kill him. Of course you can't kill him. We're not murderers. How can we kill a man?' But his hand was trembling. 'We can't kill him.'

'That's what I said.'

'But can't you just chase him away?'

'How?'

'Can't you beat him up, make him go away, do something? You've got to do something.'

'If I chase him away, the first thing he'll do is go straight to the police. Who knows what he might do?'

'Then what are you going to do?'

'Nothing. What can I do?'

'And what will he do while we wait?'

'I don't know.'

Maclachlan leaned forward and cupped his face in his hands. 'I knew it would happen,' he said. 'I knew it all along.'

'You didn't. If you had you would never have started the whole business.'

Apparently Maclachlan had not heard him. He simply repeated, 'I knew it was going to happen. Sooner or later it had to happen.'

'Then why did you start it?'

'For the sake of the money,' Maclachlan suddenly shouted, jerking his hand away from his face. 'You fool – do you think I did it for fun?'

'No, I didn't think you did it for fun,' Willem replied, equivocally.

'Money . . .' Maclachlan said.

Slowly he began to grow calmer, as Willem stood waiting before him; he even drew a little courage from Willem's indifference to the prospect of jail. And as he grew calmer he began to scheme, systematically; not with the twitching hopes that had first quivered within him, that Willem was perhaps wrong, that perhaps the man had not seen him. Those, like fear and greed, came spontaneously. But his schemes were subtler.

He looked up. 'Money – is that what he wants? Can we buy him off? How much would he want?'

'I don't know,' Willem said so dubiously that it was obvious he was wondering not about the size of the sum of money, but about the practicability of the entire plan. 'He's a strange sort of Kaffir.'

'Any sort of Kaffir wants money. He must want something otherwise he would have gone to van Schoor already. Have you offered him money?'

'Where would I get money to offer him?'

Maclachlan was thinking. When he spoke his voice was absent: 'You should have some money out of all this. What do you do with the money I give you?'

'There isn't so much of it. And I'm saving.'

'Saving!' Maclachlan said. 'That's more than I'm able to do.'

'I don't drink as much as you do,' Willem said, and when Maclachlan lumbered to his feet Willem moved back and looked at the white man with pleasure.

'You're a bloody cheeky Kaffir. Do you hear me? Don't you know how to talk to a white man?'

'I talk to you differently,' Willem said.

'You're enjoying this, aren't you?'

'Yes,' Willem replied. He could not conceal the fact, and saw no need to.

Maclachlan said: 'You're a partner with a white man.'
'Yes.'

Maclachlan stared at his own white skin on his arm. Something was stirring within him. 'You're a partner with a white man, but you're still a cheeky Kaffir.'

'I'm not a cheeky Kaffir.'

'What are you then?'

'Willem of Driehoek.'

'And Willem of Driehoek is a cheeky Kaffir. You're a Kaffir, a Kaffir, a Kaffir. And I'm a white man.'

Willem laughed. 'That won't help you. They'll put us in different jails, that's all.'

Maclachlan lurched back into his chair. 'I'm not going to jail,' he said.

Willem said nothing. Then at last he said: 'So you've got nothing to suggest to me that I should do about this man?'

Maclachlan shook his head. 'You're so bloody clever, why don't you think of something?'

'I have thought of everything, and it doesn't help. All we can do is wait. I don't know what the man wants to do, or even if he will do anything. All I know is that he knows about us, and he can put us both in jail tomorrow if he likes. I thought I better tell you the news, so I came here. And that's all.'

'Do you think he will do anything soon?'

'I don't think so. I think he's also waiting for something before he jumps on us, otherwise he would have already gone to van Schoor. Perhaps he prefers to keep us waiting like this. Perhaps he likes the thought that neither of us will be able to sleep as long as he is on the farm.'

Maclachlan cried out: 'I can't live like that.'

'You'll have to learn.'

'And what about our plan for two weeks' time?'

'Ah,' Willem thought for a while. 'I'm ready to go on with it.'

The other man looked at him in amazement. 'You have got a nerve,' he said.

'Why not?' Willem replied. He truly did not seem to care. 'If he goes to the police, we'll go to jail anyway. It will make no difference whether we stole sheep once or a hundred times.'

'No,' Maclachlan said. 'I can't go through with it.'

'Well, I want to.'

'No.'

Willem thought for a while. He said: 'I tell you what, you stay here and don't worry too much.' He smiled. 'Or worry as little as you can. And I'll go back to the farm, and watch what happens there. He might even go away without saying anything to anybody – he is supposed to leave in about ten days' time. Then, if he goes, I'll let you know that it's all right. How's that for a plan?'

'No, no. You must let me know earlier what's going to happen. I'll go mad if I just have to wait here, and wait here, and not know what's happening.'

Willem relented suddenly. 'I'll let you know tomorrow,' he said. 'I think I know what's going to happen tomorrow.'

'How do you mean?'

'That's my secret.' Willem waited, smiling, body confidently poised.

'So you think it's going to be all right?' Maclachlan asked desperately.

'That I can't say. But I hope that these things won't turn out too badly.' Suddenly he laughed; it was a jeer at Maclachlan. His game was over. 'I'm going to get some bread and jam from the boy at the back. Good-bye, Mister Maclachlan.'

He did not wait for Maclachlan's reply, but went round the side of the house, leaving the white man on the stoep.

As he sat there, the scheme came quickly and simply to Maclachlan; he wondered why he had not thought of it before. It was so simple. It could not go wrong. He sat on, absorbed, working the plan out to its last detail. He was a capable schemer – his schemes only failed because in action they became debased by the violence and slovenliness of his own feelings: he would lose himself, believing in the attitudes he had to adopt. But this time his feelings would be no danger to him. They would support him, and be believed by others: everyone would believe the lies of which Willem had reminded him.

When he was satisfied that every detail of his story rang true, he lifted himself from his chair. He called to the boy at the back of the house that he would be back in ten minutes, and began walking down the path. The sun struck at him, but uplifted by his purpose he hardly noticed it, though he wore no hat. He hardly noticed the road, or the dust scuffing round his shoes, the railway line and the truck that some Africans were off-loading, he hardly heard the noise of their cries. He walked through Dors River, carrying his portentous swaying body to the destination before it. He did not have far to walk. He passed three houses, a little shop, and then the hotel. The road swung round the corner at the hotel, and he followed it, leaving behind him the two gaunt old-fashioned petrol pumps, bright red in the sun, and the people on the stoep who had greeted him. Now before him was a stretch of veld, and the police station, a little stone building with a bed of flowers and a wire fence and a flagpole before it, with the flag hanging down in straight folds in the hot air, limp. Beyond that was the straight line of the national road to Lyndhurst, dark blue and empty but for a small glittering car that moved so smoothly it could have been standing still in the heat-tranced air.

'Morning, baas Maclachlan.' He heard a ragged chorus of voices, and stopped and stared around him. To the side of the hotel, waiting for the non-European bar to open, was a group of ragged Coloureds, the brothers and cousins and more distant relatives of Piet and Sout and Jan Blom. They stood in the shade against the wall, or simply squatted in the heat and dust. Maclachlan saw them: they were like flies to him, creatures congregating round the bar like flies around a piece of offal, all to be destroyed. He did not reply to their greetings, but stared at them, and then moved more firmly on, dazed with his purpose.

He neared the police station. The car had disappeared, the veld was motionless. The only sound in the quiet air was the fitful beat of the engine pumping water for the station – the same sound that the travellers, lying full-length in their bunks at night, unable to sleep on their long journeys to the sea, heard when the train slowed down and stopped at Dors River, whose name they did not hear, but heard only, in that island of silence after the train's rattle, the crunching of feet on the dark platform and then the beat-beat-beat coming from the night, out of the darkness and emptiness, beating like the heart of the veld which they did know still surrounded them, and would, by day or night, in all their journeys. But as Maclachlan came closer to the police station, it fell away. All fell away from him, the beat of the engine, the veld, the road, the koppies far away like vague dreams of heat and rock. He entered the office, and as he did so, toweringly, his feet on the floor boards and the sun banished, the man behind the counter looking up, already, proudly, he knew that what he was about to do was a blow not only for himself, but for all the people he knew to be his.

3   Van Schoor

Then, for two weeks van Schoor's farm was still, and during those two weeks the heat struck. It came with a wind: for three days the wind blew steadily from the north-west, blowing straight from the desert. Dust was in the air all the time; indoors there was a fine film over every stick of furniture, and a rift of dust under every door; teeth grated on dust in the bread that was eaten. And outside the world was heavy with dust. All round the horizon there hung a grey band, round the waist of the universe, that looked sometimes like a rain cloud, sometimes like the smoke of a great city, but was only and always the dust. And above all, above wind and dust and the parched earth, hung the sun – hot, dimmed by the dust, present throughout the day.

On the third night the wind slackened and dropped away and the morning came up clear. The release from the wind was a respite; waking on that morning and feeling that the wind had blown away at last, the soul stretched, expecting gentleness from the air and forgiveness from the earth. And it seemed at first that that would be granted, for after the long siege of dust the ground no longer seemed so raw, and the stillness of the air was delicate. But by ten o'clock of that morning the sun had sent a skewer through the heart of the earth, and each morning following thrust the skewer a little deeper, until at last the land was transfixed with drought. Every evening there was a movement of healing, but every morning the sun rose in the east and the crucifixion went on, methodically.

In the mornings, van Schoor sat on his stoep watching his cattle. The pan higher up on the farm was drying, and the cattle were leaving it. They grazed lower down now, and came for their water to the river. Early in the mornings the long file of beasts could be seen going down to the river to drink, standing at the river's edge and drinking their fill, and wearily beginning their trek away from the river again. Later in the day they came down in ones or twos, but always, on his stoep, looking out of the window, walking to his house, van Schoor saw them going among the burning pale rocks, hoofs clicking, their heads down, making for the water, or their bodies straining as they climbed away from it. Their condition was still good, but the farm needed rain, would soon begin to need it desperately, and the rain gave no sign of coming.

Van Schoor was used to drought: he had grown up with it on his father's farm, there near Postmasburg, a farm like the end of the world, hot and ugly and drab, with the dark metal rock that all day, all summer had shone and stung with the heat. And for the past fifteen, twenty years he had been a foreman on various farms in the district. But then the drought had been on the land of the owner of the farm, not his own. For all those years, as seasons had come and gone, summers succeeding winters, he had worked on other people's farms, branding cattle, shearing sheep, castrating young bullocks, occasionally when the owner of the farm was willing to take a risk, ploughing in the spring and watching the young mealies turn brown and wither and die of drought. He had fixed the tall steel windmills and the dams into which they had pumped their water. Cattle were dosed and dipped, sheep delivered their lambs, goats clattered up the koppie sides, season followed season.

And every time, when his contract elapsed, he had been told to move on. Not that his employers had had anything against him. But his wife was impossible. They told him that too, some of them bluntly, others more tactfully, some of them saying that they didn't mind but it was their wives who were complaining – women who could no longer bear the strain

43

of living on a farm with a woman who forced even van Schoor, who had loved her when they married, to admit to himself that she was near-mad.

Finally he could stand it no longer. He had always gone his own way, within himself, and for him all the moving around that he had to do as a result of his wife's vagaries was an irrelevance, a distraction. He was a quiet, rather soft-spoken man, a little shy because of his height; and he walked slightly bent, reducing himself; when he sat down his hands were in his way. They were big hands, with cracked and dirty finger-nails, and on the back of each finger there were tufts of long hair that had been burned golden by the sun. All the years that he had spent in work on the land rested neither lightly nor heavily on him, but seemed to have passed through him, as the soft hair thinned on his head and the lines on his face became more marked, until there was something almost lizard-like about his face in its leathery wrinkledness, its imperviousness to heat. The sun had got into him young, and it had not merely faded him as it does so many whites, but had given him strength. He had the strength of leather, of biltong, of an African's feet who walks bare-foot all his life, the strength of anything left long in the open and the sun. He had made his decision to buy a farm of his own, where there would be nobody with whom his wife could fight, and where he would be alone.

Throughout the years he saved money and cattle, money and cattle, and then went to the Land Bank, and to a businessman in Lyndhurst who trusted him, and borrowed more money from them. Now he was heavily in debt, but if the year was good he would be able to pull through – some of the cattle would be sent to the slaughter polls at Lyndhurst, and he planned to start milking soon, and sending the cream to the creamery in Lyndhurst. At the moment the cattle were simply grazing across the veld at their own free will.

And he had tackled the tasks immediately before him with energy and resolution. The house he and his wife were living in had been fixed up, and then as the first real job of improvement, he had brought Setole in to fix the kraal, so that the milking could take place under tolerable conditions – a proper milking shed would have to wait. There was so much to do on the farm that the rebuilding of the kraal, which had lain in heaps of stones on his arrival, was only a first, small job. Yet when Setole and his three helpers arrived and started work at last, he knew his power: where there had been nothing before, a few disordered rocks, something was now being made. He was making it, though he did no work, but stood at some hours during the day beside the workers, seeing the work go on. It was he who had made the stones to be brought, to be split, to be shaped, fitted on the walls that slowly grew longer and thicker under the care of them all. He had often been in charge of tasks on the other farms at which he had worked, but this delight he had never known before, because now he was alone, and it was his instructions alone that were altering the surface of the farm – he felt as though he was working with the earth itself, alone. And this isolation, even his wife could not touch. She still moved through those strange lands of hers which he knew so well by hearsay, but on his farm that did not matter.

And with his power, he knew peace, and his only grief was that he had waited so long before coming to it. Setole's three helpers said 'Ja, baas' and 'Nee, baas' with a kind of basic insouciance really, which van Schoor felt and did not mind. When he went away he knew that they made jokes about him among themselves. The Long One, they called him, and walked on tiptoe to show how long he was. He did not mind that either. The veld lay pale brown under the sun that wheeled to the west; he stood alongside and apart from his workers as the day dropped away in gold and fire on the other side of the river; he watched them finish their last mix of cement and stack their tools and trail across the veld that the sunset had fired back to their huts. He sat on the stoep in the evening; he slept all night; he woke eagerly when the first silver rays of the sun shone from the east, for another day of activity and stillness, as the veld itself was still under the sun.

But with Setole's departure, the industry and activity on the farm seemed to slacken almost to vanishing point. Sout claimed that he was a plasterer and van Schoor let him have a go at the kraal wall, but it soon became obvious that Sout was no plasterer. He mucked about with the cement quite cheerfully, and that was all, and the mix of cement he was busy with grew hard on the sheet of zinc and had to be chipped off and the broken bits thrown away to the side of the kraal. Then he used the three workers to bring soil in the wagon for the vegetable garden near the house. They worked badly, and during the dust storm did not work at all but merely sat to the side of the house and suffered audibly; once the heat had arrived they did no work during the middle of the day. Van Schoor rode over to Dors River to try to get somebody to replace Setole, but without success. He wrote to a friend in Lyndhurst, and the African they had arranged to bring simply did not turn up.

The farm was still in those days after Setole left, with the stillness of something in a trance. The veld lay as though drugged with heat, in a fever from which it could never recover. The house was quiet. The native huts seemed abandoned. Round the kraal walls there was no longer any movement; no bodies walked, bent, bowed, straightened as the work progressed; there was no longer the desultory crack of boulders being split by the ten-pound hammer which Piet had wielded so proudly and erratically.

The only movement was the shaking of heat around the walls, like something seen in a delirium; the only sound was the shrill call of the *koringkrieks,* rasping frenziedly in one dry scream. It was as though the heat, which bore down so directly upon the veld, assumed disguises, new forms: the eyes were attacked by glare, by the shaking of the veld, the ears by the scream of the insects, in an exacerbation that never let up.

Underneath the irritation of idleness and the attack of the heat, van Schoor knew anxiety. He did not think at all of what would happen if the rains did not come, if he had a bad year. Then he would be deeply in trouble, and all he had tried to do might be destroyed. But that he refused to consider: the rains would come, they had to come.

Only Willem was a source of reassurance. 'The rains will come, baas,' he said, and van Schoor asked him, 'Are you

46

sure that they will come? How do you know that they will come? Do you really think they will come?' revealing his doubts about Willem's word only in the hope that they would be dispelled.

Willem frowned and looked grave, and admitted that the heat was bad, very bad, for that time of year, so early in the season, but the rains would come, he assured his baas. He knew that they would come. And, superstitiously, van Schoor thought that perhaps Willem did know what he could not know: that there was some knowledge locked in Willem's head that he could never share, some perception that Willem's black skin had that his own would always be without.

Day came after day: each dawn brought in a spectacle of drought. Spectacular enough it was too, with the great sun shining and the land lying locked in the heat, seized with the sun like a passion; and crazy sunsets, all frozen violent colours and rays of sun flat across a continent, a world. And the suddenness with which the heat had come was frightening in itself.

A week after the dust storm, the land looked as though no rain had ever fallen there, as though no rain ever could, as though drought was in the landscape as the *koppies* were – barren, ancient, and immovable.

4   Willem

Sitting on the stoep, in the darkness of the evening, van Schoor saw a pair of unwinking straight lights, and he turned to watch the car pass, as he thought it would, along the road through the farm. He wondered who was in the car. Few people ever passed through the farm, least of all at that time of night, as he knew, for he usually sat on the stoep of his house in the evenings to enjoy the coolness. This night especially he was grateful to sit there, for he felt a cool wind upon his body. The wind had been blowing from the northeast quite steadily since the afternoon, and he knew that the chances for rain were good. The wind was the right one, and during the day clouds had hung in the sky: at first mere puffs of cloud, they had grown towards evening, deepening and changing colour. They were high up, heavy but separate, by sunset, with a great glittering stretch of dry sky between each cloud; but now still they were massing against the west. The sky was dark and there were few stars.

He turned to look for the car again, and with a shock saw the lights were not travelling along the road. The car was coming across the veld, its headlights aimed straight at his house. He stared at it in disbelief, but the lights grew stronger and closer: he saw how insanely they were bounding across the veld. Two eyes staring at him across the veld. In their light all the weaker lights of the sky disappeared, and now all shadows stretched away from that shining centre. He heard no sound: he only saw the lights shining, leaping, bucking closer. Then he heard the whine of an engine, and the lights stood for a moment. The whine ended and the lights leaped forward again. They were near. They were level with the native huts, and van Schoor saw them harshly outlined against the night, flat brown walls, all straight lines, and hollows of darkness between. And the glare of the lights caught him between the eyes, and he lifted one hand to ward them off. It was too bright, a great mechanical dazzle that filled the farm. He staggered back, arm shielding his eyes, and the flesh behind his closed eyelids was streaked over and over again with a livid white dazzle like lightning.

When he took his hand away from his face and opened his eyes, the light was gone from them. The van, it was a van, not a car, was parked in front of his house. The headlights stabbed the darkness: they shone on rock, and on the strong black line of the wire fence round the garden, they caught thorn trees in grotesque attitudes.

'Jaap? Is that you?' called a voice that van Schoor did not recognize from the van.

'Yes?' van Schoor replied.

He stared down at the van, hands hanging to the sides of his body. He did not move forward, but waited. Both doors of the van opened, then both were slammed shut, with a double metallic clank. Two men, van Schoor saw in the lights from the van, were walking up the path. He waited for them at the top of the steps.

'Who is it?' he asked. He saw one of the men was wearing a peaked cap.

'Is it the police?' he asked.

There was a laugh from one of the men walking steadily towards him. 'That's right,' a voice said. 'We have come to arrest you.'

'What have I done?' van Schoor asked.

Again there was the laugh. Then the two men climbed on to the stoep.

'Prinsloo,' van Schoor said. 'Maclachlan.'

'Maclachlan it is, sure enough. Hullo, Jaap.' And Maclachlan was up the steps, pumping van Schoor's hand in his own. Van Schoor took his hand away.

'What is it?' he asked.

Suddenly the front door of the house burst open, and Mrs van Schoor stood in the doorway. She was carrying an oil lamp in her hand, and the light that fell with a glow on her bosom sharply illumined her face, setting into prominence the frame of her cheekbones rising from her pointed chin to high beneath her eyes. Her eyes were in shadow, but they glittered blackly. Her head jerked from man to man, the black plait of her hair swinging.

'For God's sake, what is it?' she asked wildly.

Comforting her, avoiding trouble from her, was second nature to van Schoor. Automatically he said: 'Nothing, Anna.'

'How do you know?' She jerked herself towards the two men. 'Tell me what's gone wrong. For God's sake, what has happened?'

Van Schoor wanted to move to her, but found he could not. 'Anna,' he whispered.

Maclachlan's voice boomed. 'It's nothing to get excited about. We're bringing you good news. What do you say, Sergeant? Clever, that's what we were, and because of that there's good news tonight.' He threw his arm across his body in a gesture, as though he were asking someone to come with him, to a party.

'What are you talking about?' van Schoor asked.

'Well, I don't know if you can actually call it good news,' Prinsloo said more quietly.

'Bad news!' Mrs van Schoor shouted. 'I knew it would be bad news!'

'No,' Prinsloo said patiently, 'it isn't bad news either.' He spoke very slowly, as though to a child, to make Mrs van Schoor understand him. Then he turned to van Schoor. 'It's quite simple. We've caught your Willem trying to steal your sheep. We've brought him along here to show you.'

'My Willem?'

'Yes, your Willem.'

Van Schoor was silent. Then he said: 'But he isn't my Willem.'

'Isn't he just!' Maclachlan said loudly. 'Wait until you see him. It's your Willem all right – the bastard! We've caught him this time, and he'll never be able to do anything again. Not a thing,' he said delightedly. He turned to Mrs van Schoor. 'Excuse the language, hey? But you understand how we feel.'

'No,' Mrs van Schoor said sharply, and van Schoor himself said, 'No – I meant –' But he could not finish the sentence. He stood in the middle of the stoep. 'My Willem?'

Prinsloo stretched out his hand and took van Schoor by the forearm. 'It's your Willem all right,' he said, reassuring van Schoor.

This time he did not protest. He stared before him, above Prinsloo's head. Mrs van Schoor stood to the side of the men. Her dress was undone at the breast, and she clutched it together with one thin hand. The other still held the lamp, tilted, and the flame ran against the glass, blackening it.

Maclachlan and Prinsloo looked at each other. Awkwardly, Prinsloo dropped his hand away from van Schoor's arm.

Then to save the situation, Maclachlan started speaking again. 'Wait a minute,' he cried. 'Let's explain to the people. They don't understand what's going on. They don't know what's been happening, that's why old Jaap is looking as though his world's fallen in, with his mouth hanging open. Shut your mouth, Jaap, and listen to us. It's a real detective story.' No one laughed. Van Schoor's expression did not change. So Maclachlan turned to Mrs van Schoor. 'There, there, Mrs van Schoor, no harm has come to anyone.' He put out his hand and patted her on the shoulder. She jerked herself away from him. Deprived of that role, Maclachlan turned again to van Schoor. 'I tell you, Jaap, you ought to be proud of me. I've saved you a lot of trouble, and a lot of money. And you too, Prinsloo! You don't get an open-and-shut case like this every day. You ought to be grateful to me.' He swayed towards them, ponderously.

'I am grateful to you,' Prinsloo said.

'Don't mention it, man, it's my duty to you and Jacob here. We live together, don't we?'

Van Schoor saw Maclachlan's mouth opening and closing incessantly, and heard Maclachlan's voice beating against the air. But he could make no meaning of the sounds. He turned to Prinsloo, and asked, 'Tell me what has happened.'

'Well, old Mac here can tell you better than I can. He was in the business from the beginning.'

Van Schoor looked at Maclachlan. He was talking to Mrs van Schoor. Boom-boom-boom went his voice. They were all standing anyhow on the stoep. Van Schoor groped for order.

'Anna,' he said, through the hollow clangour of Maclachlan's voice, 'bring some chairs from inside.'

'Yes, Jacob.'

She left Maclachlan in midsentence. 'So you see!' he shouted after her. Then he offered the other cigarettes. Prinsloo accepted one, and they lit up. In the flare of the match van Schoor saw Maclachlan's mouth; his lips were trembling a little as they pouted over the cigarette.

Mrs van Schoor came out with two chairs, and the three men sat down around the little table on which she had placed the lamp. Mrs van Schoor stood behind her husband.

The two other men were puzzled. They had expected agitation, anger, excitement, and, in a particular secret way, fun: not this slowness to understand and move, even the desire to understand. Wasn't it simple enough? They had caught a Kaffir, one of van Schoor's Kaffirs, stealing sheep. What more did van Schoor want before he got excited? Nevertheless,

Prinsloo began telling the story, while Maclachlan leaned forward, waiting for his opportunity.

'You see, Jaap, it's like this. About a fortnight ago Mac came into the police station and told me that your Willem had come to him and suggested that they should steal sheep – your sheep – for Mac's butchery, and that they should share the profits. Well, Mac did the right thing. He didn't say no to Willem, he said he'd think about it. Then he came straight to me and told me the story. I saw quickly enough that he was right, that the thing to do would be to get Willem properly, to trap him. I told Mac to tell Willem that he agreed.' Prinsloo paused. 'I hope you don't mind that we didn't tell you about the business. It was Mac's idea, and I agreed with him.'

Maclachlan jerked his chair forward. 'It was my idea, Jaap. You see, I was bloody excited – excuse the language, Mrs van Schoor – when Prinsloo and I decided what we should do. I didn't want anything to spoil it, you see. So I thought that if we told you, you never know, but you might just let something slip that would let Willem see that the game was up. I tell you I was so damn scared that I would do it that I didn't want to see Willem again. Oh no – I was too scared he'd see that something was going on. I wrote a letter to him making the arrangements. It's a lucky thing he can read, isn't it? An educated Kaffir!' He ended in laughter.

Prinsloo continued the story. 'So I hope you understand, Jaap.' Van Schoor nodded, and encouraged, the other went on.

'There isn't much else to tell you. Tonight me and Corporal Ngkane, you know him, my corporal, got into the back of the van when Mac drove off to meet Willem. Willem was waiting for him, all right. He came when the signal was given to him, the lights going on and off. He had three good sheep lying there, with their throats cut. He and Mac started to heave them into the van – we were sitting right at the back, as quiet as anything, under a canvas, and when they were busy with the first one Mac shouted 'Now!' and jumped on Willem. We were out of the van like lightning. Willem was fighting, but when he saw us he surrendered and I put the handcuffs on him. We got him. It's an open-and-shut case – stock theft, and the magistrates don't like that, as you know. He'll get a couple of years at least, and a couple of lashes to remind him of what's right and what isn't.'

The story was ended. Prinsloo leaned back, smiling. Maclachlan too was smiling.

'Can I see him?' van Schoor asked.

'Of course. He's in the van now with Kane. We can bring him up to you if you like.'

'No,' van Schoor said. 'I'll go down.'

'This is more like it,' Maclachlan said. His smile was fixed on his mouth. 'Now we're going to see some fireworks.' He gave a short abrupt laugh, almost a bark, and stood up, leading the way.

The three men began walking down the path, leaving Mrs van Schoor at the head of the steps, with the lamplight behind her.

'Kane,' Prinsloo called. They came to the back of the truck. It was dark inside: they could see only obscure movements.

Then Willem and the African policeman appeared. They were handcuffed together: they had to move together, as though they were helping each other. They stood at the duckboard of the van. 'Come down,' Prinsloo said. Willem and the policeman looked at each other, and the policeman moved his braceleted hand in a signal, and clumsily and carefully the two of them managed to stand on the duckboard itself. They teetered there for a moment. They moved very slowly, almost sluggishly, like creatures in a dream, locked together, silent. Then Ngkane said, 'All right,' and together they jumped down, hitting the ground at the same time, almost falling, but managing not to. The handcuffs between them clattered. Swaying, still together like Siamese twins, they staggered towards the white men who gave way a little at their coming. At last they struck balance and stood.

'Baas?' the native policeman said.

There was no reply, for Prinsloo turned to van Schoor, as much as to say that it was now up to him. But van Schoor hung back at first. Then he moved slowly forward, a little. He and Willem stared at one another.

Willem's face seemed all distorted to van Schoor, and he

wondered for a moment what had happened to it. Then, of course, he thought, of course, Maclachlan and the others must have given him a hiding when they had first caught him. He looked hard at Willem trying to see exactly what had happened to him, but could not make out the lines of the man's face. All he could see were hollows and darker and lighter places.

Maclachlan said suddenly: 'There's no point in burning away my battery.' He walked away, round the side of the van.

Willem spoke: 'That man has been taking your sheep –'

Prinsloo walked up to him and his fist lifted and struck at Willem's face. This case was going to remain open and closed. Willem swayed and would have fallen if he had not been handcuffed to Ngkane. As it was he hung there, hanging by the steel links of the handcuffs grating against each other.

The lights of the car went out, and the darkness was deeper, though they had always been in shadow. Maclachlan's footsteps came back towards them.

'And what's happening here?' he shouted. Then he saw the way that Willem was hanging, and stopped. He walked slowly up to Willem and put his fist in front of the black man's face. 'Hasn't he had enough yet?' he said, still loudly. 'Do you want some more of this? Haven't you had enough of this?' He shook his fist. 'Willem, you thief, do you want some more? You black swine, do you want some more?' Suddenly, softly and swiftly, he said, 'Well, you're going to get some more,' and his fist too swung back and beat against Willem's face. 'There,' he said. 'There.'

Ngkane's free arm was across his chest and his hand had a fistful of Willem's clothing, holding him up. Willem's head lolled. They all waited in silence, and the head quivered a little. It lifted, sank again, lolling. It lifted and he managed to hold it erect.

Now van Schoor could see that it was Willem's face, though now it was horrible, so much of it featureless blood. He had watched the other men: it had been difficult to believe that those strange gestures that the men had made, like people pushing at a door or showing someone something, had actually been blows against a face. But he felt Maclachlan's hand behind

54

his back. He was being pushed towards the battered Willem. He strained back, but the pressure remained. Or perhaps Maclachlan's arm was behind his back in friendship only. He did not know. He found himself in front of Willem. He stared at him, and Willem looked back, but there was no recognition in Willem's eyes.

'Willem?' van Schoor said.

Willem seemed about to say something. His eyes moved from van Schoor to Maclachlan. He looked back at van Schoor, then lowered his eyes. He said nothing.

'What is going to happen?' van Schoor asked.

Willem shrugged.

'Ha-ha-ha!' van Schoor heard from behind him, from Maclachlan. 'He's going to go to jail. That's what's going to happen.'

Neither Willem nor van Schoor took any notice of this noise, penetrating their own closed and silent little world in the half-darkness at the back of the van.

'What is going to happen?' van Schoor asked again. His eyes and Willem's still met in the same unknowing stare.

Again Willem shrugged, slowly.

'Then there is nothing?' van Schoor said.

Willem did not answer.

'Willem,' van Schoor said, 'why did you have to do it?'

Willem did not answer.

'Why did you have to do it? Was it for money? What made you do it to me?'

Willem said nothing.

Van Schoor shook his head. 'There is nothing.' Then he added, 'I should have known that this was going to happen.' He groaned. He could not stand there any longer in front of Willem, utterly empty, defeated. Was everything a lie? Had everything been a lie?

He asked: 'And Setole? Is that what he knew?'

Willem waited for a moment, as though trying to remember the name. Then he shrugged.

Van Schoor stood silently. A question moved within him, but he did not want to give it expression. Still, it rose to the surface. He lifted one hand towards Willem.

'And where is your respect?'

Willem was motionless, and van Schoor prayed for something, even here, a cheeky remark, anything. His hand opened in front of Willem's face, with the palm naked and empty, and the fingers curled slightly inward, beseeching.

Finally, Willem shrugged.

Van Schoor's hand clenched, and he struck Willem. It was the first time he had ever hit a native not in self-defence. But when he had done it, he was glad. He drew back and waited for Willem to straighten. When Willem did so, he saw that he had hit Willem in the eye, for the one eye was closed. And when he saw it, he remembered, as though from a long time before, doing it; he remembered the feel of the eyeball beneath his fist, soft and resilient against his knuckle. Behind him, he heard Maclachlan and Prinsloo, and he turned vaguely to look at them. They were vague and distant, all seemed swallowed up in an obscure dream, the people and the van and the darkened veld, even Willem. Only near to hand was the feel of Willem's eyeball under his clenched fist.

Was that all, he wondered. He turned to Willem again, and again he slowly lifted his hand and hit, more powerfully this time. He hit against something hard too this time, and felt a sudden savage streak of pain across his knuckles like a living thing; and when he drew his hand away, it was no longer empty. He hit Willem once again, this time on the side of the face, on the cheek, and felt the softness of the flesh and underneath it the hardness of Willem's teeth.

Because he knew that he could go on now until Willem was a pulp, was no longer living, was no longer even a Kaffir, could go on beating Willem till he dropped with exhaustion and the feel of his fist on the other's flesh and bone could no longer have meaning for him, because he was not yet ready for an orgy, he turned to Prinsloo and heavily said, 'All right, you can take him away now.'

The two men jerked out of the spell in which they had lain, as though hypnotized, watching justice being executed, more than justice, right following its ritual in the dark.

'Take him away, Kane,' Prinsloo said, and the dull chained

pair turned to the van. But they could not get up as they had jumped down, and Prinsloo and Maclachlan had to help haul and shove Willem into the back of the van. Van Schoor watched them. He saw Willem's loose and incapable body being handled like a sack of potatoes.

He nursed his right hand. The skin was rough under his fingers, broken, and the bone felt bruised.

When Willem was stowed away, the two others called to van Schoor, asking for coffee and something to eat. Now that the thing was done, the appetites of life returned. And van Schoor found that he too was hungry and thirsty.

He had a last look in the van. He saw the dark bulk of the two Africans, silently side by side on the floor. Further along the dead sheep lay in a paler heap, and as Maclachlan lit a match, for one second he saw the flare of the open eye of the sheep, a green dead glint that was quenched almost immediately.

'Yes, we can have some coffee,' he said. But when he turned to walk up the garden path he saw all the natives of the farm standing in the darkness some distance away and watching silently. 'Swine!' he yelled out, and rushed at them. They all disappeared, except for Willem's wife, who fell to the ground, weeping. He could have kicked her, but he was not yet ready for that either. He walked away, he felt her weeping on the ground, and she crawled after him for a little way, calling out, then grovelled again. She lay on the ground, wailing.

'Well?' van Schoor's wife called out excitedly, loudly, above the wailing from the darkness beyond the fence. 'Well?'

'Well what?' van Schoor said. 'We want some coffee.'

Mrs van Schoor said excitedly and shrilly: 'I always hated that Willem. What did I tell you, Jacob, didn't I tell you, Jacob? And you loved him, didn't you, Jacob?'

'Shut your mouth,' van Schoor said, and strode up to her, one hand lifted. His hand trembled in the air, and Mrs van Schoor shrank, dropped her head, her neck tense. Slowly van Schoor's hand dropped to his side, and slowly Mrs van Schoor lifted her head. She hissed out triumphantly, 'So . . . so . . .' Her eyes shone, and her body remained crouching. She stayed in the lamplight like a glad, demented animal. She could spring now, tomorrow, always, all the days on their farm.

Van Schoor turned his back on her. 'We want our coffee.'

'You'll get your coffee,' she whispered.

'Then go and make it,' van Schoor shouted, body half turning towards her, and then changing. He stood firm. The stoop of his shoulders was like a hunch as he waited for her to go. He did not move until he heard the door close behind her.

Prinsloo came up the steps hesitantly, but Maclachlan was loud-mouthed. They came clambering up, Maclachlan shouting that women did not know how to take these things. 'You should have sent her inside, Jaap. This sort of thing is a job for a man. It upsets the women. You know how they are, Jaap.'

And so, Maclachlan shouting and the others' appetites quickening, they all pushed into the house. In the living-room Mrs van Schoor had turned up two lamps, and the light was harsh. In that harsh light they drank their coffee and talked and joked loudly. It was a strange sort of a meal, at a late hour, like a meal people take before going on a journey.

Outside, lightning flickered across the veld, through the darkness: the day's clouds had been true, rain was going to come after all. And in between, in lulls in the talk, van Schoor heard his wife singing to herself, chanting without meaning, unaware of the others as the brown liquid poured into the shining porcelain cups, as the men tasted its warmth and sweetness in their mouths.

Van Schoor sat, holding his injured hand. It was already beginning to swell; insistently, it was beating against his free hand.

A Dance in the Sun

To Margaret

Part 1

1

This is a story of what happened once to myself and a friend of mine, and of what we saw and heard in a house near a little village in the Karroo. We were hitch-hiking, down to Cape Town, at the time, from my home-town, Lyndhurst, in the Northern Cape.

The first day of our hitch-hike we were lucky. We made almost three hundred miles on only two lifts, both of them quite pleasant people, and both of them in motor-cars, not lorries. But the next day our luck changed. We took up our position on the road outside the village in which we had spent the night, and stood there for hours, while the sun climbed higher and grew fiercer, and the sky paled, and dust hung in the air above us. We lay in the shade under a thorn tree, getting to our feet when we saw by an approaching trail of dust that a car was coming, and signalling to the swift, dusty cars that roared towards us. But we had no luck. No car stopped. The faces in the cars flicked past us, and we turned to see a coil of dust whipping back at each rear tyre as the cars travelled away from us. There were cars, we saw from the registration plates, from all over, even a couple from Salisbury in Southern Rhodesia, people who were travelling two thousand miles for a six-week's holiday by the sea. We ate the sandwiches that we had bought at the hotel where we had spent the night; we drank cool drinks and threw the empty bottles over the barbed wire fence behind us. As the sun stalked higher, our shade shrank. And the veld was enormous and empty, and the sun seemed to have seized the land, sucking all strength from the thorn trees, and the earth, and our own bodies, leaving husks behind, husks of earth, husks of koppies, the vast empty husk of a desert.

A light delivery van eventually picked us up. A young

Afrikaner was driving it. He was quite incurious about us. He and his wife simply stared at us from their high seat, and he said: *'Klim maar op.'*

So we climbed on. The girl was wearing a cotton dress, I remember, and had a *doek* over her head and tied under her chin, to keep her hair in place. I remember that *doek* because it had pictures on it, gay pictures of trees and people walking with little dogs, and underneath the words *Café de la Paix*. I suppose those words were no more odd than they would have been in Johannesburg, but there in the desert, after those hours of waiting, one didn't expect to meet a false souvenir of the Café de la Paix. What did one expect to meet? I don't know. Something dramatic. Lion skins perhaps. Bones bleaching. All we did see of that sort was a dead horse lying by itself in the middle of the low scrub, with nothing near it except the shining railway line. The horse's body had ballooned in the heat, and the four legs were sticking out with a puny stiffness at the corners of the monstrous, swollen body. It was gone in a moment: when I looked back it might have been a rock, an ant-heap, anything.

We sat in the back of the van. We couldn't lean comfortably against the steel sides because of the jolting given the van by the road, and we had to sit erect on our rucksacks. The youngster at the wheel drove fast, and we watched our trail of dust, and shifted about to get more comfortable, or even stood up and leaned against the cab, riding high like Africans new to a lorry job. But the wind always drove us down again. It was most unpleasant, and hot even at that speed. All it did was tangle one's hair and dry one's mouth out.

Once we stopped to urinate, while the girl sat stolidly in the car staring straight in front of her and the three of us went behind a bush. Even on that most friendly of social occasions the youngster said almost nothing to us, not even to ask us where we were going. All he said was, *'Warm, ne?'*, and we, awkwardly, said, *'Ja'* – it was hot.

Then Frank, who was travelling with me, asked when we would get to Droogput, which was the village after the last one we had hurtled through, on our map.

For the first time the youngster looked at us with some

curiosity. *'Ons gaan nie na Droogput nie,'* he said. We looked at each other. If we weren't going to Droogput, where were we going? He walked back to the van, and just before climbing in said: *'Ek gaan terug na my plaas. Dis net een myl van Mirredal af.'* And he slammed the door.

Well, we weren't going to be left alone in the Karroo, miles from anywhere, in the middle of the heat and not a sign of a house or anything else in all the great plain. There was only the road, and the telegraph poles, their wires stretching and slackening, stretching and slackening, being pulled with pain across the empty veld. And a four-stranded wire fence. So we scrambled on the back of the van, and sat.

I have no idea how far we travelled. My watch had stopped and Frank did not have one. But it must have been a good sixty or seventy miles since our break before we stopped again. We passed through one or two little places: they weren't even villages, just stores with a petrol pump outside and perhaps the railway line curving towards it and then swinging away again. We ourselves seemed to be travelling along the line: we would lose and return to it in sweeps across the country. Once we saw a goods train standing at a siding and steaming idly into the sky, motionless, with no one stirring about it, as if it had always been there. The van did not stop and we did not ask him to drop us off. At least while we were travelling we were moving, even if it were in the 'wrong direction. And we did seem to be moving at least vaguely southwards, for the sun sloped down, well down now, to the right.

So the hours, miles passed. Now when I try to remember that journey I can remember of it barely one particular by which one remembers one journey from another. I remember Frank yelling at me that Mirredal was miles off the main road to the Cape, but that we could get back to it the next day by going through Suurfontein. Once the girl in front turned and stared at us through the little oval window at the back of the cab. I stared back at her, but she did not smile. Her chin was red and thrust forward a little, her lower lip remained primly sucked in. I don't think she could have been more than seventeen, or perhaps eighteen. I remember wondering why I had decided that the two in front of us were husband and wife, and not brother and sister, or cousins, or neighbours. And I remember the road being sucked away beneath us, disappearing with a roar and a rattle, like a wide white chain, and the dust, and the sun on the side of my head.

And then the car swung off the road and came to a halt in front of a gate with a final swirl of dust that eddied closely about us as the car rocked. We jumped off the back and came round to the driver's window.

'Where are we?' I asked.

'Mirredal,' the man replied. He pointed beyond me, and I turned and saw a village some miles away at the end of a grey stretch of veld. The veld sloped slowly up towards the village, of which only its trees could be seen – there must have been some sort of a fold in the ground that was hidden from us. The sun was sloping towards the west above the ragged line of trees that marked the *dorp,* and our journey with the untalkative couple was over.

I opened the gate for them, and let it swing against a bank of sand. The van ground through, and I waved at them and then dragged the gate back and put the steel link over the hook on the metal gate-post. On the post there was a sheet of flattened zinc with the name of the farm painted in black upon it: *Kameelhaak.* The driver had lifted one hand from the steering wheel – that was all. We watched the van go off slowly, bumping along the track through the veld, with its back to us. The scrub was so low and sparse that it was difficult for us to know which was the track and which simply bare veld. But the van moved cautiously on, bumping and bumping along the flat, rocky surface of the country. It was still jerking along, the only moving thing in the veld, when we turned and began walking to Mirredal.

We were stiff and thirsty, and our packs were heavy. But it was peaceful walking along the wide, empty road of sand, in the silence and heat, with our ears attuning themselves to silence after the battering they had received during the drive. The gritty earth was firm under our feet, and the emptiness of the country was not in any way alarming, for we saw the line of trees drawing nearer as we walked. The sun was brave, now, not excessive; and there was not a cloud in the sky. The nearer koppies shone, and those further away were hooded in a cowl of dark blue light. It was unendingly strange to see how the koppies rose from the veld bearing all their burden of rock upon them, and then fell back: they seemed to have nothing to do with the rest of the bare, stretched-out veld, flat under the sun, whose lines they could not alter.

Then the road turned at a gate and a cattle-grid, and sloped towards a *pan*. There was a small native location beside the *pan,* in the long hollow – the usual mess, the location, of sacking and flattened paraffin tins, stolen bits of corrugated iron, twigs, mud and cow-dung stuck together to make huts for people to live in. There was no water in the *pan,* and on its shrivelled surface half-naked brown children were playing, throwing pieces of the dried crisp clay at one another. The road sloped up. On the upward slope the village lay.

It didn't look much of a place either. The usual Karroo village with its two or three wide sandy streets: the usual police station of stone and a corrugated iron roof, a flag-staff and a bed of flowers before it, which a barefoot native convict was tending; the usual two or three general dealers' stores; the little bank with green-glazed windows and a brass name-plate announcing it as such; the lawyer's name-plate in blue letters on white enamel outside a tiny office and the list of insurance companies and agricultural implement manufacturers he represented; a garage made entirely of unpainted corrugated iron, the soil before it stained black with oil round the bright petrol pump; a tattered red and white poster giving the name of the attraction the travelling bioscope had brought when it had last visited the village. And the Dutch Reformed Church at the top of the village: a building with a nondescript butt of a body, and a rather low steeple pointing straight upwards, as if to draw one's attention to the disparity between its size and that of the space that surrounded it.

As usual with such villages, it was spread over a great area. Hardly one house stood against another; always there was a bare space between them, or a stunted orchard, or a mealie patch. The church stood in grounds the size of a couple of rugby fields. The whole village was ragged like that, with too much space for what it was. The houses were mostly of one sort – small, single-storied buildings, huddles of rooms, sloping corrugated iron roofs above white-washed plaster walls in different grades of whiteness, many of them cracked and peeling, crude red bricks showing through. Everything looked impermanent, caravan-like, and only the decrepitude of the village showed for how long a time it had been there.

The hotel at least had had sense enough not to call itself the Grand, or the Queen's. It was called the 'Mirredal Hotel', on a painted sheet-metal poster above the roof of the stoep. Once it had been called something else, and those letters still came through beneath the newer title, in a blur. The long stoep, raised unevenly above the level of the sand of the road, sometimes six inches, sometimes as much as eighteen, was quite deserted. We walked into the bar, and were met with bad news. The bartender told us they weren't putting up any more people for the night.

'The place is full, man,' he said.

'Full?' He saw us smiling with disbelief.

'Yes man, full,' he said earnestly. 'There's a big wedding on one of the farms here, and all the visitors are staying here. As true as God, we've got no room.'

'Where are all the visitors?' I asked.

He told me that they'd all got into their cars and driven to the bride's farm. 'You wait here, and you'll see them all coming back,' he offered, as proof to us.

We asked him for two beers, which he served to us. 'You'll easily find another place, you know,' he told us.

'Where is another place?'

'Well –' he spoke very deliberately now. 'You saw the church outside?'

'Ja.'

'Well, you walk past the church. Now the main road goes like this past the church, and you leave it on your left, like this.' He gestured awkwardly, constricted behind the counter. 'There's a sort of road going off. You go along it towards the river.'

'The river?'

'Yes man, there's a river just on the other side of the *opdraand*.' Seeing our disbelief, this time he smiled suddenly.

'All right, it isn't much of a river. But there's a big house there and they take people. They had plans: they were going to start some sort of a home for sick people. A sanatorium,' he said, remembering the word. 'This *dorp* is hell of a good for T.B. they say. But nothing ever came of it. Now they just take people sometimes. It's more like a boarding house, but I don't know that they got people there now.'

We thanked him for the information, and stayed on in the coolness of the bar, drinking the beer he had served us. The bartender was wearing a yellow shirt and bright blue slacks; the sleeves of his yellow shirt were rolled down and tied at the cuffs with big black and silver links, and puffed over red and black armbands above his elbows. His thin brown hair was sharply combed, the strands lying raked away on either side of the neat path. And he had a moustache too, very trim, which he would tug between thumb and forefinger every now and again, with a fierce little gesture, thrusting his head forward, as if to show us each time: there, it's real, it won't come off. He talked a great deal. He asked us if we followed the horses, and though we said no he told us that he took bets from people in the *dorp* on the meetings in Cape Town. 'And hell, you'd be surprised to see the people who come along here to make their bets. The *predikant* doesn't come perhaps, but his son does, every week. He's farming in the district here.' He was lonely and wistful in a way, for all his chatter and bright clothing, and followed us to the door, repeating his instructions on how to get to the other place. I saw his arm in its bright yellow sleeve pointing across the ragged, dun-coloured veld. 'You can't miss it. You can't go wrong from here.' He stood at the door and watched us go, with his hands in his pockets: I think he was half-hoping that we would go wrong, so that he would be able to explain things to us again.

But he had been right: we could not miss it. We stepped into the sand of the village and followed his directions. We walked past the church grounds, over the rise, and there, on the other side, was the river. The slope of the ground towards it was bare enough, but the river was something twisted on the surface of the veld, more desolate in its dryness than the ground around it. Here the rocks were gathered together, and smooth and black, lying all the way down the river-bed, and on either shallow bank. It had no water at all. We crossed it at the ford, where cattle crossed it – their tracks were like casts in the dry clay – and left behind us the round gleaming boulders, the thorn trees that grew between them in gulleys of river sand.

The house was a big, rambling place, and looked very old. We walked up the main cement path, reddened with dye, cracked with age, between small palm trees planted in old petrol tins on which the trade names could still be faintly seen. There was no one about, and the sun shone strongly in the old garden, with its few pomegranate trees and beds marked out with bricks for flowers that had not grown, and the grass that was clustered round one leaking tap. The shadows all leaned towards the house, but none of the trees or bushes were tall enough to cast it into shade. The stoep was raised a few concrete steps above the level of the garden and ran the full length of the front of the house. The same sort of palms as in the garden grew sadly from petrol tins all along its length, one every few yards. All the windows were barred against the sun by heavy wooden shutters. The place was silent, deserted in appearance, like a house that had been abandoned and left to rot and crumble away in the heat, no one caring.

Our knock on the door was not answered. From the tallest tree in the garden, a straight silver oak in the corner, a single dove called, and the ground throbbed through the still air and the yellow light, before the bird fell silent again. We stood on the stoep, dusty and sweaty and tired, and stared at one another. Frank said he would go round the side of the house to see if anyone was there. There wasn't even a piccanin in front that we could have sent round to ask the baas or missus to come. There was no one.

Frank walked away down the stoep. He was cut off from my sight by a projection in the house, where one of the shutters presented its bars to the sun. I sat on the packs and waited for something to happen.

When it did, it happened quietly and genteelly enough. I heard footsteps and turned, stood up, as a woman came wandering down the stoep towards me. 'Is there anything I can do for you, young man?' she asked when she was a yard or two away from me. She stood in front of me, with her hands hanging to the sides of her body in a rather ungainly and awkward way. That was all I noticed of her, at first. That, and a faded red cardigan she was wearing, though the day was so warm.

'My friend and I want accommodation,' I said. 'We were told that we could come here by the man at the hotel.'

'Why don't you stay at the hotel?' she asked, not moving towards me.

I was a little taken aback. 'They're full,' I said. 'So we were hoping that you'd be able to put us up.'

'We haven't done that for so long,' she said, almost reprovingly.

'Couldn't you do it now?'

She was very grave when she answered: 'That is what we're supposed to do. We are in business putting people up.'

'Good.'

She took a pace back immediately. 'I shall have to ask my husband. He may not want to. I can't really say.' She looked at me. She was thin and slight and grey, grey-haired, grey-skinned. Even her lips were colourless. But under the thin lids that she occasionally dropped over her eyes, and let linger, there were, when she opened them, eyes of the palest blue, the lightest colour, as though they too were fading, dissolving into no colour. She looked at me and her eyes seemed transparent, and there was nothing behind them: the translucence seemed more a state of mind than a physical phenomenon. She said: 'It wouldn't do if I were to raise your hopes and then tell you that you couldn't stay here after all. Would it?'

'No,' I said.

'Then you must wait here. And I'll come back and tell you.' She turned her back on me, and went down the stoep, like a swift shadow. Again I saw her hands thrust awkwardly outwards, and it was jarring to see them. The rest of her was so little there: but her hands compelled the attention, sticking out as they did on either side of her body, as if she did not want them near her. She moved quickly; she was gone in a moment round the side of the house.

I remained on the stoep, in the yellow light of the sun, and waited for her to come back. Frank came back before she did.

He said, 'God knows what's going on in this house. There's no one. There's an old African, but he didn't know what I was talking about. He sat in the sun and shook his head at everything I said. "*Nee my basie, ek weet niks*" – that was all I could get out of him.'

I told Frank that I had spoken to a woman, and that she had gone to see if we could be put up.

'They've got enough room,' Frank said. We both looked at the long empty stoep with all its shuttered windows. Then he added: 'They haven't been opened for years.' He was standing a few yards away from me, examining one of the shutters. He held up a hand to show me the dust it had collected when it had touched the shutter. Then he tugged at the shutter. It wouldn't open. The house was locked, and old, but not in any romantic way. It was old because it was falling apart in the heat and unusedness of everything, falling apart, built too rapidly, years before, near the Karroo village. But Frank desisted abruptly from his tugging when the woman came back and called to him:

'Why are you doing that?'

Frank had nothing to say for himself, so he stood guiltily with his hands behind his back. Then the woman turned her attention to myself. She spoke in a thin, dry voice, and as solemnly as before.

'My husband says that you can spend the night here if you like. Will you come with me?' I could not tell from her accent whether she was usually Afrikaans or English-speaking; her voice was neutral, South African. We stood for a moment in silence, until I realized that she was waiting for some answer from us.

'Of course,' I said. 'Thank you.'

Then she took a very large key from a pocket of her dress and unlocked the front door, tugging the handle towards her to get the lock to yield. I saw how her hand enveloped the handle, suddenly, though it was one of those round, swelling handles made of a kind of marble, and a big one of its sort. The door opened and we stepped in: it closed behind us with a bang that made every thick cube and lozenge of coloured glass in its upper half clatter.

'This way to your room,' she said, leading the way, and took us down a passage heavily festooned with buck horns that grew like creepers from the walls. Each pair was attached to the wooden plaque from which it grew by a small front of bone, through which screws had been driven. There were all sorts and sizes, from the dainty little horns of a stembuck to the solemn spiral armament of a koodoo; most of them started only a little higher than eye-level, and the smaller sets had others above. We went, between the horns, down the passage and into a kind of reception room, where there was a round table covered with a blue and yellow cloth of imitation silk, two musty easy chairs, and a portrait on the wall. The portrait had been done for the most part in dark blue and a kind of cream colour for the face and hands. It showed a youngish man in old-fashioned clothing standing to the side of a dark-blue chair, with one hand upon it, and the other hand holding a rolled-up diploma of some sort: the diploma and the hand were the same colour exactly, and at first glance the man might have been suffering from some fantastic disfigurement of his hand. His face was cream-coloured and looked like nobody special; I couldn't have undertaken to recognize anybody from that portrait even if it had been of a close friend of mine. Unless my friend had happened to have had a navy-blue moustache and navy-blue eyes in real life as well as in the portrait, in which case he would probably have been unmistakable. Above the moustache the man's eyes stared straight across the room at a pair of *wildebeest* horns, mounted more carefully than those in the passage, and bound in the centre with a piece of purple velvet which concealed the screws. We had ample time to look at the room's decorations, for the woman had disappeared, saying, 'I shan't be a moment.'

Then she came back. She caught Frank's eye on the portrait, and I think she hesitated for a moment whether or not to say anything which was not strictly to the point of our visit. Then some feeling – pride perhaps – won through, and she said: 'It's my father. It was done in Holland. He was at a university there in Leyden.'

'It's very nice,' Frank said, but she was not apparently looking for compliments from him.

'Yes,' she said shortly. She led us down another passage, and then opened the door of a room. There were two huge single beds covered with white woven covers, a washstand with a marble top on which rested a china jug and basin, a large window shuttered against the sun, a pale green carpet with a pattern of red flowers woven into it. 'Supper is at seven o'clock. If you want hot water for anything you must ask me. Or you can ask the boy.'

She left us in the room with our luggage. The first thing we did was to open the window and the shutters outside it, and let in some air. But the air that drifted through the wide-open entrance was heavy, laden with all the weariness of the late afternoon in a desert climate.

2

Beneath his eyes, on the most forward point of the curve of his cheek-bones, there were fine blonde hairs growing, in two downward-sloping tufts. They gave his face the gloss, the sheen, of the face of an animal. I think the hairs were there simply because he was lazy in his shaving, and left them to grow long and soft, all the more noticeable because of the smoothness of the rest of his face. And he half-crouched at the end of the table, low over his food, in the puttering light of the electric generator whose beat we could hear from outside. He ate little, but he talked a great deal, about all sorts of things, up-to-date things. 'Atomic power will change the surface of the globe within the next twenty-five years,' he told us. 'There'll be aeroplanes flying to London in no time at all. Liners will cross the Atlantic on a piece of coal the size of a pea. You mark my words,' he said. 'This country will be unrecognizable. They'll irrigate the Karroo. Hitler had a plan like that for Africa. In the Sahara too. They'll irrigate the Sahara with canals, once they've got the power.'

He looked us boldly in the eye. When he made a joke he laughed loudly at what he himself had said. He was not parochial or lost in the silences of the land he had come to live in;

he was of our world. 'Johannesburg,' he said, 'Johannesburg will be the capital of Africa. It's the uranium they've got there that will make it the capital of Africa.'

He talked about the world situation. There would be a blow-up, he said, between Russia and the United States. 'Ker-boom!' he exclaimed, his hands mushrooming over the white tablecloth. 'Everything smashed! Everything broken! Cities in ruins – Moscow, New York, London, in ruins. Everything radio-active. And then they'll form a world government, a government for the whole world. It'll have a capital in some place where there's never been a city before, and they'll have their police and their air force and their stock of bombs. And if they ever see anybody else trying to build up a stock of bombs – ker-boom! And that will be the end of the rebellion. What do you think of that – hey?'

We said we didn't know.

'I'm telling you,' the man said emphatically. 'Those are the things that are going to happen. You just have to read your newspapers and you can see.' He added: 'And a few books.' Then he fell upon his food as if he had just seen that it had been placed before him. But he did not maintain his attack on it for long.

The husband was the last sort of person that one would have expected the woman to have. She was so thin and wisp-like, like something stricken by drought, but her husband had a big head and smooth, shining blond hair that fell over his forehead as he talked. He looked several years younger than she, and he ate his supper in his shirt-sleeves, with his brown elbows resting on the tablecloth. Apart from his head there was nothing very big about him; his neck seemed to have some difficulty in supporting his head upright, and his arms were positively skinny. He was verbose and jovial, and had a bright brown eye that he moved in jerks round the table: when he looked at a person his gaze stuck there until – jerk, jump – his eyes were on another. He shouted sometimes.

He shouted, for instance, at the servant, habitually, without thought, without lifting his head to do so, as he at least had the grace to do when he shouted at us. But for the servant it was as though he could not be bothered to lift up his large head, that drooped a little in his normal posture, over the table. 'Bring the salt,' he shouted at the servant in English. And the servant said, '*Ja baas*,' and brought the salt. 'Where's the sauce?' he shouted. The servant looked at him, not understanding, standing to the side of the table with his tray flat and open before him, clutched in both hands. 'Sauce! Sauce! Sauce!' '*Hy's klaar baas.*' 'Don't tell me the sauce is finished. I saw the bottle in the sideboard there this morning.' He jabbed towards the sideboard with his finger, and the servant went to the drawer indicated and pulled out a heavy cruet, laden with metal jars. One of the jars was missing, and in its place there was a bottle of Worcester Sauce. The servant brought the cruet to the table and placed it in front of his master, after a moment in which he had struggled to release his finger from the ring from which the cruet was suspended. The man laughed loudly at this. 'Now when I tell you to bring the sauce you bring it, and don't start arguing with me.' '*Ja baas.*' For the servant's sake I hoped that he would remember what the word sauce meant, for he had obviously not known when the man had first shouted at him.

The man was pleased with his triumph. 'Did you see that?' he asked. 'He was too lazy to fetch it so he tells me that it's finished. What do you think of that? They're all the same,' he said, watching me brightly, 'every last one of them.' But then he had been watching either Frank or myself throughout his little scene.

And the scene reminded him of his world government. The members of the government, he said, would be a specially chosen *élite*. Perhaps they would have their own language. And they would certainly wear uniforms, distinctive uniforms, so that everyone would know who they were and have respect for them. And they would be all whites, of course, while the non-white races would be what God ordained them to be: hewers of wood and drawers of water. 'The kaffirs and the *koelies* will know their places. They'll tremble when they see one of those uniforms come. Tremble!' he said, with horrible emphasis, his own voice trembling, enacting what the kaffirs and the *koelies* would do. And then he abruptly asked me what I studied at the university. When he heard that I was studying English he asked me: 'What's the good of that? So you've learned a lot of words – does that help you?' And to Frank he said: 'Medicine? So in a few years time you'll come out of medical school thinking you know everything. I wonder how many you'll kill before you learn that you don't. Thank God they let you practise on the kaffirs. Mind you,' he added, suddenly magnanimous, 'if you were to be really good there'd be room for you in the world of government. It'll be a high honour. They won't take any pipsqueak from medical school, I assure you.'

'And can I wear the uniform, too?' Frank asked.

The man suspected nothing. 'You'll be proud to wear that uniform, my boy.' Then he turned to me. 'You'll be his boot-boy when he's in the world government. You'll be only too happy if he lets you clean his boots for him.'

'Perhaps they'll have atomic boot-cleaners by then,' Frank said.

The man appreciated that. He roared suddenly. 'That's a good one. Atomic boot-cleaners, I must remember that. Atomic boot-cleaners – what?' he shouted. 'They'll have atomic *boots* by then.'

He was all out to impress us, and eager to do so as quickly as possible. For instance, when we discussed the native problem – or rather, when he did so – the views he advanced were stale and stupid and vicious enough: 'All the educated kaffirs should be shot.' But what was odd was the way he advanced this view. Usually, when people say that sort of thing, they are serious about it, they mean what they say. But with him I had the feeling that he spoke not so much out of conviction – though that was probably there too – but more to force our assent from us. And the nature of the assent he was demanding from us was that the views had to be violent ones: if all the educated kaffirs should not be shot, then the agitators would do, or the communists, or the liberals: what was essential for his purpose was that someone should be shot. And we had to nod our heads: yes, we had to say, we quite agree with you.

We had both lived long enough in the country of our birth to know that to attempt to argue with people who talk the way that man did is a waste of time and temper, but for all that we weren't going to tell him yes, we thought all the educated kaffirs should be shot. And he dropped the subject when he saw we weren't impressed. Dropped it only to pick up another promptly. He started telling us about his dabbling in gold shares on the stock exchange, and here we did not have to give our assent to what he was saying: we simply had to admire him, marvel over his acumen. To listen to him he might have been Rhodes or Barnato or Oppenheimer, any financial wizard you may care to think of: he laid it on thick enough, about how he'd kept this packet for two years and sold it just before the shares started dropping, and how he'd bought that one in the basement and clung to them until they went through the roof. He and his wife had apparently been sheep-farming, in the district, and then, many years before, when the man's father-in-law had died they had moved into the house they were now in: like the farm it had previously belonged to his father-in-law. They had had plans for a kind of rest-house for convalescents – nothing as grand as a sanatorium. But he did not seem disturbed at all that nothing had come of their plans, so I gathered that they were sufficiently well-to-do anyway, perhaps as a result of the man's speculations on the share-market, perhaps not.

For it was extremely difficult to know how much value to attach to any of the man's words. The things he was saying – about the native problem, or finance – were cheap and com-monplace enough, really, but what was not commonplace was the energy he flung into them. And this energy went with an apparent indifference to what he was talking about: he could, as it were, change the subject, but not drop his voice. And if one topic was as important to him as any other then obviously no topic was of any real importance. No, I think all he was interested in, ultimately, was assent and submission from our-selves. He marched upon us like a marauder, and he seemed to care for nothing but his immediate victory.

He angered me a little, I must say. I could have borne with him expressing his views, I might even have been able to con-gratulate him on his financial success: what I could not stand was the personal urgency and insistence with which he thrust himself at us – while watery soup gave way to stringy meat followed by stewed dried fruit and coffee. We ate it all steadily, Frank and I; we were the only ones who gave much attention to the food. The man's voice boomed away in the closed-in room, overcrowded with furniture. Behind me there was a mahogany sideboard the length of one wall, surmounted by a mirror which ran its full length and must have been, together with the sideboard, eight feet high: throughout the meal I had the uncomfortable feeling that something was leaning over the back of my head. Behind the host there was a thick black piece of furniture to which I cannot give a name, but at least his crouched below him, and not above as mine did. Each of us had a side of the large square table to ourselves. Opposite Frank there was a mezzotint of a view across a lake, with gauzy mountains all about it, and a boat like a gondola in the middle of it. The picture was enormous and was set in a plain black frame at least six inches deep. The one small window was draped with a heavy closed curtain made of some red material. And in all the heaviness and elaborateness of the room's furniture, only the light was ungarnished, unfoiled, and the one bulb hung too low over the table, without any covering whatsoever, so that my eyes watered whenever I looked at it.

And the man told us about the share-market, the native problem, the prices local farmers were getting for their wool, which was the best magazine published in South Africa and which the worst, the service he had got out of his car, a boxing match that was due to take place shortly in Cape Town, world affairs and the imminent war between Russia and the United States – he returned to that topic a few times: it seemed to hold his imagination – and the shortcomings of the Mirredal Hotel. Only when the coffee came did he at last fall silent. His wife had been silent throughout the meal, serving from the bowls which the African servant brought to her place. 'If you please,' she had said, as she handed Frank and I our soup, or our meat, or our sweet. To her husband she had said nothing at all when passing him his plates, except once, pushing towards him the bread in a small wickerwork basket, one word, 'Here.'

We were glad enough when he did fall silent. I produced

cigarettes after coffee, and offered one to my hostess, who refused, and one to the host, who refused with a brushing-away movement of his hand. At that I asked if I had their permission to smoke, which the man granted with a nod. We had eaten food after a long day, so we relaxed, and I think they did too a little – if the man's silence was any indication. It was impossible to say whether the woman relaxed when her husband fell silent: she remained upright and flimsy in her chair, and did not speak at all. But several times she cast her eyes down to the table, and that, hooding her eyes as the movement did, seemed like a relaxation. For the blank openness of her gaze had always been disturbing; it had been as though she could afford to be open because what she was with us was something to which she attached no import-ance.

I was the only one smoking. I saw the clouds of smoke, blue when they left my mouth, greying suddenly against the light-bulb. Frank took off his glasses and played with them on the tablecloth – without his glasses his face looked bare and owl-like, with two large white circles round his eyes where the lenses had protected his skin from the rays of the sun. The man sat with his hands locked together on the white cloth; the woman's arms hung down the sides of her body. The African servant cleared everything away until the tablecloth was blank, but for a few crumbs, and the ash-tray which he had brought to my place in response to a snarled exhortation from his master. Then he went, closing the door carefully behind him. The light in the room beat in time with the putter of the elec-tric generator outside, whose noise we could hear: the flicker was exhausting to the eyes, continuously, though the beat of the engine would be lost to the ear sometimes, fading, be caught again, beating time.

The man's eyes went to Frank and myself. 'You're an intelligent pair of youngsters,' he said unexpectedly. 'Do you know that?' For the first time since we had seen him at the table he turned to his wife and spoke to her. 'Here's an intelli-gent pair of youngsters. And they're on holiday.'

His wife did not move. 'So?' she asked, in her even voice, quiet after the sound of her husband's.

The man looked from Frank to myself. Then he gave his false, loud laugh. 'Nothing.' But he kept his eyes on us.

'I know they're on holiday,' his wife said. 'So?'

'I said, nothing,' the man replied loudly.

'Then why did you say it?' the wife asked. 'Why did you say that the boys were on holiday?' She spoke so evenly it was difficult to understand why she had agitated herself sufficiently to speak to him at all. But she insisted. 'You must mean something, otherwise you wouldn't have said it.'

The man put his hands flat down on the tablecloth, and turned his face towards her. 'Later,' he said, speaking quietly. 'Later.' He waited until it became quite clear that his wife was not going to say anything again before looking at us. Then he smiled, though his mind, to put it as kindly as possible, was not exactly on the smile.

However, only a few seconds passed before he began telling us about the exorbitantly high price he had obtained in selling a piece of land to a newcomer to the district. 'He doesn't speak to me now,' he told us, proudly, as evidence of his success. But before he could work his voice up to the previous tone of braggadocio which it had held, we excused ourselves from the table: we had had enough of him to get along with.

3

After supper I went out by myself. The room in which we had eaten had been so darkened by walls and curtains and furniture that I was surprised to see, on emerging from the house, how light it still was. The sun had set already, but at the moment the sky was not merely still light, but coloured, in a soft spectrum that stretched from horizon to horizon. In the east the sky was grey, a clean night-grey, but above me it was still blue. And then, as my eye moved westwards, I saw the blue yield to green, and the green to orange, and the orange to a last violent red that marked the place where the sun had set, as the clouds, barred with black, had gathered there. But only in the far western corner of the sky was there any violence: for the rest the colours were all gentle and their graduations imperceptible, so that the bowl of the sky was luminous with a soft light, unerratic, gathering its strength towards the west without harshness. And the purity of the sky directly above me was unflawed by a single cloud; the surface of light was smooth and soft and the eye could travel about it without effort or volition.

I stood in front of the house, quite well away from it, on the far side of the river-bed. To my right the scattered lights of the village were beginning to shine feebly. In front of me a couple of lights shone from the house I had just left: one in our room, where Frank was shaving for tomorrow's journey, and the other I presumed from the room to which the couple had retired. There was a light too from the side of the house, some way behind it: a native's hut, perhaps that of the servant who had attended our meal. And those were all the lights I could see, perhaps ten in all, hardly more. Above, the sky rose sheer with its own light; below, the veld, in silence, was merging into duller colours, blacks and russets and ambers. And the greyness in the east was advancing.

Even within my circumscribed sight I could see how forlorn all the growing things were. I could see one taller thorn-tree standing up from the surface of the veld: the light pierced through its rough branches and small spike-like leaves in a thousand places, leaving it black and tangled and weightless, like something that could be blown away in the first strong gust of wind. And for the rest there were only the low Karroo bushes, barely twelve inches high, each demanding a space of sand on which nothing else grew, each low tuft islanded in a sea of barren sand. Growth here was a bitter and constricted business. The only thing that was not constricted was the sky and the space of earth. There was an immensity of space above my head, and the night gathering above could not hide the great sweep of earth away from my little summit, a lavish generosity of space given unconditionally to drought and silence.

As I watched I saw how rapidly the light of the sky was fading, and how already the little bushes were darkening, as though they were the first to be dragged down by the darkness that would later cover all that I could see. The light in the west was flatter now, sinking towards the horizon. It would soon be night: the serenity and passion of the colours would be brief, above the harsh, wide land.

I turned; I was about to walk slowly back to the house, when I heard a man's voice.

'Baas,' I heard.

I looked about me. I could see no one.

'Baas,' the voice came again. I saw an African standing on the opposite side of the river-bank. 'Baas,' he said. His voice was subdued and sure. 'Can you help me?'

It was getting dark and I did not know who he was or what he wanted of me; I would have been suspicious of any African I met like that. 'What is it?' I asked. I felt the emptiness of space behind my back like a nakedness. And he was between myself and the house. 'What do you want?' I asked, making my voice loud and unafraid.

'I want you to help me,' he said.

'In what way?' But now that the surprise was over my anxiety was ebbing. 'How can I help you?'

'I will show the baas,' he called back quietly. And then he began to cross the dry river-bed, coming towards me.

I again felt a small prickling of alarm when I saw, as he drew himself up on the summit, how big he was. His waist and chest were of a piece, tree-like, and not one of those gnarled Karroo trees either. He took off his hat as he approached me, and held it crumpled in one hand.

'What is it you want?' I asked, and as I did so he put his hand in a pocket of his overalls and brought out an envelope.

'I want you to read this letter to me, baas,' he said reasonably.

'Oh,' I said. I thought how unworthy I had been, suspecting him, when this was what he wanted. 'Of course I'll help you.'

He extended the letter towards me. 'Baas,' he said.

I took the letter and opened it. The envelope had already been torn open, and inside there was a single sheet of paper, folded. The letter was in Afrikaans, written in a small, neat hand. Only the capital letters were large with loops. 'Dear Chrissie,' I began to read. Then I looked at the name at the bottom of the letter. It was signed 'Ignatius Louw.'

'Is this letter to you?' I asked.

'No,' he said.

'Who is it to?'

He gestured, opening the fingers of one hand, saying nothing.

'Who is it to?' I asked again.

'Baas,' he said slowly, 'it's a letter to another missus that I want you to read to me.' He added, reminding me: 'The baas said that he would read the letter to me.'

'I know I said that. But I thought the letter was to you.'

'Well, now the baas has seen that it isn't. It's to another missus.'

'Did you steal this letter?' I asked. 'It wasn't given to you, was it?'

'No, baas, it wasn't given to me.'

'So you did steal it?'

He waited a moment or two before replying: 'Yes baas.'

'Then how can you expect me to read it to you?' I asked.

'It's stolen from that house,' he said, pointing across the river: he seemed to imagine that that would make it easier for me.

'That's where I'm staying,' I said. 'I could get you into trouble.'

'I know, baas.'

'Look –' I said, 'I don't want to get you into trouble. Just take this letter now and go.' I stretched my hand holding the letter towards him, but he drew back, and put his hands behind him, as if indicating that I would only be able to make him take it back by the use of force.

'Take the letter,' I said.

'No,' he replied, still with his hands behind his back.

'Very well then.' I put the letter in my pocket.

'Are you going to the police, baas?'

'No,' I said. 'I'm going to tear the letter up. You should never have come to me like this. I could get you into trouble.' My hand was in the pocket of my trousers, holding the

84

crumpled letter, and I turned away as if to go towards the house.

He said: 'The ba\s isn't going to make trouble for me?'

'No,' I said. 'You're lucky.' I must admit that I was reluctant to turn my back on him. I felt that with just one of those arms of his that dangled idly at his hips he could throw me on my back without very much difficulty. And it was getting darker. What sustained me then was his calmness of manner, and a disbelief in the possibility of violence in a veld so large and silent. The light was going rapidly: the flare in the west was orange, the bushes, sparse and dry about our ankles, black. And the air seemed immutably still, as if it were waiting for the last light to disappear before it could move again.

'I knew the baas wasn't a Boer,' the African said.

This may have been a tribute to the Afrikaans I had spoken to him, but it was rather more than that too. If he had approached me on the strength of my not being an Afrikaner, or Boer as he preferred to put it, he had been foolhardy and reckless: English-speaking whites are not necessarily more friendly to the Africans than Afrikaans-speaking whites. Surely he knew that. I said to him: 'So? Just because I'm not a Boer doesn't mean that I won't make trouble for you.'

'No baas,' he admitted. I thought he was going to go on, but apparently he had made the remark in a hope that it might win me over: having seen its failure, he abandoned the attempt without further ado.

'Are you going to take the letter?' I asked for the last time.

He turned away from me and gazed across the river-bed that flowed now with darkness in its hollow. He looked across it, towards the house in its garden of sand, with the single silver oak upright and dark before it, and the blue inhospitable veld massing in darkness behind it, under the night-grey sky. Two lights still shone from the broad, single storied house, shrinking lower as the darkness came closer around it. Barely any vegetation protected the house, and there were no other houses to measure it against: only the dark sky and the dark, dwarfing veld. Then the man turned back to me. 'I wouldn't ask you to read the letter to me if I could read,' he said.

'I know,' I said.

'I ask you,' he said. He leaned forward and stretched out his hand. I gave him the letter, and he took it from me. He took the paper out of the envelope and carefully unfolded it. He stared at the writing he could not decipher; I moved more closely forward to see if he were holding it the right way up. He was, but by the characteristically cautious way he handled the paper, and by the way he moved it from left to right within his hands, as if trying it out at different angles, I knew that he was so illiterate that he was not sure whether or not he did, in fact, have it right. His fingers were large and clumsy, and yet they curled themselves almost timidly upon the paper. I was touched by the way he handled the letter – moved with pity and guilt for him, so large, so puzzled. He stared at the paper in silence; his fingers had stopped shifting it about; apparently he had decided that he did have it the right way up. He looked at it intently, almost as if he hoped that its meaning would emerge from it if he treated it with sufficient respect. 'I can't read,' he said at last, reluctantly taking his eyes from the paper. 'I'm like a child. I'm many years older than the baas, but I have to ask you to help me. You can read, the missus can read, Baas Fletcher can read – but I – I –' He lifted his fist and shook it in front of his chest, more at himself than anybody. Though his movements had for the first time been agitated, his voice was quiet when he said: 'I've been walking round for two hours with that letter in my pocket.'

'Why do you want to read it?' I asked.

'Baas,' he said. 'I paid the servants in the house to steal this letter for me. I'm not trying to take money or things away from the house. But I must know what's in the letter. If I could read I would have read it already, and have put it back and it would have been finished.'

'Has Mrs Fletcher seen the letter?' I asked.

'Of course,' he said. 'She waits for these letters.' Then he thrust the letter towards me and cried, 'Please baas, help me. Help me to read.'

I wish I could say that it was some kind of 'political' act that I read the letter to him, or that I did it because I had been so impressed by the character of the man in front of me that I could not believe him capable of any mean or purposeless dishonesty. I did read the letter to him, but not for any such respectable reason. I read it out of pique, out of spite, out of mischievousness: it was a way of sticking my tongue out at the man who had bored and irritated me at supper. 'All the educated kaffirs should be shot' – that had been his motto. Well, here was an uneducated kaffir in difficulty because of his lack of an education: I'd lend him mine. And the fact that the letter came from the man's house was all the more a way of exercising a spite.

The letter was very brief.

'Dear Chrissie,' [I read]

I am coming home. I have lost this new job so I'm hitch-hiking back to Mirredal at the end of the week. And if your husband doesn't like it tell him to keep it to himself, or it will be the worse for him. I will see you soon.

It was signed, with some formality, 'Your ever-loving brother, Ignatius Louw.'

I read the letter in what must have been a rather high and nervous voice, and as I did so I felt that not only was I committing some sort of criminal act – which technically, I was – I felt not only that, but sank also under a sense of my own frivolousness. Here I was, reading a personal letter from one stranger to another, in the presence of a third person who had actually stolen the letter, on an impulse I hadn't foreseen, all because someone had irritated me at supper. As soon as I had finished I gave the letter back to him with an obscure hope that the shorter time I had the letter in my hand the less likelihood there would be of my fingerprints imprinting themselves upon it.

He took the letter from me, and put it in one of his overall pockets. 'Thank you, baas,' he said. 'Baas Nasie is coming back.' I think for the moment he felt he owed something to me in return for what I had done, and pondered whether or not to tell me something of his reasons for wanting the letter read to him. But I did not want his confidences: I felt they could only drive me into a deeper guilt, not only towards the people in whose house we were staying, but to him too, the thief. For whatever his reasons for wanting the letter read to him might have been, they had not been light ones – I had seen that by the intentness with which he had listened to me reading. He waited now with the side of his face to me, looking down. In profile his face was sadder than it appeared fullfaced: his jaw was humped forward ponderously at the mouth, as if speech would be a weight to him. He was tall, and his waist and chest were thick, straight up from his hips to his armpits, where suddenly his body swelled into broad, tight shoulders. His head, his short neck, his shoulders, were all packed closely and protectively together, and protective too was the way the features of his face seemed to merge into one another, without abruptness, like a rolling landscape: one felt that his emotions would be concealed in the hollows of his face, not revealed in the small eyes or the small rounded nose, or the lips that were set forward firmly and roundly around his closed mouth. His skin was bad, and under the brown outer skin there lay little lumps of flesh along the line of the jaw, under the ears, on either side of the nose. His cheeks were large and his forehead was large and both were scarred, like his protuberant jaw, again and again by his halfsecret ailment, making his face, drooping down now, more difficult to read.

Eventually, to my relief, all he offered to me was: 'My name is Joseph.'

'You'll see that the letter gets put back,' I said.

'Yes, baas,' he replied. 'It will be put back tonight.'

'Good,' I said.

He waited, uncertainly. He still felt, I thought, that he should tell me something about what was happening. I was quite determined that he should not. There was only one thing I wanted to know. Why had he come to me? How could he have dared to come to me? I asked him.

'You're not one of these Dutchmen,' he said.

I told him he was talking nonsense. And again, in the straightforward way he had, he simply abandoned that line of flattery. '*Ja baas,*' he said, agreeing with me. 'I have seen them all in Johannesburg.'

'Why?' I insisted.

'Baas,' he said slowly, 'sometimes you have to take a risk.

And then baas . . .' He paused, and looked at me, up and down, from the advantage of his height. Then he brought it out: 'You're still young, baas.'

'Is that why?'

'I think so, baas.'

'You were lucky,' I said. I had to say something. 'But it's finished now.' I waved him away. 'I don't want to hear any more about it. See that the letter is put back where it belongs.'

'Yes baas.' He lifted his hand to his forehead, giving me a kind of salute. 'Thank you baas,' he said, and turned, and let himself carefully into the gulley, going back the way he had come. I saw his powerful thick figure making its way across the river-bed, among the rocks, and then clambering up on the other side. He moved deliberately, almost like an old man, across the rough, darkened surface of the veld. I was not feeling in any way proud of myself. Watching him, I wondered if youthfulness and weakness could be seen as clearly on my figure as slowness and strength in his.

I made my way down the bank until I reached the ford, and crossed it, and went towards the house. I went up the path of the sun-blasted garden, now covered in dusk, softened by darkness, and so to the front door of the house. The last light in the west was a single lemon-coloured line, a rim of light around a flat, black world.

4

If I had not been so irritated with myself and feeling so guilty towards Mrs Fletcher I might have been shorter with her. As it was, I did allow her to talk, without getting her to say more clearly what she meant.

'What did he want of you?' she asked. 'What was he saying to you?' Her hand held mine by the wrist; we stood together in the front passage of the house. Indoors it was really dark, and it was only when she had spoken that I knew who it was who had taken me as I stepped into the house.

'Nothing,' I said in surprise. 'Nothing.'

'Why did you give him money?' she asked.

'Money?'

'I saw you giving him money. I was standing in front of the garden and I saw everything you did.'

'I gave him no money.' But I remembered what I had done: I had read a purloined letter, and the person from whom the letter had been purloined had a right to reproach me. I was only thankful that she was reproaching me for the wrong reason.

'I saw you giving him money,' she said. She spoke to me as she had done when we had been talking about the hire of the room: her voice was grave and low and humourless. But she held me tightly by the wrist, and her face was close to mine.

'I did give him something,' I said. 'But it was nothing. It was a piece of paper.'

'What kind of a piece of paper?'

'It was an address,' I said.

'What kind of an address?'

'Actually, it's the address of a firm of publishers in Johannesburg.'

'A what?'

I knew I had taken her by surprise. 'An address of a firm of publishers in Johannesburg. You see, he told me that he was trying to learn to read, so I told him there was a firm of publishers in Johannesburg who had just brought out a reading primer for Africans, and that I thought he'd find that the best thing to start with. I told him that he should write to them. Mentioning my name,' I added. 'I know the directors of the firm very well. They're friends of mine.' I thought I might as well enjoy as suffer the mess I was in. 'I told him I was sure they'd be interested in his case.'

But I had overcarried. She seized on my last word. 'Case?' she asked. 'What sort of case is that?'

'An educational one,' I gabbled. 'A very interesting one. Mature, illiterate African, Sesuto-speaking by birth, Afrikaans-speaking for employment purposes, desirous to learn to read English. It's a very interesting case.'

90

'I thought you meant a case in law,' she said. Only then did she slowly relax her grasp on my wrist. I was struck by her use of the words 'case in law'; they must have come from her father who had studied in Leyden.

'Well,' I said as pleasantly as I possibly could, 'if you'll excuse me I think I'll be getting along to my room.'

'But you mustn't have anything more to do with him,' she said. She stood directly and closely in my way.

'I shan't have anything more to do with him,' I said innocently. And I did sincerely believe that I wouldn't have anything more to do with him.

'No,' she said. I could see the grey oval in front of me moving from side to side – she must have been shaking her head. 'You must never speak to him again.'

I should simply have said, 'I won't,' but I couldn't say something to the woman which would have sounded very much like a promise from a bad boy – the fact that I had been a bad boy making it less possible for me to do so, not more. I said: 'I don't suppose I'll have the chance to, anyway. We'll be leaving tomorrow.'

But this did not satisfy her. She came still closer to me. 'It doesn't matter when you leave. You must never have anything to do with him again. Unless I ask you to. You and your friend.'

'But why?' I asked. I added: 'I've got nothing to do with him. Or he with me. I don't know what you're talking about.' This time I put my hands on her shoulders to move her out of the way – I felt that the familiarity was justified after we'd been standing practically hand in hand. Her hands came up: she held me by the wrists.

'He's a bad kaffir,' she said solemnly.

'He didn't seem so bad to me.'

The woman didn't say anything, but she kept my hands on her shoulders, tightening her grasp when I tried to move them away. Suddenly she released my hands, and as my hands fell down I could feel her turning away. 'I shall have to tell you,' she said reluctantly, 'otherwise you won't understand. Do you want to hear about that kaffir?'

I hesitated. Then, 'Yes,' I said, partly out of guilt towards her. And partly out of curiosity about Joseph. She began walking down the passage towards the yellow sliver of light under the door leading to the hall-room, and I followed her.

'Learning to read!' she said as she stepped through the door into the hall-room. 'Why should he want to learn to read?' She seemed alarmed at the idea, so as I came into the room I tried to comfort her.

'I don't suppose he ever will,' I said. 'It's so hard for them to learn when they're already adult, and without teachers.'

She glanced at the portrait of her father. 'Nowadays the kaffirs don't know their place any more. His father never wanted to learn to read.'

'Whose father?'

'Joseph's father.' She turned to me and said solemnly: 'Do you know who my grandfather was?'

'No.'

'He was the son of the first man to settle in the Mirredal district. There was nothing here, there was a kind of kaffir kraal when my great-grandfather came. He was the man who pegged out the first farm that they bought from a kaffir chief.'

'That's very nice,' I said.

'It is,' she agreed. I smiled, and looked on her face for a smile too, but failed to find one. So I stopped smiling. 'That's why they're jealous of me here in the *dorp*. And because my father was a great man. They've never had such a clever man at Mirredal. And you know how people are when they're behind the back of someone much cleverer than they are. They try to drag him down. And now that he isn't here they still try to drag me down. You wouldn't believe it,' she said – and to tell the truth I didn't – 'even the newcomers are jealous of my father. They hear about him from the others. And they hear about my grandfather. They just have to look in the church and they see his name: he was the first deacon here. There's a street named after him too.'

'Which one?' I asked.

'One of the main streets.' One of the main streets – that was something to think about. But if I may have been sceptical about the worldly greatness of Mrs Fletcher's forebears, I must add that I had no doubt at all about her own conviction as to their place and the esteem that was their due. Least of all when she added: 'You just have to look inside this house. There's furniture here that you won't see the like of in Mirredal district. No wonder they're jealous.'

'Did it all belong to your father?' I asked.

'Every stick of it.'

I looked at the table in the middle of the room, behind which she stood, hoping that I looked appreciative enough.

'So you can imagine what I have to put up with,' Mrs Fletcher said, in a rising tone: my look had apparently escaped her. 'From them all. From policemen. My father was a lawyer, and the police had respect for him. But for me – for me, they won't even chase a kaffir away from the *dorp*.'

'Who?' I asked.

'Joseph,' she said impatiently, as if there were no one else in the world to whom she might have been referring. 'I've been to the people in the *dorp* that he's working for, and I've asked them to chase him away, but they won't. And I've been to the police and told them to chase him away, but they looked at his passes and said his passes were in order. Everyone knows they put thousands of kaffirs in jail every day for all sorts of things, but this one kaffir that I want to see put in jail they say they can't do anything about. They're jealous,' she concluded simply and proudly.

'But why do you want him put in jail?' I asked.

'You know nothing,' she said, not sharply, merely stating a fact. 'That boy Joseph – well his father worked for my father. His father's name was Ben, and he'd been with my father for many years, and my father knew old Ben exactly, and they would talk and joke with one another. When Ben died, my father kept Joseph and his sister with him, and afterwards when my father died and we moved into this house we found them here. And we kept them on. We thought Joseph and his sister would be like their father.'

'Weren't they?'

She stood under the portrait of her father. She lifted her hands in an expression of slow surprise; she seemed to be supporting the portrait on the tips of her long fingers. Abruptly she closed her hands and dropped her arms, thrusting the hands under the table. 'How can you ask a thing like that? That Joseph – there was a kaffir who had everything he could ask for, and yet, one day, he comes to me and tells me that he wants to leave. I said to him, "You've got no complaints, why do you want to leave?" And there was nothing he could say. He stood in front of me with his head hanging down and his hat in his hand and could say nothing. Then I said, "Go, there's no work for you here." That's the sort of kaffir he is – he isn't a kaffir that a person can trust. He's not like his father.'

'And his sister!' She raised her voice a little, as though I might try to interrupt her. 'We had to drive her away. She was bad, bad, bad! I can't tell you how bad she was.' And she lowered her pale eyes.

I said, 'Yes, it's very difficult . . .'

'But you haven't heard it all. About six months ago this Joseph turns up again and says that he wants to work for us again. I told him that if he stayed with us we would have kept him on even if there hadn't been any work for him. For the sake of my father I would have kept him on. But after he had shown that sort of cheek, just leaving us when it suited him, and after we'd learned about his sister, he had double the cheek to come back here and ask for work again. I laughed. I said, "There's no hope."' How gravely she spoke, always: even when she said how she had laughed, nothing seemed comic to her. I was surprised that she had become so talkative, but the story itself disappointed me; I had expected something more. The story was so much one that, with variants, I had come across so often before: complaints, grievances, a well-nursed sense of injury against African servants are all common enough: sometimes one would think it's the whites who are oppressed by their servants, the way they complain about them.

'Well, you know how it is,' I said, placating her.

She came forward and leaned over the table towards me. The light flickered above her head, and I could see the pale white gleam of the parting which ran nakedly through her hair. She stared at me, as though inviting me to look within her eyes, so that I could see in their transparency there was no equivocation, for nothing could be hidden. 'And then,' she said. 'And then! Do you know what he did?'

'No,' I said.

'He stayed here. *Here*.' Her hands were clasping the table edge, and she pressed down upon them, and her elbows jutted outwards, each time, like an ungainly bird gathering strength. But she did not take off: she lapsed suddenly, her arms hanging before her. 'I told him to leave a hundred times, at first. But he wouldn't.'

'But surely you could have had him arrested for trespassing?'

'No,' she said. 'We wanted to put him in jail about the passes, but you know what happened. And he doesn't trespass, that's where he's so clever. He doesn't come into the house, or the grounds. He's always hanging around, but I've never actually seen him coming inside. Once, one evening I'd seen him hanging around before I went to bed, so in the middle of the night I got up and I went to the native huts with a torch in my hand. I shone it in each one. Ach!' the woman exclaimed, 'there were a whole lot of kaffirs who shouldn't have been there, but he wasn't among them. I wasn't interested in the others.'

I said: 'So he does no harm?'

'Harm?'

'Yes, I mean, if he doesn't trespass he can't hurt you.'

'He won't hurt me,' the woman said as if she had hardly heard what I had said. Then her eyes flared open; they were wide and pale and empty. 'Hurt me? – no. But you don't know what he wants to do. That's why we need you. Anybody,' she said. Her words were wild, but her voice remained prim and serious.

'What do you mean?'

Slowly she closed her eyes. 'Always watching, always.'

'Who's watching for God's sake?'

'Joseph. The big one. The kaffir outside.'

The light beat irregularly across her features, with a flicker that was so persistent it seemed to me to be more within my own nerves than in the single, pulsing bulb above our heads. The house was silent. Only, from outside, the generator still

95

puttered, and, like the flicker of the light in my eyes, that was a sound so persistent that it may have been my own auricular nerves throbbing. But light and sound together throbbing cast the house itself in doubt – a house, it seemed, in a dream, for nothing in the steady earth outside throbbed as this house did, like a dream, like plasm.

'There's nobody outside,' I said firmly. I too leaned forward on the table – that at least seemed solid enough under my fingers. But the blue and yellow cloth slid on the polished wood, dry, reptilian to the touch.

'Do you think so?' she asked.

'Of course.'

She moved quickly, with a sideways movement of her sharp hips, going to the door of the passage, and opening it. I followed her, and saw her fumble for a key, and then open a drawer in the passage-table. She took out a large, silver torch. Then, together, we went through the front door, into the larger, lighter darkness of the night. We moved furtively and without speaking, according the respect to the night which its silence demanded of us. It was so quiet that I could hear, separately, the drone of two sleepy *koringkrieks*, and knew them apart from one another. And then, unseen, lightless, there was the sound of a car going home in the village, and we were so far away from it that the engine's roar was no more than a susurration, a stick going through the sand.

Click! – it seemed the beam of light itself had made that noise, springing so suddenly forward. I watched the torch's beam go, silently now, across the garden: a frond of palm bobbed into sight and dipped into darkness again. The corner of a petrol tin shone stolidly like a coin, and then was quenched. Now the beam shone on the sand, and in relief each corrugation cast its shadow before it, in an ant's country of valleys and paths and passes through mountains that a scuffling foot had made. And so fingering further, where the canna leaves drooped in a cluster and lay dry and dying against the stem that had borne them, to the narrow straight trunk of the silver oak in the corner of the plot and the twisted incurled leaves that lay thinly on the ground about it. And beyond, where the light broadened, paled, lost its glitter, and diffused itself in grey and silver against the form of the man who had asked me to read the letter addressed to the woman who stood upright and lightly beside me, with the torch held high above her shoulder in one hand, like a spear that she was about to throw.

Joseph turned to receive the light where he stood, at the outermost edge of the broad cone of light. His hands were hanging by the sides of his body, and his face was lifted, and though the weakness of the light there made his figure seem misted and blurred in outline, we could see that he was un-abashed to have been caught nakedly in the beam of light. It was we, rather, the wielders of the torch, who were exposed.

The torch went out abruptly, and Joseph was lost. We turned to go back into the house; we had to grope in darkness for the door. Our hands met on the marble handle and re-treated from one another, and only then, fumbling after a little pause, did we manage to get in again.

Inside the hall-room the woman surprised me again, by her calmness. She seemed satisfied with what she had done: she felt, I suppose, that she had shown me. And if there was any doubt in my mind about what she had shown, she must have believed she had finally settled it when she said: 'There, you see that you must never speak to him again, as long as you're here.'

'But I'm only here until tomorrow morning,' I cried.

She took no notice. As an act of courtesy she opened the door into the passage that led to my room. I went through it, and she closed the door after me. Like the front one, this passage was in darkness, but I reached our room without impaling myself on any of the horns that grew from the walls.

Part 2

5

Frank was a clever little boy at school, and to this day he has retained many of the characteristic mannerisms of the boy who was much cleverer than any of his contemporaries. Which does not mean that he was pert and privately superior: on the contrary, he was timid in his dealings with people, as if he were never quite sure that somebody might turn on him with a contemptuous: 'Swot!' and so debar him finally and shamefully from making a contribution to the social intercourse of those about him. But social timidity, in his case, went with a lively interest in the things that people did, and a curiosity about the motives that impelled people to do the things that he so conscientiously observed them doing. He was shy and observant, and although as aware as anyone could be of the general nature of human motives, he was quite without one or another of the cynicisms with which most observers of the human scene usually equip themselves. He knew enough to know that he would be surprised; and each time he was surprised he displayed a freshness of wonder that might have laid him open to a charge of *naïveté*. But *naïveté* of that sort, allied to withdrawn, continual observation and comparison, is a more formidable combination, in many ways, than the brashest cynicism or the most bigoted faith. In Frank's case they certainly made him, apart from all else, an attractive travelling companion and a reliable witness.

In appearance, as well as in mannerisms, he had remained the clever boy; there was something about him that irresistibly reminded one of short trousers, perhaps his habit of belting his unchanging pair of grey flannels too high round his waist, so that he looked always as though his mother had only a few minutes before emphatically and forcibly made him decent. But his glasses too added to the clever boy effect, especially as they usually rested too low on one bump or another of his long, irregular nose. Over his forehead there always hung a lock of thin blond hair which never really looked clean. It was not his fault that he was one of those blonds whose hair at the roots is dárk, though it was unfortunate: had Frank been a woman he would no doubt have been accused of dying his hair, but I can vouch for the fact that though Frank had a keen curiosity about his body, and could regard a scab on his shin with the attention that he customarily paid to the cadavers he operated on at Medical School, his interest in his body was, neverthless, devoid of vanity. I can vouch for that, I said, and so could Frank's shoes and socks, which usually looked like those of a road-mender. His body itself was tall and rather awkwardly set together: there was a lack of proportion between his waist and hips and chest that made him move rather clumsily – the only way I can describe it is by saying that his chest was too long for his hips and waist, which does, I think, indicate something of the rolling quality of his walk. I remember once in the course of the hitch-hike the two of us trying to throw stones at a telegraph pole; Frank threw from his shoulders, with an awkward pushing movement: he must have been hopeless at games at school.

When I came into the room I expected to find him there, for that was where I had left him after supper, when I had gone out for my walk. He had been shaving, so that he wouldn't have to shave early the next morning and would hence be able to sleep for ten minutes longer; I had left him dutifully scraping from his chin the blond glinting bristle that grew so rapidly from just above the line of his collar to just below his eyes. Conscious of virtue, he had warned me that he wasn't going on the road with me tomorrow morning unless I too had shaved. For we had to maintain a minimum standard of neatness and respectability of appearance: South African motorists over the last few years have learned to be wary of hitch-hikers who accept lifts and later hit the drivers over the head with spanners or bottles or revolvers, steal their cars, and leave the drivers on the roadside to be found some time later by any other motorist whose eyes happen to stray from the road to the grass on its verges. We did not want to miss chances of lifts not because the car drivers were stingy or their cars overcrowded but because of their reluctance to load on anyone who was not an upright, clean-shaven, blazer-wearing college youth. Which was the role we played on the road with all our might: Frank had actually borrowed a blue, white and yellow blazer from his elder brother for the weeks we planned to be away from home, and curious, but respectable enough, he looked in it too.

Anyway, he wasn't in the room; and I gathered he had finished shaving by the pool of grey water that he had left in the basin. I poured it into the slop-basin under the washstand, and then sloshed a little clean water about inside the basin, to remove the last traces of his beard. I tested the jug of water that had been brought in by the African servant for his shave, but it was now only very mildly warm. However, I poured a little into the basin; I felt that I too should settle down responsibly and start shaving. But I was reluctant to do so in water as cool as that, and even more reluctant to go roaming round the house in search of the African who had brought it to us. Or of the mistress of the house. Or of anybody there, after I had opened the door, and in the large general silence of the house, heard only one sound: the voice of the man with whom we had eaten supper. He was talking quite steadily, his voice muffled and steady behind walls, as if someone had forgotten to switch off a wireless. No, I was not in the mood for meeting any of them, and the thought of facing again for even a few minutes the underhand bombast of Fletcher was enough to make me close the door and retreat into the room again. The sound of his voice – like someone shouting into a shell, it had sounded – was cut off. My room was silent. I went and lay down on the bed. I did not want to sleep, but there didn't seem much else to do, especially as the light was too dull and erratic to read by. After a few minutes I kicked off my shoes. I was too lazy to remove them from the bed; I could feel them resting idly, upside down, on the counterpane.

I think I must have fallen asleep; I know that I shuddered when I heard the sound of the front door of the house banging and all the glass rattling uncontrollably with the lead that supported it. I found myself staring at the white quilt on which I lay and I tried to decipher the pattern of raised welts on the cloth: there was a square, a diamond within the square. The light was still beating unevenly. I thought of getting up to switch it off, but was too lazy to do so. The air was so warm and still in the room, even with the window wide open; I was sweating where my limbs had touched the bedclothes. I remember feeling that I would probably be cooler if I did switch off the light – the way it flickered made it seem hotter than it would have been if it had burned steadily. But I think I fell asleep again, just for a moment, for I was startled again when Frank came into the room. I hadn't heard his footsteps in the passage.

He stood at the door with his hand on his nose, as if there were a bad smell in the room. His eyes were wide open behind the circles of glass on either side of his hand, staring at me. I stared back at him; some moments passed before I raised my head and asked him:

'What's the matter?'

'The matter!' he said. 'I've been looking all over for you.' He took his hand away from his nose, and it was covered in bright red blood. 'Oh God,' he said, and threw back his head and sniffed deeply. 'You haven't got a block of ice, have you?' His hand had gone back to his nose. 'Or a cold key?'

'No, I haven't got a cold key.'

'I thought not,' he said gloomily, much absorbed in his plight. With his head still thrown back he made his way rather blindly to the wash-stand. The jug was on the floor where I'd left it, and he groped for it all over the table.

'It's on the floor,' I said.

'Well, pick it up!' he said indignantly.

'You pick it up.'

'I can't pick it up. If I do I'll bend my head forward and then the blood will come gushing out again.' He brought this long sequential sentence out with difficulty. The blood had trickled down his hand, and lay round his wrist like a bracelet.

His eyes flashed menacingly behind his glasses, above his hand, over the blood. 'For Christ's sake,' he said. His hair seemed to be leaning over his forehead to have a closer look at the disturbance.

I got the jug from the floor and squeezed the face-cloth in the water, and gave it to him. For some minutes we did not say anything to one another; the silence was broken only by the fall of the drops of water into the jug when he wrung the cloth out, and the soft pats of the cloth against his face, and his profound sniffs.

I asked him: 'What happened?'

Between dabs and sniffs he replied: 'It's a long story.'

I went back to the bed and lay down again, while Frank continued to minister to himself. I kicked my shoes off the bed, and they fell on the floor with a clatter that made Frank start and turn and look at me suspiciously. But I lay quite peaceably, and eventually he stanched the bleeding, and came and lay down on the other bed, with his head well back over the pillow.

'What happened?' I asked again.

'I banged my nose.'

'You don't say so!'

But my sarcasm, such as it was, did not disturb Frank. 'It's true,' he said. 'I banged it against a wall.'

'How?'

'Someone pushed me. How do you think?'

I couldn't think of any other way that he might have banged his nose against a wall. I asked him: 'Who pushed you?'

'Our host.'

I sat up. 'This place is making me sick. I don't understand what the hell is going on, but I do know that I've never met a couple like this one. Do you know what happened to me?'

'Yes,' Frank said. 'You had a talk with Mrs Fletcher.'

'How do you know?'

'Fletcher told me.'

'For Christ's sake. What's going on here? Do you know?'

'A little,' Frank said. 'We've been invited to stay on here a couple of weeks.'

'Who by?' I asked in wonder.

'Fletcher.'

I lay down again. 'First he bangs your nose against a wall and then he invites you to stay here for a couple of weeks. Don't you think that's a peculiar way to behave?' For Frank's voice had hardly sounded perturbed: what irritation there was in it seemed to be directed more against myself than anyone else.

'You've got it the wrong way round,' he said. 'He asked me to stay on before he banged my nose against the wall.' Then he asked suddenly, irritated again: 'What happened to you after supper? I looked all over for you.'

'I was on the other side of the *spruit*. I was just walking.'

'You could have told me where you were going. I looked all over for you. If I had known where you were perhaps I wouldn't have had my nose banged against the wall.'

'How do you mean?'

'Well, perhaps it would have been your nose that was banged against the wall.' Frank found this sally amusing, but it was his last for some time. Apparently he had finished shaving after I'd left him, and then gone out, like myself, to get a breath of the cooler evening air. He went into the garden, but hadn't been able to see me, so he had thought that perhaps I might have been at the back. 'I went into the back-yard,' Frank said. 'I don't know if you've been there – it's an ordinary sort of back-yard, just a yard and a row of out-buildings on the other side of it. There's a garage, a room for oil drums and things, and a woodshed, and a couple of servant's rooms – you know the sort of thing – all in a row, with a little lavatory at one end.' Frank hadn't seen me there, but he had seen Fletcher, together with a servant.

6

Fletcher, Frank told me, was standing in front of the room where the generator was housed. There was a big 44-gallon drum of petrol or crude-oil on the ground, and Fletcher was pumping the stuff out of the drum into a little can: the pump was one of those with a big wooden handle that fits into the bung-hole on top of the drum, and Fletcher was jerking away at it vigorously. His head was going up and down, and his hair was flying over his face, and the sound of his breath was loud in the yard, almost as though he were pumping the stuff out with his own lungs.

An African was standing next to Fletcher, watching him. As neither of them had yet seen Frank, he thought he might be able to slip round the back of the house and come round to the front on the other side of the garden without being noticed. So he began moving across, keeping close to the house and walking as silently as he could, almost on tip-toe, in the hope that he would in this way be able to avoid renewing his acquaintance with his host. But he was only half-way across, about at the kitchen door, when the African saw him and started making towards him. Quietly and absurdly, Frank went on, but the African, though he was wearing a pair of trousers far too big for him and torn in each leg right up the calf, so that he had to flop about inside them and have them sweep the yard behind him, soon caught up with Frank.

'Baas?' the African said.

'Yes,' Frank said shortly, coming to a halt.

'Did basie get the hot water I made for him?'

'Yes,' Frank said, determined not to give the man the tip for which he was presumably angling, and beginning to walk on again, abandoning subterfuge, and simply moving fast. But the African kept alongside him, trousers trailing.

'*Dankie baas,*' he said.

This again brought Frank to a halt. What could the man be thanking him for? Because he had stopped and said 'Yes'? Or in advance, for the tip that he hoped Frank might give him? Or just because he felt that he had to thank a white man no matter what he did – for being a white man, as it were? The African responded to Frank's stare with another, enthusiastic, '*Dankie baas,*' and Frank could only decide that the man *was* thanking him for being a white man. The African had come to pay his respects. He had come to make an obeisance: the approach had been a disinterested one.

Frank was not as touched as he should have been. His gaze took in the abjectness of the man's clothing: of those trousers, of his boots that gaped at the toes, of the jacket he was wearing, that Frank thought to be surely the oldest jacket in the world, having only the lining left on the shoulders, and no lapels at all, and so many rents all over it that it looked as though someone had been at it deliberately, with a knife. The jacket was tied at the neck with a piece of wire, and below that clip seemed simply to spread out in all directions – in that unlike its owner, who displayed no physical excess of any kind. He was a tiny, wizened old man, in size no bigger than a boy, with a tiny, wrinkled, yellow face, like an apple left too long in storage. His black, monkey-like eyes acknowledged Frank's stare by blinking several times; and then, bringing his hand to his head in a salutation, and taking from his head the rag of a cap he wore, he without question or hesitation agreed with whatever it was that Frank might have been thinking.

'Ja baas,' he said with conviction, taking no risks at all.

And to his astonishment, Frank found that the man's abject manner invited harshness: there seemed to be nothing to say to him except, '*Voetsak!*' as one might speak to a dog in chasing it away. He lifted a hand, to indicate to the other that he could go, and then, seeing something he had not noticed before, he dropped it suddenly, even before the African had finished flinching. What he had not seen among the wrinkles of the man's face were the tears under his eyes.

'You're crying,' Frank said, finding it difficult to believe what he himself was saying: he had never before met so casually an old man who was crying – least of all an old man who was so humble, so ragged, so small, and so bony that it did not look possible for him to have sufficient passion or even sufficient moisture to waste on tears. 'What's the matter with your eyes?' Frank asked.

'*Niks,*' the man replied, sniffing. He brought up one hand to wipe the tears away, and the rags of his sleeve hung far down from his lifted arm.

'Why are you crying?' Frank asked.

The little man wavered for a moment. Then he looked across the yard at his master, and said: 'I'm not crying.'

But Frank had caught the glance. 'Did the baas hit you?' he asked.

'*Ja baas*.'

'Is that why you're crying?'

'*Ja baas*.'

Clearly, the man had no resistance to questions put to him in a loud, stern voice. 'Why did the baas hit you?'

'The baas says I mustn't work with the petrol.'

'And did you work with the petrol?'

'*Ja baas*.'

'Where did he hit you?'

'On the back, baas.'

'With the fist, or with the *sjambok*?'

'With the fist, baas,' the man replied promptly, and with no apparent ill-will – as far as Frank could see – towards Fletcher. It seemed almost as though the little man had found a certain philosophical consolation in the thought that the fist which had been applied was better than the *sjambok* which had not: for someone who looked as though he fought for his food with dogs, slept on sacks, drank water that cattle had pissed in, and clothed himself in rags that every possible thorn and nail and piece of barbed wire had torn – for the human equivalent of a sack-and-paraffin-tin *pondokkie* in a location – there might well have been consolation in such a thought.

But Frank neverthless asked another question: 'Why did you work with the petrol?'

'The missus said I must.'

Frank did not know if he would have gone to Fletcher and protested against the violent injustice done to the old man. Luckily, perhaps, the matter was taken out of his hands; at that moment the gasps and squeaks from the other side of the yard ceased abruptly, for Fletcher had become aware of Frank's presence. Fletcher stood upright with one hand on the drum and his face turned towards the other two. It was obvious that he could not hear what was being said, but it was equally obvious that he very much wanted to

107

know. Then he began coming across the yard towards them.

He was a few yards away when he asked Frank: 'Has he been complaining to you?'

Immediately the answer to that too was taken out of Frank's hands, for the African's voice went into a howl, half of fear and half of respect, and both of them so exaggerated that his words pattered out high and fervent, like a prayer. '*Nee, nee my grootbass, ek maak niks complaints. Ek sê net vir die kleinbaas hoe ek die water vir hom gekook het. Hoe kan ek klagtes by die kleinbaas soek? Ek het geen klagtes teen die oubaas, so waar as God. Vra net my oubaas, vra vir die kleinbaas of ek klagtes gemaak het . . .*' And as he went on pleading, he crossed his hands in front of his chest, in humility, to declare the truth of what he was saying, and he crouched his body lower to make it smaller and less assertive than it already was.

And Frank's dilemma was resolved: after what the man had just said it was clear that Fletcher would be quite capable of hitting him tomorrow, when Frank was not there, for his sin of complaining to Frank today. So Frank said:

'It's my fault. I asked him why he was crying. He wouldn't tell me.'

'Just as well for him.' Then: 'Why does it concern you?'

'I don't like to see people crying.'

Instead of becoming stiff and righteous and telling Frank to mind his own business, as he might have been expected to do, Fletcher brought his head up with a sweep of his hair and said almost patronizingly, 'You should take no notice of what this boy tells you.'

'He told me nothing. I happened to see that he was crying.'

'Him!' Fletcher said. 'Crying? He's always crying.' He turned to the African, who, while the white men had been talking, had been leaning forward to listen, despite the fear which had at the same time kept his hips shrunken well back. Fletcher waited for a moment, with the African remaining crouched before him, not daring to move. Then, with a fierce swing of his arm and a stamp of his foot, Fletcher feinted an attack that sent the African scuttling round the corner of the house and out of sight.

'See how he went?' Fletcher asked proudly. 'Did you see him run?'

'Yes.'

"What a coward he is!' Fletcher said. 'Hottentot that he is!'

'Bushman,' Frank corrected him. 'He looked a Bushman-type to me.'

Fletcher treated the correction with contempt.

'Bushman, Hottentot, they're all the same. Little yellow devils.'

'Why did you hit him?' Frank asked, and either Fletcher did not notice that Frank did, in fact, know why the little man had been crying, or else, noticing, he did not mind, but took it in as part of his pride over his exhibition of power. 'I've told him never to touch the pump.'

'Why don't you want him to?' Frank asked. 'Anyway, he told me that he'd done it only because –'

But Frank never finished that sentence. For Fletcher took him by the shirt – putting his finger in the pocket of the shirt, and pulling the cloth backwards and forwards lightly – and said, softly and craftily, 'Would you –' and there was a pause, while in silence he touched at the shirt, as though warning of the profundity that was to follow, 'trust a Bushman with petrol?'

It was preposterous. Frank disengaged his shirt from the man's grasp by leaning away slightly. 'It depends on the Bushman surely,' he said.

'Ha!' Fletcher laughed suddenly. They had been standing close to one another in the clear, sunless light of the evening, and talking rather confidentially – that had been Fletcher's manner. In another manner, equally his, was the shout of laughter, and the loudness of voice which followed it. 'Ha! That's a good one. I must remember that. You're a sharp young fellow. It depends on the Bushman!' Then he dropped his voice. Frank found that he and the other were *boetie-boetie* again, confidential. 'It depends on the Bushman, indeed.' He took Frank by the shirt and pulled it towards himself a little, and leaned towards Frank. When they were in the right attitudes of confidence he breathed out the burden of his thought: 'As if they aren't all alike!'

'That's what you think,' Frank said abruptly, to cut the other short. But Fletcher overbore him, loudly.

'That's what we all believe. You believe it too. Don't tell me that you don't. Here we are, surrounded by them: we have to believe it. What would happen to us if we didn't?'

'Perhaps we'd be better off than we are.'

Fletcher was in no mood to be offended. He merely said: 'Nonsense, my boy, nonsense. What would become of our civilization if we didn't believe it?'

'I don't know.'

'I do,' Fletcher said. 'We have faith in our civilization or else we're lost. I've seen what happens to those who have no faith.'

'Is that so?'

'That is so. With my own eyes, in my own house, I saw it happen. I've seen what happens to those who lose their faith. We are surrounded by our enemies, and if you go among them you are lost. Lost, cast out, cast asunder.' His forefinger was thrust warningly upright in front of Frank's face, and then suddenly it bent upon itself, beckoning Frank towards them. 'Would you like to have a drink with me?'

7

While Frank, who had been unable to resist the invitation, walked with his host into the kitchen, the latter made his attitude towards drinking quite clear. He was not a drinking man himself, he said, but he was tolerant towards those who were. As long as it was not carried to excess, of course.

'Of course,' Frank agreed.

Fletcher said that he saw no reason why those who enjoyed their sundowners should be deprived of them, though he was glad to say that he himself had managed without them all his life. However, he said, he did keep a small stock of sherry and whisky, for visitors, for passers-by, for people who enjoyed such things; and Frank said that that was very good of him.

By this time they were in the kitchen – a room that was

as overcrowded with furniture as any other room in the house, having in it, among other things, a tall brown dresser with rows of knobs running all the way up it, like buttons done up closely to keep out the cold, and a kitchen-table, and another small dresser, and a sink with a draining-board, and several chairs, and an enormous black stove. And everything that had a door or a drawer to it was not merely closed, but locked. Fletcher took out a bundle of keys, and unlocked the smaller dresser and took out a bottle of sherry and a bottle of orange squash, and put them on the table. Then he locked the small dresser. Then he went to the big dresser and unlocked that and brought out two glasses, which he put on the table before going back and locking the big dresser. He took the bottle-opener out of a drawer in the kitchen-table – that too had its lock which was unlocked and locked again when he had finished with it – and only then was he ready to start pouring out the drinks. And all locking and unlocking was done, as far as Frank could see, quite mechanically, quite without any perception that someone who had never been in their kitchen before might think it an odd way of going about things.

Frank said: 'You're very careful,' and to Frank's own surprise, Fletcher seemed surprised at the remark. He had been busy pouring out a drink, but when Frank spoke he paused, with the bottle still in his hand.

'Oh, but you have to be,' he said. He gestured towards Frank, with the bottle. 'It stands to reason. They get their rations. They get their mealie-*pap* and sugar and coffee and a bit of soup-meat sometimes. But they also see what we get. Of course they'd steal our things if they had their chance.' He shook his head. 'No, you can't be too careful.' And then, in a tone of contempt – and, Frank suspected, bewilderment too: 'Unless you're the sort of person who spoils them. I've heard about that sort of person. Lower Houghton hostesses whose boys eat the same sort of food as they do. I wonder what they'll say when the boys come into their bedrooms and say: "Boy eats same food as missus. Now boy want to sleep in the same bed as missus. Shift up missus." ' Bewilderment had by this time given way to almost a kind of glee, though

Frank noticed that Fletcher was careful to give him a glance to see whether or not he were perhaps sailing too close to the wind. 'Then they'll know the mistake they made,' he went on, have judged that it was safe to do so. 'Then they'll be sorry they spoilt the black devils. "Shift up missus. Boy coming between sheets. *Au!*"' he exclaimed, gaining enthusiasm in his role of salacious African. '"Lovely bed for boy! Lovely missus!" Christ!' he exclaimed. 'Then they'll be sorry.' And as the dream faded his voice dropped, and he saw the bottle in his hand again, and looked at it sourly. 'No, you can't do that sort of thing. In this house everything stays locked.'

Fletcher finished pouring out the drinks, and pushed the sherry across the table towards Frank, keeping the orange squash for himself. Frank took his drink, and remained standing, under the impression that now the drinks had been poured out he and the host would take them into one of the front rooms. But without any more ado Fletcher began sipping from his drink. He took a sip or two and then sat down. 'Sit down,' he said. 'Make yourself comfortable.'

Frank attempted to do so on the hard kitchen chair, but could not help thinking how typical the place and manner of their drinking was: to Fletcher it apparently seemed in order that one should have a house of perhaps twenty rooms, but invite a guest to drink in the kitchen.

'Cheers!' Fletcher said, to hasten Frank on.

'Cheers,' Frank replied. He sipped his drink in silence, and so did Fletcher.

And then Fletcher began to praise his guest. Fletcher said that he could see that Frank was a wide-awake young fellow. He could see that Frank had his head screwed on the right way. He could see that Frank was a lively, quick-witted, alert young man. And so on. And at some length. And while in the back-yard they had for the most part been confidential and cautious, in the kitchen they were good loud pals – or at least Fletcher's voice insisted that they were. Fletcher even praised the medical profession, and the young men who take medicine, generally; and Frank, of course, especially. When Frank finished his drink, Fletcher insisted that he should have another. It was a pleasure, he said, to offer refreshment to a man like Frank. How glad he was, he said, that the hotel had been full, and that Frank and his friend had had to come to himself.

By the end of the second drink, Fletcher must have assumed that what with the drinks and the compliments Frank would be pretty well softened up, for in the same loud tone of voice in which he had expressed his admiration for Frank's obvious intelligence and uprightness, he said: 'I've got a proposition to make to you, young man.'

'Oh,' Frank said.

'Yes,' Fletcher said. 'I have.' But he did not come out and make it. He hesitated for a moment, and then said: 'It's a very interesting proposition.'

'Yes?' Frank said.

Fletcher said: 'My wife agrees with me that it would be a very good idea. She's talking to your friend at this very moment. That's what we call division of labour – ha! ha!'

Frank said nothing.

'I've tried,' Fletcher said, 'to look at this matter from your angle too.' There was still no response from Frank. In the silence, Fletcher shot out a hand, took his glass, and finished the rest of his drink, with his head thrown back for the last drop. But from either side of the glass Frank saw Fletcher's eyes upon him.

Frank's attitude was that he had nothing to lose if Fletcher got angry; the loss would be Fletcher's. Perhaps the same thought had occurred to Fletcher, for despite the abruptness with which he had picked up his glass, and the glare Frank had caught from him while he had been drinking, Fletcher put the glass down very quietly and carefully, and then sat on in silence. The kitchen became steadily darker, as they sat, Frank playing with his glasses on the table, Fletcher watching him do so.

Eventually Fletcher began talking again, hesitantly, 'We're very glad that you came, both my wife and I. Very glad indeed. We appreciate it that you're staying with us, and that we've had a chance to meet you and talk things over.' He stopped to cast an eye on Frank. But Frank said nothing. 'It's not every day that we have the pleasure of meeting boys like yourself – educated, decent young gentlemen.' Again a pause. 'And that's why,' Fletcher said, and gathered strength for a moment before being able to bring out the rest, 'and that's why I've been thinking of asking you this other thing, which we'd both like you to consider. At your leisure, naturally, I mean. I'm not asking for a snap decision. You could let me know tomorrow morning, if that would suit you. Or any time tonight. I generally go to bed rather late and – haha! – get up rather late too. But I'm sure you'll be turning in early. You've had a hard day of it, haven't you? You've come a long way. But you've done very well, indeed you have. I admire you youngsters setting out on the road like that.'

Frank said: 'We didn't have a very good day today.' He felt he had to say something to keep the man going: after his last period Fletcher's mouth had simply opened and closed a few times, in silence, like a frog's.

'That's what I mean,' Fletcher said, most relieved to hear Frank speak again. 'Why, it could take you three weeks to get down to Cape Town at the present rate. Easily. If you had a run of bad luck you could spend days on the side of the road at one place. Couldn't you?'

'Well not days. A day perhaps.'

'Days. I'm telling you, days. Especially from here. Mirredal is an out-of-the-way spot, you know. We're well off the main road and you may have a bit of a job getting down south.'

'Perhaps,' Frank said.

'That's the way to talk,' Fletcher said. 'I like to hear you talk like that. It's the whole point of your journey, isn't it? You're after adventure, and you don't care how long the trip takes you. You've got all the time in the world. I should imagine you wouldn't even mind if it did take you three weeks to the Cape. I'm not saying that it will, not at all, I wish you the best of luck, but you must have taken something like that into consideration when you set out on the trip. And that's where you students have got the advantage over anyone else in the country: you get such long holidays. Two months, three months, sometimes even more. Isn't that so? You've got all the time in the world. You're free for the next two or three months, aren't you?'

'Well not quite. But we are free,' Frank said casually. But Fletcher seemed very satisfied to hear it.

'I thought so,' he said. 'I thought that was the arrangement with students.' Then he digressed: or Frank thought he digressed: 'I know, I've seen some of the young fellows from the farms around here who're going to college – they may be going to college but they also seem to be able to spend most of their time lounging about at home. Of course, it's different with you. I'm sure you're a hard worker. But some of these young fellows – they're hopeless. Idle, and vicious, and irresponsible, I know them all. And so often it's the older generation who have to bear the burden that these degenerate youngsters have placed on them. The youths escape, and they leave us to clean up the mess. And gratitude!' Fletcher exclaimed suddenly and excitedly, with emphasis, as if the word were new to him. 'Do you think we ever get a word of gratitude for what we've done? Never a word. Instead of gratitude, there's resentment. Instead of sorrow, there's anger. Instead of thanks, there's threats. Why? Because we've saved them from the consequences of their own folly and vices. For that they hate us, they threaten us.'

'Who?'

Fletcher bit the word out: 'Youth!'

He said it so abruptly that for a moment Frank thought that he had said: 'You!' And by the look he gave Frank it seemed that it might well have been Frank to whom he was referring. Frank – anyone – the whole world: he regarded them all with the same fear and spite. And then as though he had indeed said, 'You!' and had then remembered that he still had to placate Frank for some other purpose, he leaned across the table and put his hand on Frank's arm, and smiled, and dropped his voice. He said, with his hand on Frank's arm: 'That's why I'm asking you to stay.'

8

Before Frank could make any sort of reply to this, Fletcher was at him again. 'You said that time was no object for you,' he said. 'You said that you didn't mind if you spent another three weeks on the road to Cape Town. Why spend three weeks on the road to Cape Town when you can stay here comfortably for as long as you like? And then when you do want to go I'll fix it up so that you'll get to the Cape without any difficulty. Leave it to me, son, put it in my hands. There's always farmers going down to the Cape at this time of year. I'll go into town for you, I'll go into the hotel, I'll ask at the shops, I'll get a lift for you, don't you worry about that. And you'll be able to travel down as you should, like gentlemen.' He was carried away: Frank heard him spit out at the end: 'Not like tramps, as you come here.' He stopped suddenly, appalled.

Then he laughed that single laugh of his. 'I admire you! Don't misunderstand me! If I were twenty years younger I'd be doing the same thing myself. When I was a youngster I was also wild, I didn't care what people thought of me. No!' Fletcher said, as though he had just heard what he himself had said. He banged the side of his hand against the table. 'That's not true. I was always aware of what was decent and what wasn't. I came from a good home, down in the Cape, where you're going now. I wasn't like these modern youngsters. All filth and viciousness they are. I went to a good school.' And he told Frank the name of the school, one of those schools in Grahamstown. He gave Frank the name of the house he had been in at the school. He challenged Frank to look his name up in the school calendar, so that Frank would be able to see for himself the truth of what he was saying. That was where he had learned what was right and what was not. It had not been his fault that his father had died and that the estate had been in disorder and that he had had to make his own way. But he had, and he had not done so badly either. But he was not a snob. He repeated that he was not a snob, as though

116

Frank had accused him of being a snob, as though Frank could see anything for him to be particularly snobbish about. He was not a snob. All he wanted was decency, decency, decency, he said.

He had to stop eventually, to take in a deep breath. In the respite Frank could only wonder confusedly what was going to come next. And Fletcher still managed to surprise him. He held up one hand towards Frank. 'I know what's troubling you. Finances, that's what's troubling you. Don't you let it do that. I know the students are always hard up. I've read of these things. But don't let it worry you. I've talked the matter over with my wife and she agrees with me entirely.' Magnanimously Fletcher's hand waved above the kitchen table. 'Stay here, my boy, stay here with us. We won't press you for anything. You're our guest. How about that, hey? A free holiday, you fancy that, don't you?'

'I do,' Frank said. 'But not –'

'Of course you do,' Fletcher said, leaning back, at his most jovial. 'Who wouldn't?'

Then he was silent, waiting for Frank to say something. Or, it seemed to Frank, simply to fall on his neck in gratitude. There had been such an air of magnanimity in the way he had asked the last question, his name, Frank thought, should have been a title: Fletcher, he was, the giver of gifts. But Frank made no move towards the giver of gifts, nor did he say anything, and so the silence was prolonged – and Fletcher's joviality and magnanimity being what they were, they both withered at the touch of silence. Until, in the darkness of the air there seemed to hang, after the cadence of Fletcher's voice had faded, only the man's forlorn hope for the qualities that he had tried to display just a moment before.

But Frank was to find that not yet did he have any true idea of Mr Fletcher's moral sensibility. He said, 'But –', again, and Fletcher leaned forward, all solicitude.

'I know what you're uneasy about,' Fletcher said. 'You don't like the sound of it. You feel it's not –' and at that point his voice rose inquiringly, so that the word came out questioningly, but itself, '– right? Is that it? You don't like the idea of accepting something for nothing?'

'Actually –' Frank began, again to get no further.

'If it would make you happier we're ready to accept some kind of nominal payment. It could be anything, I don't care. A pound a week, two pounds, whatever your purse will stretch to. Mind, only if you really want to make it, and if you're quite sure that you wouldn't be able to stay here if you didn't. Because you see, apart from anything else, you wouldn't be receiving something for nothing. If we didn't need –' Fletcher paused, and then began again: 'If we didn't want you here we wouldn't ask you to stay, isn't that so? But – at the same time – I understand your scruples and I respect them. If you're quite sure you'd prefer it that way, just tell me and I'll explain matters to my wife. I'm sure she'll understand. That sort of scruple reflects credit on you. It shows me one thing: you're not like the rest of them.'

Then, for a few minutes, whatever Frank started to say was interrupted by Fletcher, or deliberately misunderstood or waved away by one hand and the words: 'No trouble at all. No trouble at all,' until Frank got to his feet and almost shouted the question at Fletcher, so that it could not possibly be misunderstood.

'But why do you want me to stay?'

Fletcher stood up too. 'We need your help,' he said.

'How can I help you?'

'I am in trouble.'

'What sort of trouble?'

'It's difficult to explain,' Fletcher said, and sat down again. Frank remained standing, and Fletcher looked up at him. 'I don't know if you'll understand.'

'Why don't you try it and see?'

'A free holiday,' Fletcher said miserably. 'I thought you'd be happy to have a free holiday.'

'On your mysterious terms? Without explanations? Do I look as though I would?' Frank said, rising to his rights the more that Fletcher gave him the opportunity to do so.

'It isn't the least mysterious really. I started to tell you about it.' Fletcher picked up his glass and tilted the last few drops of orange liquid down his throat. There was nothing else on the table that he could fidget with, apart from the bottles, and he touched at them tentatively but did not move them. He said: 'There's nothing *wrong* about it. Not about this. But it's difficult to explain.' He said hopefully: 'Perhaps you would like to speak to my wife?'

Frank felt that he could pass comment adequately on what Fletcher had said only by hitting him, or swearing at him, or throwing a glass at the top of his head. At that time he was not really so interested in finding out what Fletcher's wretched troubles were, or why the man thought he might be able to help him out of them: what filled Frank's mind was that stupid, self-absorbed cleverness of Fletcher's, that had worked out the plan, and had confirmed that it was feasible, and had then taken the rest for granted – so that his moral awareness, his interest in Frank, his magnanimity, in fact acted to reduce Frank to a puppet in a pipe-dream. It was the stupidity of it that incensed Frank, as much as the lack of consideration: he felt that he had been insulted by the other.

But Frank was really not one for hitting people, or swearing at them, or even for throwing glasses at the tops of their heads, and in the end all he did was to walk to the door and switch on the light. There was a spark from the darkness in the middle of the room, that stabilized itself into a kind of small, glowing, yellow little worm suspended directly above Fletcher's head. The worm hung in the air for a moment, and only then did the bulb go on properly, and a small, smeary, yellow light it gave; and it was no sooner on than it began winking and blinking like every other light in the house. But all the same, Frank was glad that he had switched it on. Fletcher shrank from seeming a kind of a rock in the darkness and became what he was – a man, with an arching nose and a lot of shiny, dry, blond hair waving away from his forehead. And bright eyes. His hands were on the table, clasped round a glass, and he was looking down at it, and every now and then giving Frank a glance, half-surreptitiously from under his eyebrows.

'I was going to suggest,' Fletcher said, 'that we throw a little light on the subject. Ha-ha!' he laughed, hardly so much as attempting to sound amused.

'Yes it would help.'

Fletcher stared at the glass for a moment longer. He said: 'I'm not sure how my wife would feel about this. Look, if you stay here I'll call her. Then we could have a conference together.'

Frank said: 'No. I don't see that there's anything to confer about.'

'You mean you aren't going to stay?' Fletcher asked, his voice rising, his eyes going from point to point on Frank's face.

'I'm certainly not going to if you don't tell me why you want me to.'

'Then there's no help for it. I'll tell you what you want to know.' Fletcher said this with an air of complete frankness, and then promptly fell silent again.

'All right, tell me.'

Suddenly Fletcher wrung his hands in front of his chest. 'You don't understand. I don't want you to *do* anything. I just want you to *be* here.'

'Why?'

'Because we've heard that someone is coming and we thought . . . we felt that if someone else was here there'd be less trouble for him.' Fletcher got to his feet and towards Frank, who was still standing near the door. 'You don't know what it's been like,' Fletcher said. 'There's been those letters he's been writing, awful letters, insulting letters, threatening letters. I'd a mind to go to the police with them and get the police to stop him writing them. But my wife wouldn't let me. You know what women are like – and she's just like that. Even worse where that precious man is concerned. And he's a child, he doesn't know what he's doing. He's capable of anything. And if that weren't enough, for the last six months there's been someone hanging around outside, waiting for something like this to happen so that he could strike. You don't know what it's done to my nerves. Look!' he exclaimed, and held up a hand in front of Frank. 'Look at that!' Frank saw his hand shaking with a continual tremor. 'Like an old man's,' Fletcher said. The hand that had been trembling in front of Frank went up to Fletcher's forehead and brushed his hair back. 'And I'm not an old man. There isn't a grey hair in my head. Look!' He bent his head down, so that Frank could see the truth of what he was saying.

9

Fletcher was still standing with his head down, when they heard, from the front of the house, a door being slammed, and then a man's loud voice in the passage. Fletcher did not lift his head, he remained in the posture of a penitent, humbling himself. Only, Frank saw that now his head was trembling too, at the end of the stalk of his neck: the man's head remained down because he simply did not have the strength to lift it.

Then he moved to take Frank by the arm. His voice was dry, like a whisper. 'You must stay with me. We can get rid of him tonight. There's two of us, so we'll be stronger than him.' His fingers were rubbing against Frank's arm like a shopkeeper feeling cloth. 'There's two of us,' he implored Frank. 'Isn't that so?' His grip on Frank's arm tightened. 'Please,' he said. 'Please.'

When the door behind them opened, Frank turned; Fletcher was still clinging to him so he turned too, right round, and now Frank was facing the door and Fletcher had his back to it. Fletcher had moved like a feather, like a dancer, so light was he with his fear. And the man who had come in hit Fletcher a resounding blow on the back. Fletcher collapsed into Frank's arms, like cardboard.

The newcomer laughed as Frank staggered back, with Fletcher's weight upon him. Frank pushed Fletcher away from himself, until the man was standing, and then, at what he judged to be the right moment, he let go. Fletcher stood – he did not fall as Frank had feared he might. He stood with his hair ruffled and his eyes on the newcomer's shoes and his arms reaching behind him until the fingers from each hand met one another. Then they clasped each other fiercely and fondly.

121

Frank was feeling relieved to see the man who had just come in. He was just a man – no spook or shadow or *doppelgänger* of Fletcher's: he was a young man, about Frank's age, with a plumpish face and a belt around his plump waist. Mrs Fletcher stood behind him, her face behind his shoulder. The young man turned his head sideways to her, and said, in Afrikaans, 'I didn't know you had visitors.'

'Then you'll hear about it,' Mrs Fletcher said.

The young man looked at her questioningly, but apparently thought better of saying anything to her. 'Well, everybody's welcome here as long as he behaves himself,' he said eventually to Frank. Then to Fletcher he said: 'Isn't that so? Even me, I'd be welcome here if I behaved myself – isn't that so?'

Fletcher was still between Frank and the newcomer. He had not extended his hand or said a word to the latter, but the man took Fletcher's arm above the elbow and pulled it towards himself. Fletcher's fingers tightened around one another where they were clasped behind his back, so instead of his arm coming forward, his whole body leaned forward as if he were made of wood. The other let him go.

'Aren't you going to shake hands with me?' he asked.

Fletcher said nothing. The man again turned his head and looked inquiringly at Mrs Fletcher: there was so little space in the door that their lips were almost touching. She stared ahead of her, without expression of any sort – she looked as if her husband were not in the room, let alone in the room and acting like a loon.

'Is he sick?' the young man asked. 'Hey,' he said rudely to Fletcher, 'are you sick?' There was no reply, so he leaned forward and put his face close to Fletcher's and studied him for a moment. Fletcher's face was down, so the young man had to bend a little to do so, and look up from below. It was a monkey-like, insulting peer at the man. 'Why don't you say anything?' he asked.

But for all the cheek of that stare – and it was cheek, a kind of naughtiness that he was displaying – it seemed to Frank that the man was nervous himself and was doing what he did mostly because he did not know what else to do. So he had turned it into a kind of a game, and in the game he was mocking not only Fletcher, but himself too, and Mrs Fletcher, even Frank. If he was making jokes, then, surely, his glance to Frank said, with an eyebrow cocked up interrogatively, like a comedian's on the bioscope, then there was nothing for him to worry about. *'Ou swaer,'* he said to Fletcher, *'wat makeer?'* His eyebrows climbed up even higher, and round his close-mouthed smile there were encircling lines in his cheeks; Frank wondered if he knew how close he was to grimacing. His whole expression seemed to be clinging round the wrinkles of amusement, determined not to let go.

He looked at Frank again, and shrugged. In English, he said to Frank, rather heavily: 'It's a sad case, isn't it?'

Frank did not reply.

But the newcomer and Fletcher were alike in one thing: with them, joviality covered a multitude of emotions. For the next moment his eye fell on the bottles behind Frank and Fletcher, and he said loudly: 'That's the ticket. There's nothing like a drink for a man who's had a long day.'

'Nasie,' Mrs Fletcher said warningly.

'Don't talk to me like that,' he replied, but still cheerfully. 'It's good stuff, isn't it?' he asked Frank. For Frank, too, cheerfulness was better than what might lie beneath it, so he said:

'Yes, man.' He could not help wondering if his cheerfulness rang as hollowly in the other's ears as it did in his own.

But Frank kept up the decencies, so the newcomer was able to say to Mrs Fletcher: 'There's a bloke who knows what he's talking about.' He smacked Mr Fletcher lightly on the shoulder. 'Let's have a drink.' Then his expression changed, and the smiling lines were lost in a sudden pouting. 'I forget,' he said. 'You don't drink. You've got no vices. You should have been a *predikant*. Have you ever heard,' he asked Frank, 'of a *predikant* who steals houses to make a living?' He was smiling again now that he was talking to Frank: he hung on to that smile, it seemed to Frank, as if it were all he had in the world.

It was quite clear to Frank that the kitchen was no place for him to be in. Whatever was going to happen there was

123

none of his business, and his curiosity was not so great that he was prepared to stand in the middle of the room hoping that gobbets of information might be flung at him. He moved past Fletcher and went to the door, and the man and the woman before him made way for him to go through, in silence, the man only looking at Frank quizzically as he went past, and turning his head to follow Frank with his eyes. Frank slipped past them, and then heard a scurry of footsteps. He turned and saw Mrs Fletcher and the newcomer hurled aside, and then Fletcher was attacking him. He had Frank by the arm and the neck, and Frank swung him this way and that, trying to shake him off. Mrs Fletcher and the other man grabbed at them too, and this made everything worse, for then there were four of them in the narrow passage reeling this way and that, banging against the walls and the doorposts. Eventually the other two prised Fletcher off, and held them apart.

Between gasps for breath, Fletcher said: 'Don't go away now.' And Frank, feeling utterly foolish, realized that Fletcher had not been attacking him, but merely been clinging to him. He had wanted Frank to stay. And it had been Frank who had started the fracas, not Fletcher. Probably when Fletcher had taken Frank's arm, Frank had jerked it up, and Fletcher had made a grab simply to keep his balance. Frank had felt that hand on his neck, and the fight had been on.

There was nothing that Frank could say to them. He saw a big, red drop of blood fall on his trousers, and then another, and another. 'Look,' he said, 'my nose is bleeding,' and made off down the passage. He left the other three standing in the passage. The newcomer stood behind Fletcher, holding him by the arm and the shoulder.

Part 3

10

When Frank had concluded his story, I told him as much
as I could of what had happened to myself before I came
back to our room. And when I had done so, we drew the
obvious conclusions: the newcomer was Ignatius Louw, Fletcher's brother-in-law; there was some sort of a feud between
himself and Fletcher; Joseph, the African, was in some way
or other involved in the feud. We drew these conclusions and
then found that there was nothing for us to do about them.
We were almost as ignorant as we had ever been of what
was happening in the house, and the knowledge we did have
could only tease us, no more. Yet we had been invited to stay
on in the house by its master because of what was going on,
and Joseph had asked me to read the letter to him: we seemed
to be in the middle of the affair willy-nilly. Surely it would
only be fair to ourselves to find out the reasons for the behaviour of the people who had met? So we argued to justify
our curiosity, which at that stage, and no matter what
rationalizations we might have been advancing, remained an
idle one. For the heart of the matter was that neither of us
had any intention of prolonging our stay in the house longer
than the next morning. We were on the road to Cape Town,
and despite Mr Fletcher's blandishments, and Mrs Fletcher's premature certainty that we would be staying, we
did not in the least want a free holiday. Not in Mirredal.
Not with Mr Fletcher. Or with any other member of his
family.

But curiosity itched, itched – we took turns to scratch it.
And we reassured ourselves that almost any methods we might
use to find out the truth of what was happening would be
justified: we repeated the invitations that had been given to
us, as witness of how right we were to cast about for ways of

finding out the truth. We couldn't then have known that we needn't have bothered to seek for excuses and rationalizations for our curiosity: even if we had been far more incurious than we were the facts of the matter would have been thrust under our noses. And before we were finished we were indeed in the middle of it, and at our own wish.

But we did not have the comfort of foreknowledge in our dull and flickering room. There was nothing for us to do; we lay on our beds and felt the sweat gathering in every crease of our bodies; we made wild speculations; once we opened the door of the room and listened intently to the silence in which the house, now, was plunged. I tried to read, but it was hopeless in that twitching light: Frank suddenly started to insist that I shave immediately, and we quarrelled bitterly over the hour at which we should rise the next morning. Our quarrel ended as suddenly as it had begun, leaving us both feeling a little foolish in the four-walled silence of the room, and still with nothing to do.

I closed my eyes but found it impossible to doze off as I had done before. Under my eyelids now there ran the white band of the road along which we had come; it was an endless white repetition of sand and corrugations, regular ribs of packed earth under the beating tyres of the car, slabs of earth worn smooth but for the small sharp rocks that lay embedded in it, shallow drifts of sand that lay loosely to the side of the road. Culverts rose to meet us, pebbles flew from our tyres, sand slewed from the tyres in a spray like shallow water, and at the verge of the road there was an unbroken chain of small brown bushes huddling close to the earth along the line of a jackal-proof fence. And rapidly, like ribbons, there was the waving and shaking and disappearance, the reappearance of the long marks on the road made by other tyres, other wheels, the metal rims of a laden donkey wagon that we roared past in a cry from the driver with his long whip, a shout from the surprised piccanin *voorloper* at the head of the long chain of dusty beasts, before they were swallowed in the clouds of dust that rolled insolently at our feet and behind us. And always, further away, the flat and haggard country over which we raced – gulleys, koppies, the bald stretches of sheet erosion,

126

the low surface of Karroo bushes, rocks, outcrop shining in the sun. Now curving, now straight, our road went across it, and we followed it, hell-for-leather, as if ten demons were behind us, as if beyond the pale, shaking horizon there would be no more koppies, no more gulleys, nor more bald stretches of bone-grey sheet erosion, no more outcrop shining in the sun. A roof shone, a tall steel windmill glinted, a kraal of round boulders lay shattered, no cattle or sheep nearby as if the people had trekked away with their possessions and the country had been abandoned to the sun that stalked above it. Still the road beat through it, and the whole pale land wheeled slowly and evenly around us. The road lifted a little and dipped a little, it rose to meet us, it scattered away from us, it held a pool of water in a cup of dust, before us. Easily, slightly, sickeningly, the lorry swayed towards the mirage; and when that water was all dust, towards it again, while under these yieldings, slidings, corrections, there was always the steady journeying vibration of the bald ribs of the road that were always immediately beneath us. And to the side of the road trapped beneath my closed eyelids, above the roar of our wheels, were other sights and sounds – the road itself was the torchbeam which had wandered so delicately through the darkness, and Joseph turning to meet it became the woman with her hands lifted under the picture, her voice the cries of the African children playing with the clay from the *pan,* the snarl of the voice of the man at supper, the roar of the engine of the car, the subtle patter of the sand when the car had stopped at the gate, Joseph calling me across the river-bed.

'Oh God,' I heard Frank say drearily.

His nose had started bleeding again. It was a relief for me. I got up from the bed and the whole violent day shrank to the dun brown walls of the room on which the light still flickered. But the light hung from its flex in the middle of the room, beneath the white board ceiling: this flicker was beyond my eyelids. I brought Frank the jug and took a handkerchief out of his kitbag, as he instructed me to do, and gave them to him. But this time, for all his dabbing and sniffing and muttered swearing, the bleeding would not be stanched, until he decided between sniffs that he would have to plug the offending nostril with cotton wool. The prospect alarmed me, but Frank said that he would do it by himself in front of a mirror – it was one of the advantages, he said, of being a medical student. Would I please ask Mrs Fletcher if there were any cotton wool in the house? And please, Frank added, would I not get involved in the affairs of the house while I was out of the room? He needed the cotton wool more than he did the satisfaction of his curiosity about the inhabitants of the house.

Having agreed with all he said, and delighted nevertheless at having something to do and at the opportunity of seeing the newcomer, of whom, I felt, I had read and heard so much, I went down the passage, through the little hall-room, and into the passage on the other side. There was a light under the door of the room where we had eaten, and as I came closer I heard voices, just a murmur, not at all loud. When I knocked the murmur stopped abruptly.

'Come in,' I heard Fletcher's voice.

I opened the door and was greeted in the room by a smile of sheer pleasure from Fletcher, as he leaned across the white tablecloth with which the table was still laid. He leaned towards me, pointing.

'This is the young man I was telling you about,' he said to the other man. 'There's two of them. You can see for yourself this one is a wideawake fellow. He's at the university, studying law. Isn't that what you're studying?'

'No,' I said.

Fletcher was not taken aback. 'Anyway, I'm sure you're making a good thing of it, whatever it is. I could see that immediately. Here's a pair of wideawake fellows I said, as soon as I saw them. And I was right too. Nasie, you must meet this young fellow. This is my brother-in-law, Ignatius Louw,' he said to me.

Louw leaned over the table, rising from his seat, and thrust his hand towards me. We clasped hands for a moment: his hand was small and plump and hard. Then, after he had already retracted his hand, he said: 'I'm pleased to meet you.'

'I'm pleased to meet you,' I said.

'Sit down, sit down,' Fletcher said, resuming his own seat. 'Nasie here has just been telling us about the various jobs he's had in the last few years. He's had quite a few, you know, all sorts. Some people are like that –' he said apprehensively, glancing at Louw – 'jack-of-all-trades, master of . . . them all, hey Nasie? What do you say? Yes,' he said, speaking to me again, 'Nasie's done nothing but talk. It's been very nice,' Fletcher said sincerely and nervously, his voice losing its strength, 'I hope he goes on like this, just talking, you know, telling us . . .' He fell silent. Then energetically he said: 'It's been such a surprise.'

'What did you expect?' Louw said loudly and mockingly.

'Nothing, nothing,' Fletcher hastened to placate him, with a gesture of his hand.

For a moment there was silence in the room. Mrs Fletcher was standing up, behind and to the side of her husband. Louw turned in his seat to look at me. 'What are you doing in these parts?' he asked me.

'Looking for the road to Cape Town,' I replied.

My joke went down well with Fletcher. And with Louw too, though he laughed abruptly only after looking me over for a moment.

Then Mrs Fletcher asked me, without equivocation: 'What is it that you want now?'

'I don't know if you know, but my friend's nose is bleeding –' I began. Fletcher interrupted me.

'You don't say so!' He got to his feet, frowning with solicitousness. 'You mean – still from when – but that's very serious. I think I better have a look at him. Don't you?' he asked his wife, who neither moved nor replied. He looked away from her, and gazed at his hands on the table. 'I think I better. These things can become serious if they're not attended to. I won't be a minute. I'll be back as soon as I can. I must go and have a look at the young fellow. I feel so responsible. And we don't . . .' Now he was edging himself between the table and the sideboard, the mirror reflecting the back of his head, the back of his unhappily gesticulating hands. He was still talking when he passed behind me. I took him by the arm, and he grabbed my own arm in a grip of surprising strength. 'Leave it to me,' he said.

'No,' I said. 'You don't understand. All my friend wants is some cotton-wool.'

'Cotton-wool?' Fletcher repeated, as if he had never heard of the stuff before. Then: 'Oh, cotton-wool. You mean cotton-wool. Of course I'll get some for him immediately.' Though his wife had still not made a single move, he held one hand warningly towards her. 'Don't worry, I know where it is, I'll see to it immediately. I know where it's kept.' The zeal with which he got himself out of the room – for a breather, probably – was irresistible. 'Serious,' he was saying in the door. 'Complications,' we heard. The door closed, but he opened it again and put his hand on my shoulder and pressed me down into a chair. 'You talk to Nasie,' he said. 'I'm sure you'll have lots to say to one another. Nasie,' he appealed, 'you tell this youngster some of the stories you've been telling me. Tell him the story of your last job. Tell him what you said to the fellow when he tried to cheat you of your overtime. It's a good story,' Fletcher assured me. 'Nasie told him off properly.' Again he looked nervously at Louw. 'He's wild,' he said. 'He doesn't care what he does. But it makes a good story afterwards, doesn't it, Nasie? Ha-ha!' Fletcher laughed. 'You won't miss me. I'll be back. Cotton-wool!' He closed the door behind him with a sudden sharp bang.

There was again a silence in the room after he'd left it: for a moment it was as if none of us could say anything even if we had wanted to, for Fletcher had used all the words. Mrs Fletcher leaned forward, listening so intently to her husband's footsteps beyond the door that she might have been expecting to read a message from them: they might have suddenly scurried away in flight, or broken into the rat-tat-tat of a dance step. But the sounds of his steps on the linoleum-covered passage simply receded, steadily, one after another, until the house absorbed them into its own silence.

Mrs Fletcher moved quickly to the door. She stood with her back to it. 'This is the young man, Nasie,' she said. 'I must tell you before he does. I've asked them to stay here until you leave. He has also, but he doesn't understand. He thinks it's for his sake, Nasie. But it isn't. It's for yours. Truly it is Nasie. You must believe that I don't want to help him. I want to help you.'

Louw said: 'Yes, yes.' He said it in English, though his sister had spoken Afrikaans to him: I assumed it was his way of warning her to mind what she said in front of me. As for me, she could have been speaking any language in the world – I hadn't understood what she'd just said.

'And then you must go Nasie. Without delays or excuses. You must go and never come back. You've been lucky this time, breaking your promise like that. But next time you won't be so lucky and then what will happen to you?' She clasped her hands in front of her chest. 'To us all?' she asked. She still spoke quickly and softly in Afrikaans.

Louw's eyes were on the table, and I was sure that he was embarrassed by what his sister was saying to him in my presence, and the hurried and furtive way she was saying it. I got to my feet. 'I'm interrupting,' I said. 'I'm sorry.'

'Of course you're interrupting,' Louw replied. He looked angrily at his sister. 'But it's just as well.'

I turned for the door, but Mrs Fletcher didn't give way. She said to Louw, still hurried, and, I think, a little bewildered: 'But he must be here, otherwise he won't understand.' She lifted one arm crooked at the elbow, the hand leaning forward at the wrist, bird-like, a gesture of restraint and interrogation. 'Or don't you understand?' she asked. I did not know of whom she was asking her question. Her eyes went equally from Louw to myself.

'Nobody understands,' Louw said irritatedly. 'You're all making a fuss. There's nothing to make a fuss about.' Though I could see he really did not want me in the room he leaned over the table and tried to manoeuvre my chair so that once again it was behind me: apparently he felt that it was better to have me there than to be alone with his sister. 'Sit down man. There's no need to run away. You aren't really interrupting anything important.' And again he gave his sister a puzzled, bullying glare from under his eyebrows.

'There is,' she said. 'There is a need. Tomorrow you must run away. Then these two boys can go too. Then there'll be peace again. As much peace as he lets us have.' Every time she said 'he' she emphasized the word as though there were only one person in the world to whom the word could possibly refer.

'Did you hitch-hike here,' Louw asked, ignoring her.

'Yes,' I replied. I felt I was being paid off for my curiosity. I was most uncomfortable.

'How did you come?' Louw asked. He was patiently making conversation, but I was grateful to him for doing so. I even felt that in what he was doing there was the desire not only to restrain his sister from raising topics uncomfortable to himself, but also an act of courtesy, to save me from embarrassment.

'I don't know,' I replied. I told him how we'd been picked up and brought to Mirredal, almost without our knowledge. He listened with attention that was divided only to the extent of now and then glancing at his sister. But for the most part he kept his eyes firmly on me, as if what I was saying was of any importance to anybody.

'Funny that,' he said, when I'd finished. 'I was going to say that nobody comes to Mirredal because he wants to.'

'What about yourself?' I asked.

'It's different for me,' was the reply. 'This is my home.'

'No!' His sister came forward and leaned across the table. When I turned my head my face was almost against the faded yellow print of her dress. 'You musn't talk like that, it's not your home.'

For the first time, Louw was drawn into what she'd said. 'Whose is it?' he asked, scowling. 'Your husband's?'

'Why don't you listen to me?' Mrs Fletcher asked, straightening. 'I've told you why you can't stay here. With that man outside – how can you think of staying? I'm not talking about your promises, Nasie, though you gave them like a man and should stick to them like a man. I'm talking about the danger that you're in.' She touched me lightly with her hand. 'He's seen him. If you don't believe me, ask him. He's talked to him. He knows what he's like. And for months it's been going on. Every night the same. He knows, Nasie.'

Louw said: 'That's enough.' But he could not let the matter go. 'He'd do nothing, anyway.'

'He would, if we weren't too many for him. I'm frightened of him, Nasie. You don't know how frightened I've been the last few months. And then your letters telling me that you were coming! Didn't you get my letters? But thank God, it will be all right this time. We're too many for him.' And again she touched me on the shoulder. Her words were distrait, but her voice was level and grave, though she spoke so quickly, hurrying all the time as if she had only a few minutes in which to say everything. I think she feared the return of her husband.

'Does everybody know?' Louw asked. 'Do you know?' he asked me. 'Have they told you everything about me?'

'No, Nasie, no,' his sister said. 'Nothing.'

I said: 'We don't know what's happening. All I know is that Mr Fletcher asked us to stay here for as long as we liked. He said that there was some sort of trouble – I don't know what kind it is.'

'That's what he thinks, Nasie,' Mrs Fletcher said. 'When he came to me and said the boys should stay it was because of you, Nasie. He was frightened for himself. He was frightened of you. But I said yes not because I cared what would happen to him but because of you Nasie. I thought the more we were the safer we were. Why didn't you read my letters? Then you would never have come. You would have known who's outside, waiting for you.'

'Look,' I said. 'We don't want to get involved in anything illegal.' It sounded so weak and foolish that I fell into silence even before Mrs Fletcher said:

'There'll be nothing for you to do. Nasie's going tomorrow morning, I promise you. Then you'll be able to go too. We won't charge you anything for the night.'

'That's not the point,' I said.

'Take it!' Louw said. Unexpectedly he grinned at me. 'Take a free night's board and lodging. What the hell have you got to lose?' I was surprised: I was quite beginning to like Louw. In the first instance he was younger than I had ever thought he would be – and it was a relief after the mustiness of the house and the uncanny youth of Fletcher and the fadedness of his wife, to come across someone really young. Not merely young but thriving too, physically, with a collar tight around his thick

133

neck and his shirt-cuffs tight around his wrists. His jacket was hanging over the chair behind him, and he sat with his arms extended on the table. He seemed, compared to everyone else in the house, plump, relaxed, and trim. It was a pleasure to see his tie hanging neatly down from a tiny knot, and for all his plumpness and the way his body swelled out the shirt at the shoulders and chest and neck, it did not do so flabbily but with a tautness of the flesh; a positive display of vigour it seemed to be in itself, in that decaying house. His face was round and ingenuous in appearance, but he wasn't, I thought, nearly as simple as he looked. He had round eyes, and his sister's small nose and small mouth, only his nose and mouth were set not among the lines of a thin and shrinking face, but in the healthy curves of his cheek and chin, and his eyebrows were cocked alertly above his round eyes. His brow was well-formed and smooth, except when he himself would crease it in interrogation or dismay or humour. He was not as I'd imagined him to be, though I was to see soon that his intelligence was inseparable from a kind of wilfulness, and that his small mouth could set easily enough into a sulk. He said: 'That's more than I'm getting – a free invitation. All they've invited me to do is leave.' He looked at me as though inviting me to share his sulk if I cared to. And then he added, 'I may be an expensive visitor for them, all the same,' and in that remark there was no room for me or anyone else.

Mrs Fletcher was still leaning across the table, listening to every word her brother said – she leaned lower, inquiringly, when he fell silent. 'Nasie . . . ?' she began.

But he was too quick for her. He spoke to me, ignoring her. 'So you've been impressed with Mirredal?' he asked.

'It's not a bad little *dorp*,' I said.

Louw laughed. 'No, it's not too bad if you come here on a visit. I used to hate the place, but now that I've been around a bit I can't say that I mind it so much. It's funny, when you're a kid you think anywhere must be better than the place you're in, but when you're grown-up you decide that one place is so like another that it's hardly worth moving. If the other places are different they would only be worse, you think, not better, so it's better to stay in the place you know best. Like me,' he said. 'If anybody had told me that I'd *want* to live in Mirredal I would have laughed at him. Me? Live in a place like Mirredal? I was much too good for Mirredal. I thought I was going to be something special – I suppose most kids do. And look at me tonight –' he opened his hands, and beckoned inwards, towards himself – 'here I am, come to settle in Mirredal after all.'

'Nasie . . .' his sister said.

'And what town did you say you're from?' Louw asked me.

'Lyndhurst.'

'A bigger kind of Mirredal?'

I smiled. The description was accurate. 'Yes, I suppose it is.'

'And would you like to settle there?'

'I don't know,' I said. 'Sometimes I think I would, other times I feel I might as well bury myself alive as settle in Lyndhurst.'

'Take it from me,' Louw said, 'in a few years time you'll be only too glad to bury yourself alive in Lyndhurst, if you've got a place to live there, a place to sleep, people you know, food to eat – all the things you don't think about until you've had to do without them. Look at me,' he invited again, with that flick of his fingers. 'Here I am.'

His sister took his fingers in her own. 'Haven't you heard a word I've said? Must I say it all again?'

Louw sat back in his chair with exaggerated alarm. 'No, for Christ's sake don't do that!'

The humour of it escaped his sister entirely. 'You'll listen to me before I'm finished,' she said. 'You'll see that I'm right.'

'O.K. I will,' he said; he still mocked her, though: 'Just you let me know when you're finished.'

I stood up. 'I'll be off now,' I said. I really did not want to stay in the room with the two of them any longer – Mrs Fletcher was too much for me. 'I must see how my friend is getting on.'

11

Fletcher was standing idly in the passage, as if it had been a street, and he were waiting there for a friend to come out of one of the buildings along it. He came sliding up the wall towards me. 'You're not leaving,' he said, when he was still a few paces away from me. 'I've just asked your friend to join us.'

'In the passage?' I asked.

'No,' he said. 'I was just going into the room –' he gestured towards it. Then he must have felt that I'd seen the way he had been hanging around outside, for he added, 'I was just thinking by myself for a moment.' An even better explanation occurred to him. 'I was waiting for your friend.'

'But he can't be coming,' I said. 'His nose –'

'I know all about his nose. It will be all right in just a few minutes, you wait and see. I've brought him the cotton-wool and a new cloth – you'll see, it'll stop bleeding in no time.'

'I better go and see all the same.'

'I'll come with you,' Fletcher said eagerly. 'We'll go together and see how it's getting on.' He looked thoughtfully at the door a few yards behind me, then, 'No,' he said, 'we'll leave the two of them. They've got lots to talk about. My wife's been like a mother to that boy, and they haven't seen each other for a long time now.' We were moving side by side down the passage. 'Worked harder for him than a mother could, she did, so that the family wouldn't be let down. It was a burden for her, she was just a young girl when she was left to look after that boy, all by herself.'

He stopped walking and stared at me for a moment, 'That's the way it is,' he said. 'I'm not saying she's been adequately rewarded for the work she's done. But she's given of her best.' He shook his head. 'Misguided!' he said sadly. 'Misguided . . .'

'Have you seen my library?' He took me by the arm. With the other hand he opened a door that I had not hitherto seen opened, and switched on a light. He stepped into the room first. The room was shuttered and stale, and overfurnished like every other room. Like ballast the furniture in that house was, weighting the people down, giving them a solidity they would have lacked without it. There were bookcases all the way round the walls of this room – high, heavy bookcases, some of them with glass fronts, others without. And there was an old-fashioned roll-top desk, and a small brass table bearing on it an enormous brass pot – Benares-ware, I think the stuff is called. I didn't have a chance to look at the books with which the bookcases were crammed: they seemed to be a pretty dusty and unused collection. In the brass pot there were rolled up copies of various magazines, *Spotlight* and *The Outspan* and *Die Huisgenoot*, cylinders of them thrust into the pot as though they were flowers. A large old-fashioned radio stood in the corner. When he saw me looking at it Fletcher explained, 'Battery model. But we don't listen much. There's atmospherics. There's interference.' His voice trailed away. He stood next to me, on the verge of the room, with the open door just behind him.

'Books hey?' he said suddenly, lively again. 'I bet you'd like to lay your hands on some of these books. There's old books here, valuable some of them. Most of them belonged to my late father-in-law. Books he got in Holland when he was a student there. Law books. Books on science. Encyclopaedias. He was a great reader. His wife, you know, died when she brought that youngster into the world. After the funeral he went straight into his room, didn't take part in the funeral lunch, and when they sent for him they found him reading a book. That's what I heard in the village when I first came here. And the farm went to ruin but he didn't care. He said he had to live in the village because of his legal practice, but a fat lot of practice he had by the time he died. Yes, he died, you know, leaving my poor wife with the burden of the farm and this house, and that young brother of hers. She did her best. She brought that boy up – she was mother and father to him. She is all he has in the world. And the things I had to put up with from him. Cheek! Impudence! Lies! Insults! But he had to come to me in the end. I had to drag him out of his troubles.'

From the way he was talking he might have been under instructions to keep me busy while some shady scheme were being carried out in another part of the house. He gestured around him at the room, overweighted with unused books and paper and furniture, mouldering things half-dusted, a surfeit of possessions. 'I do my accounts here. But any afternoon you care to have a look around just let me know. You can have the run of the place. I'm sure you'll find a lot of stuff that will interest you. History – are you interested in history? There's real history in this room. Papers from the time of my father-in-law's father and before that.'

'Yes,' I said. 'Hadn't we better be getting along to see how my friend is?'

'Of course,' he said with alacrity. 'Funny thing,' he said, as he switched off the light and we stepped into the passage again. 'Funny thing, family pride. You should hear my wife on the subject. Her father! Not that it's helped them much,' he said with undisguised malice, squeezing my arm above the elbow. 'We've got no children, and that young fellow in there – all he could ever do is bring disgrace on the family.'

He stopped in the middle of the passage to tell me: 'She had plans for him. Oh, such plans! She was going to marry him to one of the richest girls in the district. Ten thousand morgen the Noordhuizens have got, and only one daughter. You must have passed their place, Kameelhaak they call it – it's along the main road, about a mile or two away from the village. And who's going to come into those ten thousand morgen? Not Louw, not him. Nobody had ever seen young Meneer Bester until the Noordhuizen girl met him on holiday. At the Strand she met him, and now she's Mrs Bester. And what is there so special about Bester?'

'Is he a young chap?' I asked. 'Hasn't got very much to say for himself? Drives a brown Ford van?'

'That's the one,' Fletcher said.

'I think he's the one who gave us the lift here,' I said.

But Fletcher did not seem surprised at the coincidence; he did not even comment on it, except to say, 'Yes, he's always running around. Well, he can afford it. And it was Nasie who could have had all of it: the girl liked him, any fool could see that the girl liked him. But he had to leave, and she took another, and I'm not going to say anything against Bester just because he married a rich girl. People say that he's unfriendly, and they say that he doesn't want to talk to anyone because he's ashamed – he thinks everybody believes that he married the girl just because of her money. But people are always saying that sort of thing. Some people even said it about . . .' He dismissed that thought with a wave of his hand, and reverted to an earlier one. 'But that marriage was the end of some fine, fine plans for this house. Maybe for the Noordhuizen girl too – who knows? – she looks glum enough nowadays, whenever I see her in the *dorp* . . .'

So he talked apace, while we made our way down the passage and into the bedroom I shared with Frank. We found Frank lying on his back, with a trickle of blood across his cheek, slanting down from his nose. It was dry though, and Frank was fast asleep.

'He seems all right,' Fletcher whispered in my ear. 'We had better leave him.'

'Yes,' I said. 'It does seem better.' I turned to him. 'Thank you for your help, Mr Fletcher, I appreciate it very much. And now if you don't mind I think I'll be turning in too.'

'Turning in?' he asked incredulously. 'Turning in too?' He whispered his surprise in my ear. I saw his shining face close to my own, and the electric-like blond hair that grew in a tuft under his eyes. 'I won't permit that. No, no, you must join our little party. After all, it isn't so very often that we have so many guests at one time.'

'Yes,' I said. 'But we've had a long day and I'm very tired, so if you don't mind . . .' I gestured him out of the room with my hand. But his legs didn't budge. Only his body leaned towards me, and he was whispering in my ear again.

'You'll be able to rest tomorrow. You'll have breakfast at eleven in the morning, if you like. There'll be no limit. You're not anxious about your breakfast, are you?'

'No,' I truthfully replied.

'Well then.' He lengthened the last word out to a breath. 'You'll come with me.' He switched off the light in our room, and closed the door. We stood in the passage again.

I immediately opened the door. He tried to prevent me, simply by putting his hand on mine where it rested on the handle. His touch was surprisingly dry, on such a warm evening. I closed the door again. I did not want to wake Frank.

'Look,' I said. 'What the hell is going on here? If you don't tell us, I don't understand how the hell you can expect us to help you.'

'Didn't your friend tell you?' he asked.

'He doesn't know. You haven't told him either.'

The man said a little grudgingly, 'I thought I had given him to understand that his presence here was for ... was for ... what would you call it.'

I thought he was simply groping for a word, but he fell silent. 'I don't know,' I said. It was only when I said the words that I realised his question had been a device to find out how much I did know.

He was disappointed, anyway. 'I would have thought you'd have gathered by now. You're educated young people. What is it that you go to university for if not to sharpen your minds?'

I was certainly not going to answer that question, so I remained silent while he looked at me from under his thick blond eyebrows. Then he threw his head back. I knew that was coming, and waited for it. It came – his harsh laugh, like the fall of an axe against wood.

'No offence meant,' he said. 'And none taken.'

'No,' I said.

'That's the spirit. Come,' he said. 'We'd better be going back.'

By that time I felt not only that I had lost my curiosity about what was happening in the house – I felt something else too – I wouldn't call it fear – it was nothing as grand as that. Deserted would be a better word. Or lonely. Miles from any place I knew, and with my companion asleep. It was a kind of homesickness, I felt then, but it was a sickness for a home I had never had, for a single cultivated scene, for a country less empty and violent, for people whose manners and skins and languages were fitted peaceably together. The lorry on which we had hitched a lift from that young couple, whose little history I had just heard, had hurled us towards the man next to whom I stood, and whom I had never seen before, across endless countrysides of heat-seized, silent veld; now we stood together for a moment before the next day would hurl us apart again. And so Louw himself had come, and Frank who was sleeping, and the African outside who had been to Johannesburg – a multi-tongued nation of nomads we seemed to be, across a country too big and silent for us, too dry for cultivation, about which we went on roads like chains. We were caught within it, within this wide, sad land we mined but did not cultivate.

Fletcher looked at me anxiously. 'Everything will be fine,' he said.

I stared at him as though he were a mind-reader who had read partly right, but drawn the most hopelessly wrong conclusions from what he had read. 'Fine?'

'Yes. Haven't you understood? I thought your friend would have explained to you. I was expecting trouble when that young brother-in-law of mine came here but now everything will be fine. He won't start any trouble when he sees how many friends I've got. You see, we didn't know exactly when he would be coming, and that's why I invited you to stay as long as you cared to. But now he's come and he'll be going again soon, and then you'll be quite free to go or stay, as you please. Not that you aren't free now.' He had me by the elbow again. 'Of course you are. But if you go after he's left your consciences will be absolutely clear, and you'll know that you helped a friend of yours when he was in trouble. You won't have let me down. I knew you for a pair of winners as soon as I set my eyes on you.'

'What's wrong with your brother-in-law?' I asked.

'Everything. What isn't wrong with him? That's why I asked you to stay. He won't dare start anything with me when he sees that I've got two friends here.'

'Why should he start anything with you?'

'Because he thinks I've wronged him. Wronged him! I've saved his life. I've saved his name and the name of his family. But now he thinks I've wronged him. Do you know that he's threatened to stop my mouth forever?' He stared at me in all seriousness, his mouth slowly closing, after bringing out the phrase. 'Those are the words he used in one of his letters.

What kind of language is that?' he asked me, still seriously, as if I could give him any sort of an answer. 'But with you here he'll be as meek as a mouse. You mark my words. He'll be leaving soon. But you must show him that we're friends. He must see that I've got friends on my side, and then he'll understand that this is no place for him.'

'How did you wrong him?' I asked.

He let my elbow go. 'You ask me that?' he demanded. He scowled at me, his head hanging down at the end of his thick neck, with all the weight of hair on it. 'You're my friend and you ask me that.' He swung his head up. 'I *never* wronged him. He wronged me. And his sister – think what he did to her! And I – I –' He struck his chest with an open palm, so that the flabby slapping sound was loud in the constricted passage. 'I was the one who set matters right.'

'Why does he think you wronged him?'

'Because I sent him away. He came to us and told us what he'd done. He came with his cheeky manners and loud voice – and his lip trembling. This one,' Fletcher said, and seized his own lower lip and waggled it between finger and thumb. 'Like that he was, in terror, for all his shouting and bravado. And I knew that it was my chance. I told him that I'd fix the matter up, and save him and his sister and every white man in the country from disgrace – you too, and your friend who's lying in the room asleep. You must remember that. What I'm asking from you isn't a favour, it's a payment for what I've done for you as a white man.' The man softened his voice and came closer to me. 'From him,' he said, 'from that Nasie I insisted on payment down.' One finger tapped against the palm of the other hand. 'No payment in a year, or ten years, or twenty years, maybe never. Down payment. A hard bargain.'

'What was the bargain?'

'That he leave. That he get out and not come back. That we never see him again.'

'Did he agree to it?'

'Didn't I tell you the state he was in? He was only too grateful when I told him I'd fix the affair up for him. He would have agreed to anything. Oh, I knew the state he was in when I

142

offered him my bargain. I'd been watching him, when he didn't know that he was being watched. I saw how he carried on when he was alone.'

'What was it that he'd done?' I asked.

The man said very softly, 'That I'm not prepared to say.'

'In that case,' I said, 'I'm not prepared to help you. And I can speak for my friend as well.'

'What difference does it make to you?' he asked. Then he added: 'Friendship doesn't ask questions!'

'Doesn't it?'

'No,' he said earnestly, shaking his head. 'If you're my friend you wouldn't be asking such questions. And you are my friend. You and that boy asleep in that room – we're together, aren't we?'

Should I have disabused him of that idea? He was in earnest in asking for our friendship; and though the request was shabby, ill-nurtured, devious, even malevolently-motivated, it was a kind of trust that he was – I felt – asking of me. I didn't yet have the heart to refuse it. Not abruptly, in so many words, a few inches from his face.

12

I walked with him to the door of the room in which Louw and his sister had remained. At the door Fletcher said: 'They haven't heard us yet' – whispering the words to me. And the murmur of voices that we had heard did not in fact slacken off, as it would have had the people been expecting the entry of others into a room. It went on. The voice was Louw's. Suddenly it rose into a single, inquiring word:

'You?'

'Yes. Who else?'

The voices dropped again. We were just about to enter, when there was a loud rasp from Louw, and Fletcher checked my movement towards the door with his hand. Louw shouted: 'I'm not scared.'

Fletcher nudged me with his elbow. 'Did you hear that?' he

said. He had no shame at all about eavesdropping in front of me: perhaps because we were friends, now.

'You are,' Mrs Fletcher said abruptly, also raising her voice.

I put my hand on the door-knob, but Fletcher pulled it away. 'We must listen,' he said. He whispered something I could not catch: he was being very careful. His voice trailed off. I heard the word '... interesting.'

Mrs Fletcher said: 'Have it your own way. I'd like to see you face up to him. He knows something.' Then she said: 'Thank goodness those two boys are here. I don't know what would have happened if they weren't here.'

'And you were the one who wanted to keep everything so secret,' her brother said.

'But it is. They know nothing. They aren't going to get anything out of me.'

'And that husband of yours. Do you trust him to keep quiet?'

'He has so far.'

'He's had no one to talk to.'

'You talk like a child,' Mrs Fletcher said. 'He also has his reasons for keeping quiet.'

'Of course,' Louw said, mollified. Then angrily again: 'Why hasn't he chased Joseph away?'

'How? You know we've tried.'

'By giving him a hiding. That's the only way to treat them.'

'Can you see my husband giving Joseph a hiding?' Mrs Fletcher laughed at the thought. It was the first time that I'd heard her laugh: it came out in a thin chatter, a rattle of sound in a high voice. Then she added something which I could not make out, and her brother replied:

'It's disgusting. What sort of man is he?'

'Don't ask me that. His own sort, I suppose.' Again there was the rattle of her laugh: apparently her brother's presence brought out certain gayer elements of her character which were at other times concealed. Though gay is hardly the word for her laugh.

'He was man enough once,' Louw said morosely.

'He was. He was the man who saved you.'

It was only when I heard that that I dared for the first time to look at Fletcher. He seemed to have forgotten that I was with him; his face was no more than an inch or two from the blank piece of wood before it; his mouth was open. I could have given him the smallest shove with my hand in the small of his back – a friendly, joking kind of shove: one of those he had given me numerous times in the course of the evening – and he would have lost a couple of teeth. And for the first moment he would not have known where the shove had come from, so rapt was he in hearing the voices of his wife and brother-in-law say discreditable things about him.

Then Mrs Fletcher said: 'You always hated it here. You always said you wanted to get away.'

'Of course I said that sort of thing. I was a young boy – I didn't know anything.'

'You knew some things only too well.'

'I was young,' Louw repeated.

'You weren't so young.' Then Mrs Fletcher's voice spoke rapidly, the words pattering out in her monotone. 'I'm not going to say the things that I've already said to you a hundred times. I have said them, though you've never heard me. I've said them to you at night when I can't sleep, in the mornings when I wake up and walk around the house where you no longer live, when I drive in the car with him to the village, in the evenings when neither of us talk to one another and I go on to the stoep and stare at the darkness and try to remember what you looked like and what your voice sounded like. I dream sometimes that I'm telling you these things, and I wake up and I could cry that you aren't here for me to tell you these things.'

'It's just as well,' came the heavy mocking voice of her brother. 'They don't sound such pleasant things to me.'

'How could they be? After what you've done.'

'And you?' Louw asked. 'Do you think that you have done the right thing?'

There was a silence. I'd been watching Fletcher, who was now actually leaning against the door, with his forehead against the wood, as a man in a fever will lean against a wall or a pane of glass to cool his brow. But though his eyes were closed I was sure that he was listening not with anger but with a kind of delight, almost of glee, to the things that were being said. And the delight was not only that he was hearing his wife and his brother-in-law without their knowledge, and so playing some sort of trick on them, but more immediate and intense: it was obvious in his attitude that he was finding some justification for his own behaviour in the laughter and scornful voices and references to him that had come to him through the closed door – though now in the room there was a silence so deep that it was as if the voices had dropped out of hearing into a gulf. We stood purposely, like sleepwalkers, out-side a room in which there might have been no people but only the beating light on heavy, untenanted furniture. Fletcher, however, did not move from his position: he remained devout against the door.

'I tried to do my best,' Mrs Fletcher said eventually. She spoke very slowly.

'Your best?' came Louw's harsher, more rapid voice. 'Your best for whom? For your brother?'

'Yes, for my brother. For myself. For my father.'

'Your father's dead.'

'He is not dead as long as his children are alive. I was in his place. I asked myself what our father would have done if this had happened while he had been alive. There was only one answer, Nasie. But I know – I know –' her voice fell silent again. 'I understand,' she said. Then: 'I could never have done it if he hadn't said that those were the terms on which he'd help us. We could do nothing. Do you remember what you were like when you came and told us what you had done, Nasie? Do you remember how you shook? How you cried that you couldn't go to jail?'

'I remember,' Louw said. 'And I remember how you lis-tened to him telling us his plan without saying a word. I wanted some message from you, but you stood without moving. You stood silently when he made me swear that I would never come back. I thought: how can she stand there silently when her brother is swearing never to come back to his house? But I swore: there was nothing else I could do. I swore, and I went away. And before I left, when I was packing my things, did you come and help me? Did you stand in the room and talk to me while I was still in your house? Did you walk with me to the gate? Nothing. I went like a stranger. Worse than those two chaps who came here tonight.'

'I was frightened,' Mrs Fletcher said.

'What of?'

'Of seeing you. Don't you understand? I try to imagine what you must have felt like, but you don't ever seem to make the effort to understand my feelings. You had done wrong, Nasie, and we were in trouble. If I'd been a man I would have sent you away, for my father's sake, because I was in his place. But I was too weak, and I knew I was too weak. And when he came with his plan how could I refuse when I believed it was the right thing to do? I was grateful to him, Nasie, grateful for doing what I was too weak to do.'

'But why did he do it?' Louw asked.

'That doesn't matter. He was doing what I had to do, and his reasons didn't matter. I bore the guilt: he made me expiate it. What could I do but obey him?'

'Bear the guilt? You still live in this house. I'm the one who has no home.'

'And what do you think this house is to me without you? It's a prison, not a house. I brought you up the best way I knew how, and you were hardly a man when you brought shame on your father and me. And on yourself. And I had to live without you.' She dropped her voice. 'But I was grateful to him, all the same.'

'You *were*!' Louw seized on the word. 'And now?'

'I hate him.' The words were without expression.

'And don't you think I've been punished enough by now?'

'Nasie,' Mrs Fletcher said soothingly, 'you can't live here now. Even if I did think you had been punished enough there'd be no place for you. Joseph is here, Nasie. He's waiting for you. He can kill you Nasie, for what you did to him. I know how the kaffirs feel about their families. He thinks you took his sister away from him.' Her voice changed suddenly. 'I think he's mad. He's a madman. You can't live in the same *dorp* as he does, Nasie. Do you know that when you came walking up the path with that one little suitcase of yours, there was someone standing in the darkness, not moving, not afraid, not saying anything, not thinking –' her voice rose on the last word – 'watching, watching, watching you. As he's been watching this house for months and months.'

'He's got nothing to connect me with it,' Louw said. But her words, to judge from his voice, had impressed him. He sounded sulky again, half-beaten.

'He doesn't need anything. He knows. Don't ask me how he knows. Perhaps he met his sister somewhere. Perhaps she told him what happened.'

'No!'

'Why did you say no? Do you know? He knows, that one, outside. Don't think that he doesn't. He's been waiting for you. You must leave tomorrow.'

'No,' Louw said, like a petulant boy.

'Yes,' his sister insisted gravely. And then they were silent again.

Fletcher had stepped back. His expression was as somnambulist as ever, but now the distant, obscured glee had been replaced by an expression of distaste. He frowned a little, with a vague distaste on his features, as a dreamer will frown seeing or hearing something in his dream that the dreamer does not comprehend. His head moved neither to the right nor to the left, and his forehead was creased and his mouth turned downwards: how could this unpleasantness, his expression asked, be any concern of his? Why had it been thrust under his attention? But when Mrs Fletcher spoke again, dream-like he leaned forward to listen.

'You ask me,' she said, 'why I stood silently when he made you swear never to come back. Why didn't I help you pack your things, or walk with you to the gate. Haven't you thought at all? Have you ever tried to put yourself in my place? Didn't you understand, even then, that I didn't do them because if I had – if I had seen you pack, if I had walked with you to the gate, if I had spoken when he was making you swear that you would never come back – if I had done any of these things I would never have let you go? If I had walked with you to the gate I would have gone beyond the gate, I would have followed you to the village and beyond. If I had watched you packing your things I would have gone to my room and packed my own things so that I would be ready to leave when you left. If I had spoken when he was making you swear that you'd never come back, I would have sworn that I would never come back either. Nasie, have you had no thoughts for your sister? Have you never thought that I loved you?'

Louw was silent.

'Do you understand now?' Mrs Fletcher said.

There was still no reply from Louw.

'Will you ever forgive me?' the wretched woman called.

The room was silent: there was not so much as a creak from a chair, a groan from the ageing floorboards.

'Nasie! Why don't you look at me?' This time we heard a piece of furniture being flung aside, and then again Mrs Fletcher's voice, muffled now, as if her head were in her hands or she were embracing her brother. 'Nasie, can I come with you? I can't live here any longer like this. I can't bear this house without you. Nasie,' she implored him, 'please let me come with you. We'll expiate your sin together.'

Shockingly, Louw laughed. 'That,' he said, 'sounds like a hell of a life. No thanks. No thanks.'

'You won't stay here,' Mrs Fletcher said. 'And you won't go by yourself. I'm coming with you.'

Louw was silent for a few moments. When he spoke his voice was calm. 'Christ!' he said. 'I want a drink.' There was no reply from Mrs Fletcher so he wheedled her: 'Go and fetch me a drink, Chrissie. Go on.'

I waited almost with anxiety to hear how Mrs Fletcher would respond to her brother's carelessness, his sudden disregard, his flippancy. And she promptly and shamelessly flirted with him. 'Drink without food will make you so drunk. You think I don't know you? Your head would swing on a thimbleful: do you think your sister knows nothing about you?'

'Never mind,' Louw said. 'Go on, *ousis*. Bring the bottle here.'

'And you'll have only one?'

'Maybe two . . .' Louw replied, in the same rising tone.

'Then I won't bring the bottle,' she said.

'Oh yes you will.'

'Oh no I won't.'

'If you don't bring it,' Louw said quickly, cajolingly, 'I'll go and bring it myself.' He waited; he was sure of his victory. 'You bring the bottle and we'll see how many I have.'

'I'll make some sandwiches too,' Mrs Fletcher said. 'You haven't eaten a thing.'

'Ach, I've had some chocolate,' Louw said, deliberately gruff, like a tough twelve-year-old.

'Chocolate! That's not enough for you.'

'You're telling me. All right, Chrissie, you bring the bottle and make some sandwiches and I'll wait here for you. How about that?'

'Yes,' Mrs Fletcher said. 'Yes, Nasie, it's so nice to have you here again. It's been such a long time since I last saw you. I'll bring your food now. I'll be happy to watch you eat.'

They were silent again: perhaps clasping hands, perhaps embracing. Then we heard footsteps approaching the door. Fletcher said loudly to me as he stepped back lightly in the passage:

'Your friend is all right now, isn't he? We fixed him up, didn't we?'

I stood for a moment stupidly, and then said: 'Yes,' as the door opened and Mrs Fletcher stepped between us in the passage. She looked at me and her husband, her expression blank. 'Thank you. Good night. Good night, Mrs Fletcher.' I left them to go to my room. Fletcher made a grab at me, that missed. I went on down the passage.

But Mrs Fletcher came after me, leaving her husband at the door. She said seriously to my retreating back, 'You can leave tomorrow. We're all leaving tomorrow.' I turned to look at her. She was as grey and faded as ever, but one large hand was extended towards me, palm up, exposed like a present. It was empty. I did not understand the gesture until I realized that, as her eyes did, her gesture promised me that there was no concealment: she displayed to me even the awkward and ugly hand that usually she carried thrust away from her like a guilt.

Part 4

13

In our room our packs were lying open on the floor, disgorging their contents in a mess of towels and billycans, a Penguin book stained with shaving soap, a pair of dusty boots. The place looked about as permanent, for us, as an army-billet, and as well cared-for. We hadn't used the enormous dark-brown wardrobe that cast a tiny shadow about itself on the pale carpet, nor had we sat on the velvet-covered armchair in one corner, though the seat sagged as though someone had just got up from it. And the bulb beat in light and shadow against the dun wallpaper that was marked with stripes and the outline of faded leaves, and stains, and an indecipherable frieze below the picture railing, from which no picture hung. Our beds were disarranged, Frank lolling on his while he listened to my story. We were both in shirt-sleeves, but I could feel the sweat slowly and continuously gathering in my armpits and under my bent knees as I sat on the bed. And when I wiped my forehead I was doing no more than brush one moist surface with another.

At the window the shutters we had opened yawned down from their hinges, a weight on the metal screws that held them. In hope of finding it cooler there, I went to the window and leaned out, my elbows on the sill. The paint on the sill was coming away in hard angular pieces that were brittle to the touch, and I tried to think what the flakes of paint reminded me of, and then remembered the *pan* outside the location, and the African children who had been flinging the flat cakes of dried clay at one another, as we had walked past. I remembered how each cake had burst into fragments with a puff of dust when it had hit the ground, so dry and brittle they had been. And no wonder with a sun shining on them like the one under which we had travelled to the village.

Outside, now, the blaze of the sun was gone, and gone too was the first thick darkness in which Mrs Fletcher and I had shone our torch and found Joseph, the African, at the end of its beam. Now there was a half-moon up, riding high in the sky, and round it the blackness of the sky was softened, weakened, watered into a blue-grey mist through which the stars around the moon could only feebly shine. Lower down it seemed that the light of the moon had less effect, and there, towards the horizon, the sky remained almost as dark as the earth that was tilted sombrely towards it. Nearer, the light lay meagrely upon the ground, without the lambent smooth glitter with which the full moon would invest it.

How still the air was – curtain-like it seemed to hang, down from the moon that held it together like a clasp. Over the shadow-shapes the air rested, on the ground it lay, motionless, unstirred by a hand. But though the air was so still and warm, the warmth and stillness were not stifling together, perhaps because of the dryness and clarity of the air in the lungs, perhaps because of the simple respite from the shining of the sun that the night seemed to be. And one could look up and see the height of the stars and the moon, and see the spaciousness of what had otherwise seemed to have fallen soundlessly and closely upon one. When a sleepy *koringkriek* trilled one long note the sound came through the air as sharp as a drill before fading unexpectedly into silence, as if the air hardened to let no sound through.

There was no rustle of any dry, falling thing. The garden did not move, and the black veld that lay beyond might have been a chaos, without form. That was the way we had come, to where we were now, to where, in the moonlight I could descry the borders of the faded garden, and the outlines of a row of low trees. Before me the light from the room cast an oblong of yellow light on the stoep, in the middle of which lay my own dark shadow on the cracked cement of the stoep. The nearest palm showed its leaves in a fan of hard green spikes that bristled almost a full circle round. But the spike-tips were wilting, languishing into thin brown whiskers. They did not move: the hairs hung in the air downwards as they had fallen, or trailed back and lay lightly on the motionless leaves. To my right and left there was the darkness of the house, where rooms in darkness were thrust forward on the stoep, their shutters closed. No light shone into the garden, other than the one behind me: the parapet around the stoep was in darkness, and the wooden pillars that at regular intervals held up the roof above the stoep. And all round lay the uncultivated veld, the country in darkness, the land which human hands had barely touched, putting up a barbed wire fence here or a windmill there, but barely scarring the surface, scratching the rock-outcrop which so much of the Karroo was. I could not see it, could not even see the rocks along the line of the river, and the lights of the village did not show – they had all gone out by this time.

But I had forgotten that in that rough darkness there lingered someone who was watching the house and must have seen me leaning out of the light. Out of the darkness that gathered itself in the garden where I knew the gate-posts to be, a shadow detached itself and began moving up the path. For a moment, forgetting, I thought it to be an animal, for what person at that hour would be wandering around the house so thrust in darkness as the one we were in? But no, it was erect, and tall: it was a man. I heard a man's booted step on the cracking concrete path, coming closer, without pause. They were on the stoep. A stone skidded away from the boot with a tiny scream across the concrete. The man had turned towards the window, and was coming closer.

I withdrew. Frank too had heard the footsteps, and was standing up between the beds, looking towards the open exposed space in the wall through which our light had shone on the surrounding night – so feeble the light had been, so open our window, so large and unoccupied the night.

Out of it there emerged a hand. A single, cracked-skinned brown hand rested for a moment, by itself, on the shattered white paint of the sill.

'Joseph,' I said, for reassurance.

He stood there, the frame of the window cutting short his legs at the knees, but the rest of his body centred with the square of light, his face high up in the open space, his hand on the sill. The light shone on his brow, on his flat, forward-pursed face beneath the heavy brow.

'Baas,' he said gravely to me. Then he saw Frank, and greeted him too: 'Baas.' He lifted one hand from the sill, then placed it flat down again. He spoke to me, not to Frank, whom he did not know. 'Baas, will you help me again?'

He waited for a reply. 'I don't know,' I said.

'I need help again, baas.'

'What kind of help? Have you stolen another letter?'

He withdrew his hand. He paused. Then he replied to my question. 'No.' He waited: he was giving me another chance.

'What kind of help do you need?' I asked.

'All I want is you to tell me what you have heard in this house,' he said.

'Will that help you?'

'Yes.'

I said: 'We've heard so many things in this house. We can't tell you anything – unless you tell us what it is that you want to know.'

He looked at me closely, without moving, trying, I thought, to see if I were mocking him or telling him what I believed to be the truth.

'We don't understand what we've heard,' Frank said. 'So we can't tell it to you. If we understood we could tell you.' Joseph turned his attention to Frank, the newcomer, the one he'd had no dealings with. 'Do you see?' Frank asked, his voice as calm as his pose, where he stood with his hands in his pockets.

'The baas is right,' I said.

Joseph still hesitated. Then he said to me: 'I hear the baas had a talk with the missus?'

'Yes,' I said.

'And this baas,' he said, lifting his hand a little, barely pointing towards Frank, 'talked to Baas Fletcher?'

'Yes,' I said. I was curious to know how he had found out about these talks. 'How do you know?' I asked.

'There are other people in this house,' he said briefly. It was with a kind of wonder that I remembered the spindly-legged

154

African who had served our supper, and Frank telling me about the little Bushman who had scampered away when Fletcher had stamped his foot at him. Spies, each one of them. Were there others, I wondered.

'Baas, if you will tell me what the missus said to you I'll be satisfied,' Joseph said. With less assurance he said of Frank: 'And if this baas would tell me what Baas Fletcher said to him?' I saw his hand grip the sill. 'Baas,' he said. His hand did not relax. 'Baas, if you will tell me what I ask you, I'll pay you.' He said the last words abruptly.

'What!' I said. I was shocked, almost insulted. 'Do you think I'd take payment from you!' And even Frank collapsed back on the bed, with his hands still in his pockets. Lying on his back he whistled at the ceiling.

Joseph said: 'I have the money. How much would the baas want?'

'Stop talking like that!' I said.

'Why, baas? I have the money,' he repeated.

'I don't care how much money you've got. I'm not going to take any money from you.'

'Why not, baas?'

'Because –' I started angrily, and then stopped as impetuously as I'd begun. I couldn't say to him that I wouldn't take money from him because he was black. I was silent. I think he saw how distressed I was, because he insisted.

'Why not, baas?'

'You know damn well why not,' I said. 'As well as I do.'

With the same almost careless honesty with which he'd admitted that the letter I'd read to him earlier had been stolen, Joseph asked me now: 'Is it because I am a kaffir, baas?'

'No,' I said. 'I wouldn't take money from a white man either.'

'But it's worse because I'm a kaffir?'

'Yes.'

'And for this baas too?'

'Yes,' Frank said quietly.

I made a kind of joke. 'We have more money than you.'

'You don't know how much money I've got,' Joseph gently reminded me.

'No,' I said. There was no way out: he had exposed the

tenacity and duplicity of my own feelings of white *baasskap* – my own 'liberal' intolerances, my own assertion of where his place should be, and where mine. And to my surprise I saw that for the first time in all my dealings with him, Joseph's stiff and deliberate manner had relaxed, as he bowed his head and smiled doubtfully, bowing almost as if he were waiting for a reproof. I stared at him, failing to understand, and as I did so, from beneath his furrowed, lowered forehead, he gave a glance that lingered on me for a few seconds, though he kept it concealed. And when he saw that I'd caught the glance he did not lift his head, but remained in concealment, both covert and unabashed. I saw all the grooved brown skin of his face relaxing, and his arms hang downwards unclenched, unused.

'Baas,' he said softly. 'Will you help me now?'

I felt that we had at last discovered his weakness. If that is the word; if it was a weakness that he should have hungered for acceptance, for approval. And not acceptance on some special terms of his own, not acceptance on the basis of his overwhelming physical strength, not acceptance because of a guilt towards people of his colour that he had somehow managed to divine in ourselves, certainly not acceptance on a simple man-to-man basis unimaginable, perhaps to him, in a country where it is the rule of life that a white man is a white man and a black man is a black man, and each has his place as though given to him by God. It was none of these. This African, Joseph, who had asked my help in a scheme which he could not disclose, who had exposed himself to rebuff and far worse with the aloof air of someone granting a favour that I could not but accept, this man hungered for us to accept him as he was to everyone else in the country – as a black man. To do that I had to be what I was to everyone else in the country – a white man, a baas.

'All right, Joseph,' I said. 'Tell us your story. And then we'll be able to see if we know anything that can help you.'

'*Dankie, baas,*' Joseph said. I think both he and I wondered why we had not been able to have immediately and with less discomfort, at our first meeting, the relationship which was now between us, straight and firm in our hands, like the heft of

156

an axe. I know I did – and that I blamed those liberal scruples of mine, which, while preventing me then from establishing with him that trust which I believed we now shared, had also protected me from going to his former employers in a state of white and righteous indignation to inform them of what he had done. Now, I thought, we had the best of both worlds, and certainly the discomfort with which we listened to his story was not occasioned by any crudity of the relationship in which we found ourselves – that was mellow, that was history – but by the bitter content of the story itself.

14

He told the story too in a way that I recognized with a feeling of nostalgia: I remembered, as I listened to him on that evening, the strangeness, distance, and wonder of the lives of the household servants who had told us stories when we were children as he now was telling us his story. The stories of the servants too had been of their own lives: of marriages and adventures, of the farmers for whom they had worked and the brothers of theirs that had run away to the mines and been killed in accidents, of places we had never visited but whose names we knew – Slypklip, Gong-Gong, Taungs, Draghoender, all the sunbaked railway sidings, R.M.S. bus halts, little *dorps* lost in the emptiness of the short-grassed Northern Cape, where sandy, declining Lyndhurst was a metropolis, and Koopmansfontein or Lohathla a centre of traffic. We had sat in the kitchen in the evenings, or on the ground in the back-yard, where nothing grew and the sand reddened our restless fingers, while we listened through sunny afternoons, when the sun shone from an absolutely clear blue sky and the air was lucid – listened without fatigue or involvement to tales from servants, strangers, dark people whose language – even whose second language – was not ours, whose lives crossed ours in ways we did not understand but simply accepted as we accepted the lucid air, and the house we lived in, and the town around our house where streets and other houses spread themselves lavishly on the flat, dry, unkempt, uncared-for veld. The servants came and went by the mysterious ordering of their lives, and we watched the newcomers who were all shy and silent at first, as they worked in the front garden in the afternoon, or polished the stoep floor in the morning. Time passed in the garden, in the stoep, in the back-yard, while we trudged to school or idled holidays away on our bicycles, and shyness and silence gave way to talk and stories of pleasures that were so distant from us that we knew they could never be ours, of griefs so great and distant that we could not understand how the person who had borne them should be standing in front of us with a spade or a broom in his hand, talking evenly, as if the earth had not swallowed up his mother's body, as if the farmer who had beaten him so that he could still show us the scars on his arms and shoulders were not still alive and perhaps doing the same thing to another. And already there stirred within us the first uneasy strivings towards guilt and pity – the guilt and pity that were later to hunt us and shame us in our own country.

But that was in the future: they were stirrings, no more, and our youth and distance, the small compass of our imaginations, our very skin that surrounded us and that had given us our large house and the servants, protected us, held us warmly, cocoon-like, while we listened to the African voices. The stories lulled us more than they disturbed us, lulled us in our childishness, so that in the end even the stories of grief and hurt and pain were soothing, and there was as little that we could do about what had happened as we could about the sun that shone charitably in winter and fiercely in summer upon us. This was part of our security: to have dark servants who were adult and yet under our command, who were adult and yet talked lingeringly or passionately to children while they worked, who were strange in language and colour and led lives in rooms we hardly ever entered, lives of which we knew only what they chose to tell us – though the rooms were in our own back-yard, and the house they lived in was ours.

Joseph spoke to us as these servants had done: the language he used, the turns of phrase, his very voice, were those of the people I had forgotten.

Four years before we had come to Mirredal, Joseph had left the service of Mrs Fletcher. He did not go in search of adventure. Nor to better himself, for there is no way that an illiterate African can better himself. Nor in search of a kinder master, for he did not complain about the treatment he had received from Mr and Mrs Fletcher, or from Louw, who was still living in the house at that time. He had simply gone, on an impulse, packing his bag of things, telling the Fletchers that he wanted to leave, and taking the train to De Aar – where the railway lines that run north to south cross the line that runs westwards to South West Africa, eastwards to the coast at Port Elizabeth, and where soot of engines lies crudely and strangely on the desert earth, on either side of the rows of flat and shining tracks: where there is a village built around the railway lines, with one bioscope and several general dealers' stores and a lawyer or two, a double-storied hotel at the end of a square of sand, that leads from the railway platforms, and on which absolutely nothing grows. And in De Aar, inevitably, Joseph worked for the South African Railways. He worked in the railway shunting yards. The work was hard, and the place was hot: even Joseph, born and come to adulthood in Mirredal, found De Aar hot.

But he stayed there, for six months, for a year, for eighteen months. Then, at the end of his eighteen months in the shunting yards at De Aar, perhaps he thought he had seen the world, and that it would be as well for him to go home now, back to Mirredal, sunk some two hundred miles away in its own stretch of the Karroo, smaller than De Aar, without any railway lines at all, let alone a whole junction of them, but his home-*dorp* nevertheless. So he came back to Mirredal.

Came back to find his sister gone. Gone as he had left – suddenly, leaving no word. She was the only member of his immediate family still alive: his father and mother, his brothers were all dead. There had been only himself and his sister, and both of them had worked for the Fletchers. She had been working there when he had left. All the time he had been away he had not heard from her, though he himself had sent one letter to her after he had been in De Aar for some time. This letter had informed his sister that he was working for the

S.A.R. in De Aar. The letter had been formal in style and brief in content, for the scribe whom he employed to write the letter charged by the length of the letter, and would not allow any deviations from his standard pattern of phrasing.

Where was his sister? Where had she gone? He asked Mrs Fletcher, for he was puzzled that she had left without informing him of this by means similar to that which he had employed. And more puzzled yet that, having left, she had not written him where she now actually was. He asked Mrs Fletcher, and was told abruptly that she did not know. Mrs Fletcher said that his sister had simply announced to her, as he himself had once done, that she wished to leave. Mrs Fletcher had accordingly let her go. Mrs Fletcher now added, for Joseph's benefit, several remarks about the ingratitude of the kaffirs for past favours they had received, of their readiness to leave as soon as they thought they could better themselves, and of their disregard for the length of service they had had under one particular missus, or even under the father of the missus. Mrs Fletcher grew shrill in references to these unpleasant and apparently congenital characteristics of the Africans, and her complaints widened to include not only their unsatisfactory behaviour as servants, but also their uncleanness and immorality. Joseph listened in silence to the harangue which was louder in tone and wider in reference, but otherwise very much the same as the one that had been delivered to him when he had told Mrs Fletcher of his intention to leave. Then he thanked Mrs Fletcher for receiving him and listening to his inquiries.

Joseph inquired of the household servants if they knew where his sister had gone, and was told that they too did not know. He was also told that she had given up her job not as the result of some unexpected impulse, but because she was going to have a baby. This was something that Mrs Fletcher had omitted from her harangue, as a particular, though no doubt the generalities about immorality had included it. Though the servants did not know where his sister had since gone, they did know that she had had the baby in Mirredal location. After some inquiry Joseph found the woman with whom his sister had lived after she had given up her work to have the baby. The woman remembered his sister without any difficulty: she remembered the baby too. It had been what she called a yellow baby. A little girl. Not an African baby, but a baby whose father had either been a white man or a Coloured.

Naturally, Joseph asked, who the father of the child was. He was told that no one knew, and that his sister had refused to divulge to anyone who the father was. And no one in the village – or in the location itself – had come forward to claim the parenthood of the child. The woman told Joseph that she had repeatedly tried to find out who the father of the child was, and had suggested numerous names to his sister, from all sections of the community. But every name had been met with a denial. The woman had finally suggested to his sister that perhaps the father of the child had been a stranger to the village, and his sister had agreed to this: yes, the father of the child was a stranger, someone who had passed through once, nine months before. But, the woman said, she personally was quite sure that his sister had agreed to this suggestion only for the sake of peace, and that she had not merely known who the father of the child was, but where he was too. Looking at the woman, Joseph was quite sure that she had made her inquiries as assiduously as she now claimed to have done, and was not surprised to hear a note of bitterness in her voice when she referred to his sister's evasiveness. And he understood clearly enough how his sister might have said, yes, the father of the child was a stranger, for the sake of peace.

At the end of the story Joseph asked if she knew where his sister had gone. The woman did know. His sister had gone to an aunt of hers who lived in a village some forty or fifty miles away. She had left a few weeks after the child was born, taking the child with her and a bundle of her clothing and possessions. How had she gone? Joseph asked. The woman did not know. All she knew was that his sister had left one midday, taking a lift into Mirredal village with a man who had a donkey cart. The woman did not know how his sister had proceeded further. And the man with the donkey cart? He came from yet another village, some fifty miles away, and had happened to be passing through on the day his sister left. A stranger he had been – the woman said – like the child's father?

But Joseph left the woman at that point. He now at least had a destination, an address towards which he could work. He wanted to find out what had happened to his sister and her child, and what had happened before the birth of the child. He wanted to know who the father of the child was – not that he had any idea of restituting a wrong, forcing a reluctant male to acknowledge his guilt and responsibility – nothing like that. But he wanted to know, all the same. Just as he wanted to know how his sister was managing. So he walked to the village in which his aunt lived. He walked forty miles across the bare veld, in two days, sleeping at night in the huts of farm Africans whom he passed on his way, and on the end of the second day came to the farm on which his aunt lived, where she worked for a white man.

He asked his aunt if his sister were there. No, she said. His sister had been there. But she had taken the train, saying that she was going to Cape Town. Had she taken the child with her? Joseph asked.

What child? the aunt asked in return.

Joseph replied casually that he had heard in Mirredal that his sister was looking after a child, an orphan from the farm where she'd been working, but apparently there had been some mistake and the story wasn't true. Though his aunt persisted in asking questions about this child Joseph headed them off, or ignored them, until the subject was dropped. Then he spent another two days, walking back to Mirredal.

He went to the woman with whom his sister had stayed. All those stories – he asked – had they been true? Had his sister taken her child, saying that they were going to her aunt? Yes, the woman replied. Had she seen his sister leaving with the child? Yes, the woman replied. She had seen his sister and her child getting on the stranger's donkey cart and riding off to Mirredal village. What was the stranger's village? The woman did not know, but she gave Joseph the name of someone in the location who was the stranger's cousin. Then the woman wanted to know why Joseph was asking all these questions of her. Had something gone wrong? Had his sister not arrived at his aunt's? Where was his sister? Where was her child?

The man whose name had been given to Joseph knew where the man with the donkey cart had come from. He gave Joseph the name of the man, and the village where he lived. He had come to Mirredal, the cousin said, over the matter of some goats which he claimed were owing to him.

It took Joseph three days to walk to the village of the stranger who had given Joseph's sister the lift into Mirredal village. When he found the man, he found too that the man remembered clearly that he had given a lift into Mirredal village to a woman with a small child. Had they gone further with him? Joseph asked. No, the man said. He had dropped them opposite the Mirredal Hotel, near the veranda of the Mirredal General Trading Stores, where the woman had said she had some things to buy. He hadn't seen her again, because he had left immediately: he had had a long way to come home. Yes, Joseph said, he knew that the man had had a long way to come. The man then inquired after his cousin, whom Joseph had seen a few days before, and went into the matter of the goats. He claimed that his cousin had repaid half the number of goats due, and yet had refused to pay the remainder – five goats – on the grounds that the debt was a false one. But if the debt were a false one, the man asked Joseph, why had the cousin admitted liability to the extent of repaying half? Joseph couldn't answer. The man then gave him messages about the goats to give to the recalcitrant cousin and three days walking took Joseph back to Mirredal. He was certain now in his own mind only that his sister had left the location with her child, and reappeared on the aunt's farm forty miles away, without the child. Could she have left the child with some other woman?

At the end of a week's guarded and hesitant inquiry, Joseph had established that all the children of the age his sister's child would have been could be accounted for. Every last bastard and orphan could be accounted for, and his sister's child wasn't among them. He spent another month walking to every farm in the district on which lived any African woman whom he knew his sister to have known, in the hope that she had perhaps made a detour on her way to her aunt and left the child with friends. He appeared always as someone

163

making his way to a further destination, and always he asked if the people he met had seen his sister lately. He said nothing about a child, about her visit to his aunt, nothing at all about her except that he wasn't sure where she was, and that someone in the location had said that he had heard that she was going to visit this farm or that farm, another farm, the fourth, fifth, sixth farm, until he had been to just about every farm in the district and found that none of the people on any of them knew anything at all about his sister. None of them had any exciting stories to tell either, stories about how a child had been found on the roadside, here or there, by this person or that, about how a strange child was growing up on yet another farm in the district: they had no stories, even when Joseph fed them with a story of his own manufacture about how he had heard of a child being found on the roadside near De Aar, when he had been working there, and the way the child was being brought up by the people who had found it. None of them could bring forth a corresponding, recent story. And Joseph knew that no one in Mirredal had such a story: if there had been one he would surely have heard it from the busy lips of the woman with whom his sister had stayed while she was having her baby.

So he returned to Mirredal as he had done twice before in his search, before all the days and nights of tramping on the bare veld, knowing only what he had known before: that his sister had left Mirredal location with the child and arrived at his aunt's without it. He walked to his aunt's place again, simply to make sure that it was Cape Town to which his sister had gone, and to ask if his sister had left any indications of what she was going to do when she got to Cape Town. His pretext this time was that he himself was going to Cape Town, and would like to get in touch with his sister when he got there. His aunt confirmed without hesitation what she had said the previous time he had been there. His sister had definitely said that she was going to Cape Town, and the aunt herself had gone to the station with his sister to see her on the train. But Joseph, after the dry weeks of searching, could take nothing on trust. Had it in fact been the train to Cape Town which his sister had boarded? And if it had been, did his aunt in fact

164

know that his sister had bought the ticket to Cape Town, and not to some other destination along the line, or simply to the nearest junction where the local rail joined the line that went not only to Cape Town, but also northwards to Johannesburg? He received no satisfaction in his queries. His aunt did not know; to her the departure of a train, bearing someone she knew upon it, was in itself so great an action that it swallowed up any consequences or destinations the action might have had for the protagonist.

Joseph did not now know what to do. Always he was afraid that his presence and the inquiries he had made, for so long now, in Mirredal and the district around it, might be causing too much wonder, and might begin to cause suspicion. He was particularly afraid of the woman with whom his sister had lived in Mirredal location. And there was another reason why he could not go on as he had been able to hitherto: he had no money. He would have to find work.

He used almost the last money he had walking back to Mirredal from his aunt's house, and as he walked he did something on the way that made the journey take not the two days it had when he had first walked the distance, but more than a week. A week of walking and digging. Whenever he saw on the side of the road a piece of earth that looked as if it had been disturbed not too long before, he dug into it with a stick that he carried, digging in as deep as the earth had been disturbed. Whenever there was a clump of thorn bushes, with younger bushes growing closely around it to form a barrier round a circle of earth, he went into it, and looked carefully within it to see if the ground had been lifted. He could not cover the whole wide country, but he could cover the road his sister must have taken on her journey to her aunt, and he did so, as he moved slowly back to Mirredal. All the weaker wood had splintered away from the stick in his hand, and the harder was smooth and shone as though it had been polished by the time he reached Mirredal. His digging had been of as little avail as his walking. He had found nothing. Nor did he find anything in the two days he allowed himself in the little natural quarries in the veld around Mirredal, where among the rocks and thorns and embedded in the hard earth he found only rusting tins and dung and papers and rotten sacks, the dried detritus of the village.

So though he could search no longer, his search was not yet over, and as a last desperate effort he returned to the house of the Fletchers. He wanted to speak to the person he referred to throughout as Baas Nasie. As he walked to the house he did not know what he would tell Baas Nasie, or how much he would tell him, but he did know that silence and space and his own illiteracy and ignorance had defeated him. He had no money. The distances between even the nearest village to which he had to walk to save money were too great. The people he spoke to were as illiterate and ignorant as himself. His sister had disappeared into the distance like a tree. He could not write to her: he did not know what ways there might be to set about finding her. He had reached the end of what he could do by himself.

He had now, he thought, to ask the help of a white man. A man who could read. A man who had a motor-car. A man who called policeman by their first names. A man who could write letters, send telegrams, put through phone calls, a man who had been trained for the world which his fathers had built, which he himself was expected to continue to build in his turn, and in which Joseph was an illiterate and poverty-stricken servant for whom the police and all the mechanisms of the ordering of society held only danger – even when all was well and his conscience clear, and of whose workings he could think now only with horror when he did not know where his sister was or what she had done with her child.

It was only when he was already sitting in the kitchen of the house, waiting for Baas Nasie to come to him, that he decided what the requests that he would make of Baas Nasie would be. He would simply ask Baas Nasie if he could help him in the task of finding his sister, who, he would say, had gone to Cape Town without leaving a word. Perhaps Baas Nasie would be able to suggest a way: those in authority and light had means of power and recall which Joseph had before seen easily produce results which he could regard only as little short of miraculous. And he knew that Baas Nasie would understand his shyness in calling in the help of the police – assuming the police would be at all interested in helping to trace the whereabouts of a single African woman among so many millions, when there was nothing against her which would interest them at all. But Baas Nasie would not question what Joseph felt about the police: what white man didn't know how the Africans felt about the police? Perhaps, Joseph thought, Bass Nasie would write a letter for him to the officers of the Department of Native Affairs in Cape Town, asking them if the record of his sister's entry into any of Cape Town's locations had been registered in their books. Joseph did not like the idea of an approach to the Department of Native Affairs, but they were better than the police. Perhaps Baas Nasie would suggest a notice in the newspaper which might catch the eye of someone who knew, or employed, his sister. Surely Baas Nasie, a young man, in the authority and light denied to Joseph, would know what to do.

Among all the white men he knew Joseph had chosen Baas Nasie to help him because when Baas Nasie had been a child, it had been Joseph who had told him stories, played with him, hunted hares and meerkats with him: Joseph had once killed a puff-adder, upon which Baas Nasie had almost stepped, with the single throw of a stone. Not that Joseph did not know that childhood was childhood, and past: he was not stepping out of his place, no more than he had done even within the larger freedom of childhood, when the white boy had been allowed to lead more often than his years had warranted, and Joseph had followed. He sought no reversal now. On the contrary, it was the very masterhood, the *baasskap,* of Baas Nasie to which he was now appealing. Only, as he heard the footsteps of the servant whom he had asked to call Baas Nasie returning with those of another, and as he stood up and took his hat from his head so that Baas Nasie would be greeted formally and with due deference, Joseph did hope that Baas Nasie would remember that youthful companionship kindly. It was that hope that had brought him there.

Baas Nasie, however, did not come into the room. The servant brought Baas Nasie's sister, Mrs Fletcher, and Joseph saw immediately that she was not pleased to see him and resented his presence in the kitchen. She asked him what he wanted. He told her that he had come to see Baas Nasie. She replied that Baas Nasie was not in the house, speaking with a great abruptness, which Joseph assumed to have stemmed from her previous anger over his leaving her service, and the subsequent departure of his sister. But as deferentially as he had greeted her, Joseph asked where Baas Nasie was, as he wished to see the baas. Baas Nasie, he was told, no longer lived in the house. Joseph asked where he was. Mrs Fletcher replied that he had gone, gone, far away, too far for Joseph to be able to find him. Joseph asked when he would be coming back. He would not be coming back, Mrs Fletcher replied. He had left even before Joseph's last visit to the house, and would not be coming back.

Joseph said that he was sorry to hear this as he had hoped he would be able to speak to Baas Nasie. There was no reply. After a pause in which they had both stood in silence in the kitchen, with the two new, strange servants looking on, Joseph said that he hoped there was nothing wrong that had made Baas Nasie go away. It was a remark made in innocence, for he knew that Baas Nasie had planned to stay in the house, and he knew too how much Mrs Fletcher loved her brother, and how little she had wanted him to leave, even when he had left for college. And by the word 'wrong' he had meant no more than an occurrence beyond the control of Baas Nasie, no more than an undesired change of plan. But whatever he had meant, Mrs Fletcher shouted loudly at him: 'What makes you say that?'

Joseph was surprised at this reaction, but he stood his ground firmly. He explained that he had meant nothing, that he knew nothing, that the last thing he had had in mind was to accuse Baas Nasie of having committed a misdeed. He made his position clear, expecting Mrs Fletcher to chase him away before he had done. But to his surprise she became calmer while he talked to her. Though she stood as stiffly upright and hostile as she had done before she did not shout at him, and seemed to listen with care. And when he had finished, she asked him – almost as if she herself might be able to take the place of her brother – why he was looking for Baas Nasie.

Joseph told her that he had thought that Baas Nasie might

168

be able to help him find his sister. And again she screamed at him. 'What makes you say that?' were her first words, and then as Joseph listened to the words of abuse of himself which poured from her lips, interspersed with commands never to come near the house again and invective against his sister, and as he watched the expressions of rage and fear which twisted her features, Joseph knew, knew without hesitation or anger, that he had at least found out who the father of his sister's child was.

15

So far Joseph's minor-keyed African voice, with that hoarse and plaintive scrape at the back of the throat to which I had so often listened before, telling me stories which had in common with this one only those elements of heat, distance, and the difficulties of poverty and ignorance – the earth of the country on which we had built our houses and roads. And one other thing which I recognized too, and which I responded to with as much respect as I had as a child: a profound family feeling, an acceptance of involvement in the lives of those to whom he was related by blood.

Perhaps I can most clearly indicate the nature and tenacity of this feeling in Joseph by mentioning that not once during his telling of the story did Joseph refer to his sister as anything but: 'my sister'. He did not once mention her name. In part, I think this arose from the fact that he did not know what his sister had done with her child, and was trying to make sure that we would be no more able to trace her, no more be able to help the police, than we would have had we never heard the story. But though that might have been a reason, it is equally true that the mode of phrase he used came fittingly to his tongue, and indicated precisely the quality and kind of feeling he had in the affair – beyond any reasons there might have been for the adoption of the circumlocution on that particular night. Other names he gave us: the name of his aunt, for instance, was Sarah, and the name of the man who owned the donkey cart, Klaas. But his sister was nameless, defined by one attribute only, the condition for her being mentioned in the story: she was his sister. 'My sister' – that was her title. In the same way, he never referred to his sister's child by any other appellation but that of 'my sister's child'. Never 'the child' or 'the little girl' or 'the baby' or even 'her child'. Always 'my sister's child'. And when he talked of the two of them together, it was always in a way which was long-winded and difficult to say: 'my sister and my sister's child'. Throughout the story that was how he referred to them. 'The woman said that my sister and my sister's child had ridden to Mirredal in a donkey cart' – like that. It would have been formal and self-consciously hierarchical if he had spoken in this way with any self-consciousness, but there was not a trace of it in his voice or manner. The way he referred to them was simply what they were: 'my sister' and 'my sister's child': his, and his responsibility.

The profundity of this family feeling of his did not arise, it seemed to me, out of pride, or dynastic ambitions, or a desire to protect a self-regard extended in an unwarranted manner to the members of his family. Nor was it merely an obedience to an imperative from an almost forgotten tribal past, whose commands were to be grudgingly heard and grudgingly carried out. It was not even a matter of love – the protean emotion that excuses as many evasions as it encourages selflessness. The precepts that he was obeying were those of his own morality – a morality that acted on its own level, almost wordlessly, without fuss. In its closeness and unquestioned necessity it presented itself simply as a part of life: what he was doing was the act of living.

After this moment of illumination with Mrs Fletcher, he retired to Mirredal location, to think matters over. He knew who the father of his sister's child was; he did not know what had happened to the child or where his sister was. All he did know was that she had been seen at one point with the child and seen later at another without the child, and that she had not thereafter mentioned the child to anyone. She and the child had disappeared: and it was at that point that Joseph decided that so far as he was concerned his sister was dead.

170

Dead to him. Gone away. Swallowed up by Cape Town or Johannesburg or Port Elizabeth or Durban as surely as by the earth itself. All her actions showed that she had no intention of coming back. He reproached her for her death as little as he mourned for her. He accepted it. She was gone.

But this certainty of knowledge of her final departure from him did not end his search. It settled one matter. It left the other insisting as urgently for settlement as the other had done. He knew who the father of the child was, and he knew that his sister would not come back, but he did not know what had happened to the child. What he did know – what came to him with as little possibility of doubt as the earlier intimation had done – was that Mrs Fletcher knew what had happened to the child. And if Mrs Fletcher then almost certainly Mr Fletcher too. It would be the Fletchers who would tell him what he wanted to know – they or no one. Like life, like the life of the child, the duty persisted.

He had no redress in the matter, no proof, no status, no one to whom to appeal. More than that, he had a great fear of perhaps bringing a trouble on his sister whose nature he could hardly dare begin formulate; and he knew that dead though she might be to him, if the police wanted her for inquiry they would almost certainly be able to find her, and bring her back to life; he knew certainly that under such circumstances his sister would not thank him for bringing her back to the life she had left. And he did not in the least want to bring any trouble to her; whatever she might have done that was not his purpose at all.

Surprisingly, he left Mirredal then. The reason was that he knew that he would not be able to get work in the village which would pay sufficiently well for him to be able to save money. The high wages, he knew were being paid in the towns. So he went to Johannesburg, and worked there. He worked for a builder in Johannesburg, and earned almost eight pounds a month – a wage for an African unknown in Mirredal. Though eight pounds a month in Johannesburg was not as much as it had seemed to be in Mirredal, nevertheless he managed out of that wage to save a pound or two every month. He did not know what he would do when he returned to Mirredal, but whatever it might be, he wanted to have money to be able to do it. Two years work brought him savings, in all, of some thirty pounds. With that reserve of cash in hand he returned to Mirredal.

His purposes had been undeflected by the time that had passed, and, as a first step, and with very little hope, he went to the Fletchers and asked them to give him work, as Mrs Fletcher had told me he had done, in her garbled version of the events. As he had expected, they drove him away, so he got a job in the village. And he waited. He watched, taking up his position outside the house in the evenings, over the week-ends, at night sometimes. Out of his savings he suborned the servants of the house to tell him everything they overheard in the house, and to purloin any letters they could lay their hands upon. Until, after months of waiting, we had come, and Baas Nasie, together, and Joseph knew that he had to risk asking for our aid. He had to have some proof with which he could confront the Fletchers, so that he could force them to tell him what had been done to his sister's child.

I asked him how he thought he would be able to force this from them, and he did not answer. I don't think he knew, that evening. I asked him why he had asked the Fletchers for work when he had come to Mirredal and again, he did not answer. I would not say that Joseph had at any time lost sight of the purpose of his search, but it did seem that his insistence on being near the house, if possible *in* the house, was the expression of a desire that was bounded on one side by the whereabouts of his sister's child, but on the other only by the very frame of his imagination, the world in which he had grown up.

That was as it might be. In the meantime Joseph did have particular proofs to establish. He ended his story as he had begun it, with a request: 'Will you tell me what you have heard from the people in this house?'

16

'You're a lunatic! Don't do that! Don't *do* that!' The shouting of these words was followed by a tremendous thump
within the house, that made the floorboards shiver beneath our
feet. Then a door slammed, and we heard a rushing of footsteps. More doors were slammed and the footsteps came
rapidly down the nearest passage. Our door burst open, and
Fletcher stood within it. He stared wildly about the room
before closing the door behind him and leaning against it.
His hand groped beneath the door-knob. 'The key,' he
shouted. 'Where's the key?'

Deeper in the house we heard a door being slammed, and
then Louw's voice. He was shouting in Afrikaans. 'Once and
for all', 'This time is the last time', 'The end of the story'.
And each disconnected phrase was followed by a crash. Again
and again the flooring boards under our feet shook, until
after each shiver there was a faint sigh that seemed to come
from the heart of the house itself.

Fletcher turned round and looked at us for a moment.
'Lean against the door,' he commanded, before he swung his
face towards the door again, as if the danger lay in his not
watching it. It was only then that I remembered Joseph, and
turned towards the window. But the window was open and
empty to the still night outside: we might have dreamed the
big dark man standing there, dreamed his voice, and his
hands on the sill. I remember feeling relieved to see that
he had fled, as I presumed he had: there was more than
enough to deal with at the moment without Joseph being
there too.

Within the house the sounds of rampage grew louder, and
came more quickly. There was barely time now to sort out
one sound from another, and the floor quivered continually,
until even one of the beds in the room began to shake and
the brass caps with which the bedstead was decorated started
to tinkle delicately. All we knew was that things were being

ripped from walls, hurled down passages, ground into splinters on the floor, torn open with a cry of cloth. Something skidded and hit an outside window with a crash and a patter of glass on the stoep outside: with a characteristic dry gasp, a light bulb exploded. Then there was a roar that bewildered me until Fletcher shouted: 'He's in the library!' Again there came the roar of sound, and I realized that he was overturning the bookcases and the books were cascading in cataracts upon the floor. Something beat a rapid tattoo on wood, until the wood splintered and cracked apart with a sharp report, like a pistol shot. 'The desk,' Fletcher moaned, 'it's an antique.' A door slammed and footsteps retreated down the passage. Again there was the splintering of wood and then pots rang, stricken metal, against one another, and cups and plates and glasses burst furiously against the wall and fell with a clatter of china on the floor. There were loud and clumsy creaking noises – 'He's got the dresser,' Fletcher said to us.

'He'll break that too!' Within seconds the dresser hit the ground with a great, resonant boom. 'What next? What next?' Fletcher whimpered.

Next there were a few more desultory sounds, as the man roamed around the further wing of the house, apparently destroying whatever he could without the expenditure of too much energy. Then he started coming nearer again; we could hear him tearing down the buck horns on the walls in the front passage, and then in the passage that led to our room. He came still closer. He went into the room next to ours and started banging away inside it with great vigour. The window of the room went as the others had done, with a crystal tinkling of the glass on the stoep outside, and the marble washstand broke heavily, almost like wood. 'Once and for all,' Louw was still saying. 'No more of this ... I've had enough.' His voice did not sound wild or enraged: he grunted the sentence out, almost with the sound of someone on a difficult and tiring job. The drawers in some chest or other in the room screeched out of their places and followed the various other articles he had thrown out of the window and on to the stoep. 'Finish it off!' Louw was saying. 'Enough is enough!'

Fletcher had by this time left the door and was now standing between Frank and myself, near the window, where we had taken up our position, ready to flee through the window should the man come into the room with a club in his hand. Fletcher held one of my hands in his: perhaps he was doing the same to Frank on the other side, but I could not see. He said: 'He said he was going to kill me. That's when I ran.'

'And Mrs Fletcher?' I asked.

Fletcher looked at me in surprise. 'He won't do anything to her.'

Our door-handle rattled, and Fletcher lost all thought of others. 'It's me he's after,' he said, tightening his grasp and staring at the door with his eyes wide open. Though the door was not locked Louw was having a little trouble opening it, so despite the fact that it would hardly help him with the lock, with a single crack he kicked open one of the lower panels in the door. Then he tried the handle again, and after all the noise he had been making the silence in which he opened the door was positively eerie.

He looked much as he had done when I had last seen him, though now his face was darker, and his tight black hair a little disarranged, with one wavy lock lying over his clean rounded brow. His shoulders rose and fell, but when, after a moment's silence, he had recovered his breath, he guffawed loudly at the three of us.

He laughed uproariously and experimentally, watching us closely. 'You should see the place,' he said. 'I've smashed it up. You can have a look if you like,' he invited us tentatively, and gestured with his hand behind him.

But none of us moved, and Frank said patiently: 'Don't smash anything here. We want to sleep here tonight.'

Louw hesitated. Then he said mildly: 'I've got nothing against you.'

'Good,' Frank said.

Louw was clearly not as drunk as he was pretending to be. His face was darkened and he swayed a little on his wide-planted legs, but there was nothing befuddled about his eyes, and the way he used his eyes to watch us. When he looked at Fletcher he said nothing: he smiled without opening his lips. Then he said to us defiantly: 'I bet you this is the most smashed-up house in the Cape Province. You should see what I've done to it. You should go into the kitchen. The kitchen! They won't be cooking food there for a month.' He stopped abruptly to stare at Fletcher, who said nothing. So Louw could go on. 'I left out the bathroom,' he said regretfully. 'I didn't think of the bathroom. There's mirrors there! Do you think I should go back to the bathroom?' he asked. 'Make a proper job of it?' He seemed to wait brightly for our answer, but I was quite sure that he had no intention of going back to the bathroom, whatever our reply might be, so it was safe for me to say, in as confident a voice as I could summon:

'I don't think you should do that. You've had enough fun for one evening, haven't you?'

'Fun!' Louw said. 'Fun! It's the best fun I've had for years.' He began to swing his arms from side to side, in front of his body. 'Kerrash!' he shouted. 'Smash! Bang! Boom! Tinkle-tinkle-tinkle!' He put two fingers in his mouth and whistled piercingly. 'That's the way to do it.' He bent down suddenly and came up holding a chamber-pot. He held it by the handle for a moment and then swung it neatly through the air; with his eyes wide open he watched it sail away from him. It hit the water jug on the wash-stand, and both the china vessels burst simultaneously. There was a splash of water from the jug, on the floor, all over the wash-stand. Some of it splashed our kit. Frank went forward and dragged the kit-bag away from the path the water was likely to take. 'This is our stuff,' Frank said.

'I've got nothing against you,' Louw said.

'Well, just remember that next time,' Frank said, straightening. 'We don't want to get our stuff mucked up.' He spoke very casually: it seemed to be the right tone to adopt for Louw listened without taking offence. Then Frank stepped back and Fletcher took him by the wrist. This was seen by Louw.

'Don't hold his hand,' he told us. 'You'll get dirty if you do. And you!' he said to Fletcher. 'Holding hands like a girl. I'll kill you if I want to, and if I don't I won't. There's no help for you in holding anyone's hand. I'm just making up my mind now.'

This was so obviously a joke, of sorts, that even Fletcher was able to take courage and say: 'You won't get away with this.' Louw lifted a lip in reply: it was enough to make Fletcher quiver violently, as if it were only his grip on my hand that prevented him from leaping backwards through the window.

Then we heard footsteps coming down the passage. Louw leaned back and put his head through the door. 'Here comes Chrissie,' he announced. 'Come to inspect the damage.'

Mrs Fletcher came into the room looking unchanged, as though there had been no flight, no argument, no destruction since we'd seen her last. 'I heard what you were doing,' she said to her brother, 'and then it got quiet.' She looked round the room, apparently checking that everyone who should have been there was present. 'I was wondering what you were doing. It got quiet so suddenly.'

'Nothing,' Louw said. 'We were talking. Just a friendly conversation between me and your husband.'

Mrs Fletcher said reprovingly to her brother: 'You've broken everything.'

'Not everything,' Louw replied modestly. 'Only the things I could get my hands on. I forgot the bathroom.'

'You can't stay here now,' Fletcher shouted unexpectedly. 'I've got the right to call the police and set them on you.'

'Call the police! Do you think I want to stay here?' Louw clapped his hands suddenly. 'You know,' he said, 'once I'd decided to go, I was happy. Then I could smash everything. It was marvellous. You should see where I've been,' he said to Frank and myself. 'It looks like a bomb dropped on the house.' And though he was taunting Fletcher, and, I thought, his sister too, there was no doubt in my mind that he was speaking the truth. He had enjoyed what he had done: the plump, neat, candid-faced young man carried with him a devil of destruction. And it hardly mattered to him that what the devil destroyed might have been his own. 'And look at the jug,' he said to his sister. 'One throw with the pot, and both of them – crash! Most of the house is like that.'

'I've seen,' his sister said.

'You hear?' Louw said to us elatedly, having proof with

him. 'I smashed what I could.' He advanced towards Fletcher, who shrank away between us. 'You wanted this house,' Louw said to him. 'Well now you can have it. All smashed up! Oh!' he cried, throwing his hands to the ceiling. 'I wish I had a gang of kaffirs. In an hour we'd have it down to its foundations.' His eyes were alight with his destructive will, and he threw his head back and guffawed. He walked round and round in circles, stamping his booted feet upon the floor, and the laughter came out in jerks of sound: 'Ho! Ho! Ho!' like a war-cry, in time with the stamping of his feet. He threw his head forward and back, and the lock of hair on his forehead danced too. He stepped behind his sister and suddenly gave her a push with his hand in the small of her back, so that she almost fell forward on top of us. I caught her in my arms, but she pulled away. She had her arms around his neck and her face thrust close to his own.

'I'm glad you're going,' she said. 'You'll be safe. And Nasie, I'll come with you.'

Louw swayed his thick shoulders from side to side, and his sister's body moved with the swaying as she clung to him. 'I'll be safe,' he said, squinting down at her, his chin tucked in and his eyelids lowered to see her in a kind of hellishly merry wink. 'You talked me into it. And let you come with me?' He stopped swaying, and reached up behind his neck and took his sister's fingers in his own. Her grip tightened, but despite her strength he managed to lever her hands away, and slowly bring them down, until they were level with his ears, where he held them for a moment, before again beginning to push her hands down. He had a better grip on her wrists, and could do it more easily. He did not jerk or shake her; he pushed steadily until she stood with her bosom braced against his and her arms spread out in an inverted V. 'Let you come with me?' he asked, and let her hands go.

Immediately her arms sprang towards him again, but he was as quick as she had been, and caught them in front of him. In silence they resumed the struggle, he still quite steady in the pressure he was putting on her, she now jerking a little in her effort to overcome his greater strength. But she could not, and he brought her arms down, and let go again. Her

178

movement towards him this time was smaller and more easily checked, and when he let go of her she did not move, but let her arms hang where he had left them, away from her body. Only her hands hung straight downwards, drooping heavily at the end of her wrists. Louw stepped away from her.

'Take you with me?' He simply shouted his scorn, his head thrown back, his eyes closed like the eyes of a new-born child. 'Ach!' There were no words in what he shouted. It was a sound, a yell of derision.

He had to stop to take a breath, and when he did so he marched upon Fletcher. 'Take him!' he shouted. 'Stay with him! How can you think of leaving him? You've got to have some kindness for a thief like him.' He punched Fletcher on the chest; he did not care if the blow had hurt the man or not – his contempt was too great; no sooner was it done than he turned to his sister, not seeing Fletcher reel back from the blow. 'And what would I do with you?' He brought his next words with care: 'Expiate my sin?' He shouted at her again, like a man possessed by a guttersnipe demon: 'Aaach!'

Fletcher turned to me, protesting and gesticulating: 'He's always been like this. He's always made mock of me. He was always saying that I'd married for the sake of the money and the house and the rest of it. I'd married for money! What had he done to throw that in my face? Six months in jail people get for doing what he did – there's a law against having anything to do with a kaffir woman, and he knew it. And the disgrace of it! I had him like this,' Fletcher said, clenching his fist. 'Wasn't I right to drive him away? Wouldn't you have jumped at the chance to make him go? It was the best day of my life,' he said passionately. 'I'd do it again if I ever could.' He was so carried away that he had not noticed that Louw was leaning forward, and had listened to his last words.

'And this has been the best day of mine,' he shouted. 'I'd do it again if I could.' He shouted at his sister: 'You talk about the family. Where is the family? You've got no children, he couldn't even make one.' He jabbed at Fletcher. 'Or you,' he said to his sister, 'were you too old already?' He waited, though no reply could come to a question as cruel as that. 'And me?' he asked. 'What did we do when I made one?

179

Did we want it? It would have been yellow. Did you hear that – yellow? The little one, yellow and wrinkled like a stone, did we want it? Didn't you say the mother mustn't know where the child is, and the child mustn't know where the mother is, or who the mother is, so that they could never come together again? Weren't those your words? And didn't he come with his lump sum for this one and his lump sum for the other one and the lump sum for the ones who came in the motor-car? So don't come and talk to me about family. If you want a family go and look for it.'

Mrs Fletcher moved away from her brother and stood in the middle of the room, alone. 'I wish,' she exclaimed in a sudden, frantic prayer, clasping her hands and lifting them high up where they shook, so tightly were they clasped, until her whole torso shook too, 'I wish this whole house would fall down. So that there would be nothing left.'

And suddenly her brother was quiet. 'It will,' he said. 'It's our choice.' He turned to Frank and myself, and his body rose silently with a laugh that made no sound, and then sank again. 'I've done my bit,' he said. 'I did what I could.' He asked his sister: 'You know what I feel like?' She stared at him without speaking. 'I feel as though I've just been with a woman.' He leaned to her. 'When I was with her. That's what I feel like.' He was able only to breathe out for a moment, having said what he had to his sister. He nodded, though, confirming what he had just said. 'And wanting her!' he said. 'I've never wanted anything the way I wanted her. It was sad inside me, wanting her. Sometimes I'd stand next to her and I'd be afraid that if I moved I'd fall down in a heap – that was what it was like. And then one night I was drunk. Like tonight. And afterwards I felt as I feel now. That I've *done* something.' He had been speaking quietly: when he lifted one clenched fist and struck it with all his force against the palm of the other hand, the sound was single, sharp and, in its abruptness, pained, in the otherwise silent room. 'Afterwards,' Louw said, 'after the times I'd been with her . . .'

'Stop! Stop talking, Nasie!' Mrs Fletcher shouted, the words choking themselves in her throat. I thought it was because she could no longer bear the recital of her brother's fall into what they all regarded – even he himself – helplessly and finally as shame. But it was not for that that she had called him to stop. She had just seen Joseph at the window.

17

Louw was the first to move. He moved to the door, and only when he was there did he say to Joseph, without surprise – he was beyond surprise – and almost without fear, 'You can do nothing with me. I'm going. I'm finished with this place.' And he turned and fled. We heard his footsteps through the house, running, and then we heard them beating down the garden path. Joseph could have headed him off quite easily, I think, but he made no effort to do so; he stood at the window without moving. Louw's footsteps clattered on the path, and then were dulled suddenly on sand. We heard them sharply again among the stones on the river-bed, and only when he reached the other side of the river did they disappear from our hearing. That was the last we heard of him: the silence and the darkness of the veld shut him finally from us, then.

And when the last sounds had faded Fletcher asked Joseph: 'How long have you been there?'

'All the time,' Joseph replied. 'Since you came to the room.'

'And what did you hear?'

'Everything.'

Fletcher looked as though he would like to follow his brother-in-law into the night and out of hearing and sight: repeatedly his glance measured the distance between himself and the door. Then he said: 'You heard nothing.'

'I heard everything.'

Fletcher bit his lip caressingly, letting his lower lip slide forward between his teeth, reflectively. But he was a man of resources: out of his shaggy, shiny, bewildered head, even then, he produced a reply. 'Prove it,' he said. His eye again measured the distance between himself and the door, just in case, perhaps, the card he had played were not trumps.

But he gained courage from Joseph's silence. 'Prove it,'

he said. 'Tell us what you heard – and then prove it.' He waited, with his head alert, his legs straddled towards the door.

Joseph stood silently at 'the window. By the way he was standing I could see that it had not been accidental that Mrs Fletcher had seen him when she did. He must have risen up deliberately, having heard enough.

'Well?' Fletcher said. He cocked his head to one side. Joseph remained silent. 'What have you got to say for yourself?' Fletcher waited again. 'Nothing?' Joseph still did not speak. 'You thought you were clever sneaking around outside and listening to what the white baases had to say. And now you tell me that you heard everything they said. Well, tell me what they said – and then prove it. And to anyone else you want to tell your stories to.'

Joseph did not say anything. He listened in silence to Fletcher, who stood withindoors, lower than Joseph, looking up at him, his head jerking in little aggressive twitches. Joseph watched Fletcher closely; but I did not know what he was thinking; I could not read the expression on his forward-humped face.

Fletcher, however, believed that he could. 'That's given you something to think about, hey? You hadn't taken that into account, had you, hey?' When Joseph raised a hand Fletcher stepped back a pace hastily and said: 'No, you don't. You wouldn't dare start anything here. We're too many for you.'

Joseph's hand fell back. 'Thought better of it, have you?' Fletcher snapped. 'Now listen, Joseph, you've been making a nuisance of yourself for too long. You've been getting cheeky. You've been forgetting your place. You've been trying to get on top of the white men. You're old enough, Joseph, to know that you can't do that. And you're old enough to know what happens to kaffirs like yourself who try. They get punished, Joseph. I'm not alone. I've got all these people here, and the police are just at the end of the telephone wire. They'll come quickly enough when I tell them that I've caught a trespassing kaffir. So? Hey? What have you got to say for yourself? Still nothing?'

Joseph did not stir.

'I'm giving you your last chance, Joseph. You tell me now that you're never coming back to worry me, or I'm phoning the police. They'll settle your problem once and for all. Trespassing, burglary, those are the charges I'll lay against you, snooping around the house at all hours, trying to get in through the windows. And don't think that you'll be able to tell the police some cock-and-bull story about the things you heard while you were lying outside the window. Who'll believe your stories? Who'll believe the word of a stinking, ignorant kaffir against the word of a white man like myself? Hey? Answer me that. I've given you your choice: either you promise never to come to this house again, or else I phone the police. Which do you want? Answer, man. And don't you forget that you're a kaffir and I'm a white man and the police will believe what I say, not what you tell them.'

Joseph said: 'They will believe what I say. I have witnesses.' And he pointed at Frank and myself.

Part 5

18

I shall pass in comparative briefness over what happened the rest of that night, though several hours were to elapse between Joseph's appearance at the window and the time when I finally managed to fall asleep. My own memory of those hours is patchy, blurred, distracted: I remember periods of confusion and activity, and other stretches of time as being quite without incident, as though we had all been silent and unmoving in the room, like open-eyed, dumb sleepers, caught in one another's dreams. And then more activity – Fletcher talking, Fletcher pacing up and down the room, Fletcher gesticulating to himself in a corner, Fletcher biting his lip in the soft, caressing way he had under strain. I remember that vividly – the way he bit his lip – his teeth closing suddenly and savagely on his lower lip and then relaxing to let the lip slide away, as if he could not bear it that any part of his body should suffer any kind of pain. And the yellow light fidgeting about the room as the antiquated machinery outside beat in spasms, in shakes, slapping away at the silence of the black veld around us.

And Fletcher talking. Fletcher hung over the foot of my bed, his arms dangling over the high metal bedstead, his shoulders hanging, his hair dangling, his head drooping: he looked as if he had been made of an elastic substance that had been held above the foot of my bed and allowed to sag downwards of its own weight as far as it could. And from the haggard face almost level with the drooping shoulders there came words – so many words, in such different combinations, in two languages – English and Afrikaans – in all the tones and timbres that his voice could compass. I don't know for how long he remained like that but it seemed to be for hours, the face and the words inescapable, as though I'd slept and dreamed and woken and fallen asleep into the dream again. Then I remember the same man hanging at the foot of Frank's bed and talking to him as he had talked to me.

I remember how he fell silent, and walked about the room, gesticulating. He held his hands open in front of himself; he closed them into two clenched fists which he brandished in the air before him; he flung his arms to the ceiling. His lips moved, but made no words. He started suddenly, one foot poised, as if he had just heard a faint important sound, he resumed his pacing as if he had never stopped. Sometimes he seemed to be measuring things with his hands, gauging their weight, their height, their distance from him. He cocked his head reflectively, or let it sag down as far as it could upon his breast; he pointed one finger straight into the air and looked at it fixedly; he stood under the light-bulb and gestured towards it, so that he stood like a torchbearer; he shuffled about in misery; he kicked his heel against the floor. And then, again, he would come back to us.

He tried everything he had. He talked until he was exhausted. Bodily exhausted, with the words coming out more and more slowly and his movements being made more and more heavily, and his voice growing more and more hoarse until it finally ground itself into silence. He talked until there was no further way in which he might have appealed to us. He caressed us and flattered us. He threatened and swore. He wheedled and complained. He defended himself, he accused us. He declared that nothing made any difference, that he was an old man now and would be glad when he was dead. He coughed, he ranted. He orated at us. And he appealed not only to us as we were but to the 'better natures' within us that he was sure were struggling to find expression. He described those better natures at some length, and told us what a disaster it would be if we failed them. It would be a disaster for us, as people, and it would be a disaster too for white civilization in South Africa. On us, in Fletcher's mind, there seemed to depend the future of that white civilization, western civilization, all that was noble in our heritage. Phrases like that come easily in South Africa – every trashy politician talks about white civilization, western civilization, the fortress against bar-

186

barianism, quite casually, as if everyone in his audience will know without any difficulty what he is talking about. Fletcher did the same. Wasn't he a white man, he asked us. Weren't we white men, he asked us. Shouldn't the white men stick together? Weren't we proud that we were white men? Did we know, he asked us, what the kaffirs were like? He asked me if I wanted to have my throat cut by a kaffir in the middle of the night. In the darkness, he said, my skin would shine in the night – a target for the creeping kaffir. It would happen to me, it would happen to Frank, it would happen to every white man in the country, if we didn't all stick together. And then, he asked, where would white civilization be?

Whose word, he asked us, would we trust? His, or that of that kaffir Joseph? Who would we see discomfited, him or, again, that kaffir Joseph? Who was educated and civilized, him or that kaffir Joseph? Would we, he asked us, like our sisters to marry a kaffir like Joseph? He called us to duty: even if we didn't want to, he said, we would have to stick by him: it would be our duty as white men to do so. He said that he could well imagine someone disliking him, Fletcher. But what had dislike on a petty personal basis to do with an issue in which a civilization was involved? He even invited us to hate him – he did not care, he said – because hatred would be as irrelevant as love where duty was involved. And our duty was to stick by him. That was one phrase that remained unaltered – he brought it out whenever he could. Stick by him, we had to stick by him.

But he never defined what that phrase would mean. I don't think he knew. Sometimes his mind seemed to run on midnight oaths of loyalty on bibles, at others to courts of justice in which we would appear to throw his enemies into confusion and all South Africa – white South Africa – at our feet. He talked sometimes as though sticking by him would involve no more for us than an open house and royal entertainment in Mirredal, at others as though we might at any moment have to *opsaal* and ride in fury upon Mirredal location in a crusade for right in which no quarter would be shown to the heathen. A little later, he would be speaking as though the house we were in was a besieged blockhouse where each man's duty was at the loophole above the body of the fallen comrade. Often enough the fallen comrade was himself – piteously he described himself as an old, ¹sick man who had given his life in the service of right and justice and white civilization.

He said he would break our necks. He wasn't afraid of us, younger than him though we might be. He would take us on one by one – if we were sportsmen, he said, we would come only one by one – and he would clean us up once and for all. He jerked his head, he marched about the room with a high kicking step, he threw our things together – towels, shirts, books, being flung through the air and landing in some sort of heap on the floor. 'If you make your friends with that Joseph there's no room for you in this house. Come on, out! Quick march! Double time! Both of you, all of you, out! Go to your black friend Joseph. Out! Out!' He kicked the billycans and sent them flying to clatter against the wall. He went to the window and shook his fist at the night. 'Why doesn't it rain?' he cried. 'If it was raining you'd know what it was like to spend a night in the open.' Frank quietly began packing our things in a more orderly way, and Fletcher watched him. 'It's a warm night,' he said. 'That's why you're so cheeky. If it was raining you'd sing a different tune.' Frank went on packing quietly, so instead it was Fletcher who sang a different tune. 'Hey?' he said. 'You didn't think I was serious, did you? I wouldn't put you two boys out in the middle of the night. I don't do that sort of thing to my friends.' Frank stopped packing, so Fletcher said, 'Of course, I knew that you boys would help me out.'

'What did you do with the child?' Frank asked.

Fletcher took him by the throat. 'Don't you ask me that sort of question. Let the kaffir ask those questions.' He twisted Frank's shirt just below the collar, pulling the collar tight. Frank pulled away and the collar tore. Fletcher gave a cry and let go immediately. He had plenty of khaki shirts, he told Frank, and he'd be glad to replace the one that had just been torn. He offered Frank a shirt, and sherry and whisky to both of us, and the use of his car for our holiday. He offered us some of his gold-mining shares. He told Frank that he was one of the handsomest men that he, Fletcher, had ever seen. His voice grew hoarse and he refreshed himself by splashing on himself some of the stale water from the basin in the wash-stand in which I had washed myself when I had returned to the room, and which had escaped the destruction wrought upon the jug by his brother-in-law. The water stained his shirt-front and brought some of his fine, blond hair into spikes that stood out startlingly above his ears. He said he was leaving Mirredal that night, and going to England. He still had people, he said, in England, in Stockton.

He was pitiable, but I was desperately fatigued and sleepy, and as the night dragged on the man's antics and words be-came duller and duller to my sight and hearing, and I became more and more bored with what he was doing. Bored, dulled, stupefied, bored to the point of indifference, bored to the point when he could thrust his face as close to mine as he liked and open his mouth as widely as he could and I did not hear his words and closed my eyes to the sight until the noise receded and I knew that I could safely open my eyes again and stare in comparative peace at the ceiling. Steadily my eyes grew heavier, and my limbs more and more reluctant to move. And the man went on. I wasn't talking and I was exhausted: I wondered what resources of nervous energy he had managed to plumb that night. It was infinitely wearisome. For, quite apart from anything else, at no time during the night did I feel the slightest flicker of desire to 'stick by him'. I was prepared, if necessary, to be thrown out of the house and to spend the night on the veld, but I no more thought of sticking by him than I did of walking back to Lyndhurst. I cannot say that the idea of sticking by him was unthinkable, because it did occur to me once that we might say we would – not remotely meaning it, but simply in order to get him out of the room and to give us a few hours of the sleep we needed so much. And one look at him disabused me of the idea, promptly. I could never have done it: I hadn't the heart to deceive him: he was too near the end of his tether. He was boring and foolish and fantastic, but it would have been cruelly unfair to him, in the state he was in, to deceive him. And as the only discomfort we had to suffer in an attempt to be fair to him was some boredom and noise, it was better to be fair. We could afford it.

And Fletcher went on talking. At no time in all his talking did he get any closer to making clear what he meant by 'sticking by him'; and it did occur to me then, and has often occurred to me since, that perhaps Fletcher was asking in his wild way for nothing but moral respect. If he had done nothing wrong, criminally wrong I mean, in the affair with Louw's child – which is a possibility, which is something which we still don't know – then the only explanation of his behaviour that night is that he was a man who felt himself to be utterly alone and unsupported. 'Nothing but' moral respect I have said, but what greater need could Fletcher have had? He was abandoned: he had been cast aside by everyone: even his wife had wanted to leave him, and offered him now no support at all in his anguish. He had been jeered at and cursed and a kaffir had worsted him: no one had come to his defence, attempted to deflect the accusations and insults that had been flung at him, no one had shown any pity for him. He was alone, in a monstrous loneliness that was great enough to warrant threats and promises and flattery and appeals to white civilization to the two young men who were in his house but implicated in none of the other miserable relationships with which he was surrounded. So he bludgeoned and bludgeoned away at us. If we gave him friendship, then he had a friend. If we feared him then he was still powerful enough to make someone fear him. If we were moved by his appeals to our white skin, then he, like ourselves, would have a status among people. If we were attracted by his promises, then there was someone who looked to him for gifts and munificence. Anything, in his position, would be better than nothing: he could not afford to discriminate, and so he could change in a moment from wheedler to bully, from bully to statesman, and see nothing strange in what he was doing. His objective remained the same throughout: the moral respect of another human being.

I think in this at least I have been fair to him, even though we both steadfastly denied him the support he was seeking. More than fair, for I have omitted so many of the things he did that night. I must say that towards the end of his long harangue, to my tired sight he had almost ceased to be a man and seemed to have become a piece of paper, a puppet, a balloon that was alternately inflated and deflated, that sank and rose in and out of my sight as the air dandled it and let it fall, a thing of gusts and intemperate movement, without depth or permanence, the image of a man that a hand could have crumpled.

Mrs Fletcher did not stay in our room as long as her husband did, though she was there for a good part of his harangue. She sat, for the most part, in a chair in the corner of the room, with her head held straight and her hands in her lap, her feet crossed beneath her. She kept her gaze on the wall before her: she did not seem to hear the commotion that her husband was making. But it was in one of his rare silences that she spoke for the first time since Joseph had left us. While Fletcher paced about the room gesticulating fiercely and silently, Mrs Fletcher rose to her feet and walked to the window. She stretched her arms squarely in front of her body through the vacant frame, leaning out, as the light itself leaned into the darkness. She stood like that for a few moments, while behind her her husband continued his prowling about the room, as unaware of her as she had been of him. The light lay for only a few feet beyond the reach of her arms, but she threw her voice beyond it, over the stoep in to the decaying and dried garden in the sand.

'Nasie,' she called. 'Why have you left me here? Come back for me, Nasie.'

But from outside there came no reply. No stir, no murmur, not so much as a ripple in the dark, warm air. All was still. The air was as relaxed as it always is on a summer night in the Karroo, unruffled, undisturbed, without limit above the unpeopled earth. Mrs Fletcher waited with her arms stretched out before her: she wavered as her arms moved up and down a little in the strain of keeping them up: eventually she was forced to drop her arms. Not even the wind had answered her, no sign had been given to her, no token had come that she could be released from her attitude of desire, nothing had come from the darkness beyond the uneven oblong of light.

The silent world was indifferent, exposing only by indifference the folly of what she had hoped for. There was ignominy in this last defeat.

Ignominy and horror. We had seen much that was lonely and violent and pitiable in that evening, but I remember only one thing with horror. That is what we saw when Mrs Fletcher turned to face the room again. We had already seen her calmness go, her expression distorted, her silence broken, but it was only then, at the very last, that we saw her eyes crack. Those narrow ovals of light blue that had always been transparent and expressionless were suddenly flawed, split in two, while we watched: we saw the light that before had sunk in them without discomposure caught on the surface and broken there; her eyes shivered and glittered, they shone like an animal's when it is caught in the veld by a beam of light and stands dazzled, shining, and helpless, before the approach of its enemies. Mrs Fletcher's eyes quivered blindly in the light for a moment, until the first shivering, reluctant tear fell from them, leaving her eyes blue again, until the next tear broke them. Then she wept without sound, without wrinkling her features for concealment from our sight, without wiping the tears away that were still leaving her eyes and running down her sun-withered cheeks, when she walked out of the room, moving upright, with her hands hanging stiffly and shyly away from her body.

19

It is not perhaps surprising that we overslept the next morning, though I know I was shocked to see, on awakening, the sunlight splashing itself lavishly against the wall opposite my bed. But we had been up late the previous night – and not only through the efforts of Mr Fletcher. For even after he, in exhaustion, had at last fallen in silence into the armchair which his wife had vacated, and after Frank had approached him and stirred him awake and suggested he leave, which he had totteringly done, without a word – even then we had not fallen asleep. Alone in the room at last, we had had a long discussion about what we should do next in the affair.

What emerged most clearly from the discussion was that whatever had been reluctant or involuntary or idle in our involvement previously, had been swept away after the events of the evening by a determination to give Joseph every help that he might need. This was something that each of us had resolved upon independently: we were willing now to stay on in Mirredal for as long as Joseph might want us to. We were children no longer; and we could not merely listen to his story of hardship and bewilderment.

I suggested at first to Frank that we should, in the morning, go immediately to the police at Mirredal, inform them of what we had heard, and insist that they thrash the affair out as thoroughly as they knew how. But Frank pointed out that Joseph feared that his sister might be involved – criminally involved – in the disappearance of her child, and, that being so, he would scarcely at the present stage, wish to go to the police in the matter. I suggested then that we should consult a lawyer, but again Frank vetoed the idea, on the same grounds as the first. His plan – which was the one we agreed on, after casting around without success for an alternative possible action – was that, together with Joseph, we should confront Fletcher and bully or blackmail him into telling us what he had done with the child. If the child had been got out of the way by some underhand but not necessarily vicious means, and if Joseph wanted to recover her, then we would help him to the best of our abilities. If the facts of the matter were uglier, or if we got nothing at all from Fletcher, we would consult with Joseph on what we should then do next. But whatever happened, we were determined not to let go.

We knew whose side we were on, without reflection. And though we shrank from the prospect of further scenes with Mr Fletcher, of police actions, court cases, explanations and the general exposure of ourselves to public gaze which we could not but foresee, we were determined, nevertheless, not to betray the trust which Joseph, we felt, had placed upon us by telling us his story and by calling upon us as his witnesses. In the normal course of events there were a great many duties which we, like any other citizens, were prepared to waive; but the duty we had towards Joseph was a limitless one. Guilt and pity, I have said, were hunting us out of country: here was an opportunity to expiate both. It would be an injustice to say that we were flushed with righteousness, but we were determined to do our best to see that Joseph got what he was looking for.

And I must say too that we looked forward to Joseph's gratitude. He had called upon us as his witnesses, and then had left almost immediately, before any of us could recover from the surprise that his remark had caused. He had left with a salutation of his hand: we had heard his footsteps slowly retreating into the darkness. In the solitude of our room, after Fletcher had left, we decided that Joseph had left when he did because though he had called upon us, he had not done so with any belief that we would in fact help him. It had been a way of silencing Fletcher, for him, no more – and he had left in the silence of what he had said, before he could be disowned. We were going to surprise him with the truth of what he himself had not dared to believe.

We knew that if the knowledge that Joseph was seeking should be unpalatable to him, we would then be faced with another, almost unthinkably difficult problem: we would face that when it came up. And in the meantime we were comforted by the fact that – ugly as the whole business undoubtedly was – it seemed definite from what Louw had said that it did not include the possibility of Joseph's discovering what he had most dreaded to discover. Frank even said contemptuously that Fletcher could never have had the courage; and he believed without question, from the way Joseph had spoken of her, and despite Joseph's own fears, in the innocence of Joseph's sister – though not necessarily in her ability to withstand bullying and bribery. A lump sum here and a lump sum there, and the complete chaos of record in any of the African locations at any of the major urban centres, would together all have served Fletcher's purpose. This, compared to what we had at times feared, was comfort. I was comforted by what Frank said, and also, I suppose, though I was only to realize this later, by my own lack of awareness.

We were adults now, and ready and determined to act, but, insuperably, strangeness and distance from the story Joseph had told remained: I was as white as I had been as a child and now, as then, the barriers in my own imagination protected me from a realization of our task as intimate as it might have been had Joseph been white.

So, under the circumstances, it was in tolerably good heart that we finally fell asleep. To oversleep was not an auspicious start to a day of activity, and as I lay in bed, staring at the ceiling that was white with the harsh morning glare reflected from the wall, I did allow myself to be tempted away from our purpose. With longing I thought of the journey that still lay ahead of us, through the dry country, through the *dorps* where little whitewashed cafés faced on streets of sand and no one stirred in the mid-day heat, through the empty mountains along a dark blue road, out of the Karroo, and at last into the Western Province. There the country would still be sparse and scattered and sandy, I knew, and the higher slopes of the mountains untouched by the few people who lived in the valleys in isolated white houses; there all would still be pale-coloured, pale brown of earth, a pale sky, the faint blue of mountains. But in the valleys that the mountains enclosed like clenched fists of rock, out of the rock a trickle of green would run: young wheat, peaches, pear trees, the low dim vines that would run in regular rows away from the roads along which we would travel. The vines would wheel like spokes in the centre of the turning land, and beyond them the land would always be opening up further; beyond the valleys, beyond the mountains, other bulks of earth would be shrugging away, right to the margin of the sea.

But even as I allowed myself to be tempted by the thought of our desination, in the act of imagining our journey, I knew that we would not leave until we had helped Joseph. And the mountains would still be there, days later, and the vines, and the sea. Would we be able to enjoy them at all if we had failed Joseph when he was in need? – though with good luck we could have been in Cape Town that very night, with moderate luck over the mountains at least.

I leaned over and woke Frank. It was time for us to be

going. We would not stay for breakfast – even if breakfast were to be served to us, which I greatly doubted. We dressed and packed our things rapidly. Frank suggested that we should leave the money for the night's lodging on the wash-stand, and clear out through the window, but I was curious to see what the house looked like after Louw's visitation, and persuaded him to come with me. So we shouldered our packs, and left the room through the shattered door.

20

We had to pick our way down the passage towards the hall-room. Our footsteps crunched and squeaked on glass everywhere, as though someone had scattered sugar all over the floor. Horns from the walls lay on the floor at all angles and in all corners: only one set was still on the wall, and the curving horns were hanging upside down, pointing down in a gesture of fantastic and silent negation. I looked into the room next to ours in which Louw had rampaged: I noticed particularly the bed he had turned upside down, and from which he had then, for some reason, smashed all the legs. The metal showed grey and jagged, twinkling with tiny points of light, where each limb had been truncated. The legs themselves looked pathetic, lying about on the floor with the little wheels still uselessly clasped at the end of each amputated limb.

The hall-room looked as though a bomb had burst within it. The doors were all smashed, the armchairs lay on their sides, ripped open, disembowelled, with tufts of a grey, woolly substance hanging out from each. The picture of Louw's father was lying across one of the armchairs, upside down, showing the plain brown back of the canvas. The frame was broken in several places: it was the canvas itself which was keeping the picture together, like the poles and pegs of a collapsed tent. Curtains were tumbled in a heap on the floor, and the curtain rod was hanging outwards and downwards from one hook only, ready to fall at any moment.

The front passage was like the other through which we

had passed. Some of the outer sheaths on the horns had cracked apart when they had been flung on the floor, and the white bones that had been revealed lay like newly-stripped sticks that children had left after playing. The front door gaped open in its upper half, where the glass had been: the lead which had held the glass was twisted into all sorts of shapes, from some of which a fragment of red or blue or green glass still hung. The little passage-table, out of which Mrs Fletcher had taken the torch, leaned towards the floor like a slide, with its front legs couched before it. We carefully left the money on the floor in front of it. A blue and yellow cloth was spread over the nearest palm tree, in the silence of the stoep.

Nobody had stirred as we had made our way out of the house. Not a sound had come from anywhere in the house. We might have been the first revenants to a house through which an army had passed, wrecking everything that the troops could not loot and carry along with them. No one watched us, called to us, asked us what we were doing: there was not so much as a creak from the rest of the house. It was a relief to get out of it, into the silence and heat of the stoep.

Outside the arid daylight of the Karroo poured down from the sky, without stint. We stepped into the blaze of sunlight that lay just beyond the lowest step into the garden, and immediately the sweat started under the straps of my pack, as though I had been touched there.

The sky was high, and had that grey, glazed look that comes with the heat. Low down, near the horizon, there was a streak or two of cloud, thin stuff, crumbling away on either side into a few small marbles of white. There were no other clouds: we moved under a shining sky, without colour, all colour drained into the flame which was its centre. And though the flame itself was golden, an irradiation of colour above, where we walked the light was like that of the sky, hard and colourless, striking at the earth with an intensity that bewildered our eyes, and kept them fixed on the hot, orange-coloured path before us. The path looked as though it had not been dyed by hand for decoration, but simply thrust under the sun and left to be fired, kiln-like. I saw the sides of the petrol tins glinting, and where the concrete path had cracked apart to one side and fallen into a decline into the bare dust, the grains of sand glinted, so grey under the strong light that they looked almost green, lying loosely: they would have been hot to hold in the hand.

If we had been able to look up we would probably have seen Joseph before. As it was, we almost stumbled on him. He was lying on his back under one of the bushes to the side of the path – I think it was an oleander, and the clustered stems of the plant, and its dark green leaves, cast a ragged island of shade in the bare, unrehabilitable sand. He was lying on his back, with his stained felt hat serving as a pillow. He got to his feet when he saw us coming, though he had not, I think, been asleep, and must have heard our approaching steps.

We were most relieved to see him. We had thought that he would probably be coming back to the house in the morning, but we had not been sure, and had foreseen, as our first task, a visit to the Mirredal location, where among battered huts and ragged children and suspicious stares we would have had to ask for him. And under a sun as hot as this, it would have been so much less a pleasant task. But here he was, as brown and big and furrowed as ever, dressed in the same dusty overalls.

'Morning, basies,' he said to us.

'Good morning,' we replied.

'*Soe! Maar dis warm vanmore, my basies!*' he exclaimed emphatically. He was holding his crumpled hat in his hand, and with it still folded he wiped the sweat that was trickling down his forehead. With every movement he made I saw the patches of sweat on his overalls, at the armpits, and round his waist where the overalls were belted. The drops of sweat lay too on the crown of his head, clear round drops, larger than the shaven curls of hair.

'It is hot.'

'When do you think it's going to rain?' he asked.

I laughed. 'I don't know. You're the one who lives in Mirredal. You should know.'

'*Nee baas.*' He shook his head. 'I don't know.' He gazed up at the sky. 'It must come one day,' he said.

'Ja,' Frank said. 'But I hope we won't be here still when it does.'

Joseph looked our packs over very carefully, first Frank's, then mine. He asked: 'Are the basies going away this morning?'

I said: 'I don't know when we're going.' And Frank: 'That's what we want to talk to you about.'

'Talk to me?' Joseph asked. He moved his head back a little, and stared at us. His lips moved towards a smile, but he did not smile. 'Me?' he asked again.

I was both proud and afraid as I answered, letting us both in for it, irrevocably, now. 'Yes, you. We aren't leaving until we've given you all the help that you need. And that's what we want to talk to you about.'

Joseph said slowly and inquiringly: 'The baas says that he wants to help me?'

'Yes,' I said. 'We're going to help you. You aren't on your own any more. We're ready to do whatever you think best to help you find out the things you must know.' I thought I understood Joseph's incredulity, and Frank too threw in his voice with mine:

'We agreed last night that we would help you. We talked it over and we decided to do whatever you wanted us to do.'

Joseph dropped his head. I could not blame him for being incredulous: what an ugly history, I thought, lay behind that incredulity. We waited for a word from him. Eventually, he said: 'You mean you want to help me in last night's business?'

'Of course that's what we mean. You said to Fletcher that we were your witnesses. Well, we are. Here we are, now. And we're not only going to be your witnesses for what you already know, we're going to help you find out what you don't.' His incredulity could only strengthen our determination to help him.

Frank asked: 'What do you think we should do first?' He added: 'We've already decided that the best thing would be for us to ask Fletcher what he did with the child. If we all three ask him he might tell us. Even if he doesn't want to, we might be able to make him.' He waited for Joseph's approval of the plan. Then he added: 'You needn't be afraid of Fletcher.' Then with a gesture of apology, a smile of admission, having been guilty of thoughtlessness: 'You haven't been afraid of Fletcher up to now. But think,' Frank said, 'how much stronger your position is now.'

'*Ja baas*,' Joseph said, after a pause, though he had hardly seemed to have been considering what Frank had said to him. He looked from Frank to myself. Then he said again: '*Ja baas*.' There was a guardedness, a neutrality, in his voice that made me ask:

'So? What do you think?'

'Nothing, baas.'

'What do you mean you think nothing? What do you want us to do?'

Joseph shuffled his feet, like a stupid and humble African. 'Nothing, baas,' he said.

'You want us to do nothing?' Frank asked, his voice rising.

'*Ja baas*.'

'But you must need our help!' I exclaimed.

'Help baas? I don't think so, baas.'

'But we are your witnesses.'

'*Ja baas*,' Joseph said. 'Last night baas.'

'And this morning!'

'And this morning also baas.'

'So?'

'So nothing baas.'

'You mean you aren't going to go on?' Was he a coward, after all? I couldn't believe it.

'Go on, baas?'

'Yes, go on with Fletcher.'

'*Ja baas*.' He agreed with me promptly: I no longer knew to what it was that he was agreeing. I couldn't have told from his tone of voice either, for he produced his agreement automatically like what is known as a 'good kaffir'.

'How will you go on with Baas Fletcher?' I asked. Only when I'd asked the question did I notice how I'd phrased it: the man's manner had demanded it.

'I want to work for Baas Fletcher, baas,' he replied.

'But what about the trouble?' Frank asked.

'The trouble, baas?'

'Yes, the trouble last night. You know what I'm talking about.'

'Baas,' Joseph said earnestly, frowning, his head a little down, as if he were trying to reassure us on some point about which we were, inexplicably, anxious, 'I don't think there will be any more trouble, for you.' He added helpfully, 'I think the trouble is finished for you, baas.' His voice was kind and humble, and it undercut everything we had thought we would feel at this meeting.

'I don't understand,' Frank said, a little indignantly.

'Understand, baas?' His own lack of comprehension was profound, his voice implied.

'What are you going to do?' I asked.

He shifted his weight. 'I'm going to stay here, baas.'

'In Mirredal?'

'Yes, baas. In this house, baas.'

'They won't let you,' I said.

He made no reply. He simply shook his head. 'I don't want any more trouble for you, baas,' he said after a pause. He looked down at our white, upturned faces, his own face a shadow in the sun. We dropped our gaze. 'Are the basies going a long way to-day?' he asked.

'We have got a long way to go,' I said. 'But —'

He looked up at the sun. 'It's getting late, my basies.'

He pointed towards the sun with a small gesture. 'And it's still going to get hotter today, basies.'

'So you think we should go?' Frank asked abruptly.

He was humble and careful in his reply: 'Baas, if the baas has still got a long way to go today then I think it might be better if the baas left now.'

I clung to what I knew we had over him: we were his witnesses. I said: 'You'll need our addresses.'

'Addresses, baas? I don't think so.'

Frank took out his wallet, and tore off a piece of paper from a letter that was folded within it. He used the wallet as a pad, and wrote his name and my name on the piece of paper, with our addresses underneath, his in Johannesburg, mine in Lynd-hurst.

'Here,' he said.

Joseph took the piece of paper with care. He folded it slowly between his work-thickened fingers, and put it in a pocket of his overalls. 'Thank you, baas,' he said noncommittally.

'You'll write to us if there's any trouble?' I asked. And Frank said:

'We'll be your witnesses if you ever want us to be.'

Joseph's head hung above us. I saw him smiling, with a reluctant wrinkling of the rough skin about his mouth. 'Write, baas?' he asked me. 'I can't write, baas,' he said gently.

'Well, you can always get someone else to write for you,' I said cheerily. There was no other tone I could adopt. Certainly there was nothing more we could do with Joseph. I hitched my pack higher to take the weight off the small of my back. 'Good-bye, Joseph,' I said.

'Good-bye,' Frank said.

'Good-bye, baas,' Joseph said. 'Thank you, baas,' he said, lifting his hand in his formal salute. 'I hope the basies have a nice journey.'

We began to move down the path again. But Joseph was unrelenting. He followed us to the gate, and jumped in front of us to open it, and then stood aside and waited while we went through. He might have been the boy who had made our beds or cleaned our shoes, and who still hoped, even at this late stage, that we might, before leaving, fumble in our pockets and bring out for him a sixpenny tip.

21

When we were through the gate we looked back, and saw Joseph stretching himself in the shade again. It was then that Frank suggested that we should hide ourselves somewhere and see what would happen when Fletcher came out. We were both smarting under the treatment we had just received, and the knowledge of how we had exposed ourselves to it, and in the end, when we decided that we would wait, we did so not out of any feeling that Joseph might yet need our help, nor out of a simple curiosity, but more out of respect for Joseph. After what he had just done to us, we wanted to see what he would do to Fletcher.

Finding a place near the house in which to hide was not at all easy, for we wanted to be within sight and hearing of the house, and yet concealed from view, and in all the hot, flat veld there wasn't much vegetation that would have given cover to anything larger than a *dassie* or a rock-rabbit. Eventually we settled down among some rocks on the nearer bank of the river. A thorn-bush grew between the rocks and gave not only some concealment, but also threw a necessary shade where we lay. We agreed that whatever happened we would wait there only as long as there was shade for us to lie in. It would have been impossible to lie nakedly in the sun when the shade had been cleared away.

We waited in our hard little nook of rock and thornbush for some time. Long enough, at any rate, for our heads to begin swimming in the heat, and for every little ribbing and tussock in the earth to imprint itself familiarly upon us with a steadily-growing sharpness that seemed to be, in our heat-dazed state, merely another pain, a different kind of heat. And the place stank a little with a smell that I could not identify, the smell of something small and dead and dried-out, as if the desert had laboured to produce an extra little discomfort, a mouse of a stink. The heat came off steadily from the water-smoothed, glittering rocks around us; I don't think we could have remained much longer among those untouchable rocks.

And when Fletcher did come out, and Joseph spoke to him, we found that we could not hear what they were saying: we were too far away. After all we had just been through in order to overhear the conversation, we were not to be baulked, so without thought, without consultation, and with no further attempt at concealment, we rose from our hiding-place and simply walked across the sparse, rock-littered veld, to the fence round the house, where we stood on one side. We stood there in the sun, and neither Fletcher nor Joseph took the slightest notice of us.

Fletcher must have been exhausted from the previous night. He was broken, we could see, even though the first words we heard from him were:

'No, you can't work for me.'

'Baas,' Joseph said, 'I am going to work for you.'

'How can you work for me?' Fletcher asked.

'I am going to work for you.'

'Don't say that to me!'

'I want to work for you, baas.'

'I'll set the police on you, that's what I'll do.'

'No,' Joseph said, shaking his head. 'You won't set the police on me.'

Then they were both silent. Joseph stood with his body stooped forward a little, towards the man he was determined should be his master. And Fletcher stood wearily, sideways, with his shoulder to Joseph, unable to look at him.

'You think,' Fletcher said, 'you'll be able to find out something from me?' He waited for a reply. But Joseph did not speak. 'If I tell you that – if I tell you that I hurt nobody – will that be enough?' Still Joseph made no reply. 'Then by Christ,' Fletcher shouted, 'as long as I live not another sound about it will cross my lips.' Joseph did not say anything. 'I'm telling you,' Fletcher said weakly.

'Baas,' Joseph said, 'I'll bring my things this afternoon. Then I'll start work to-morrow.'

'And what will you do if I don't let you?' Fletcher asked. Joseph did not reply. For the first time Fletcher looked at him, his head shaking – no, no, no. But all he said, after the silence, was: 'There's no work for you to do in the house.'

'I'll find work.'

'What do you want of me?' Fletcher asked, with his hands lifted in front of his chest. 'Can't you leave me alone?'

'No, baas.'

Again they were silent. 'All right,' Fletcher shouted suddenly: 'Bring your things! Work for me! I'll make you work until you drop!' He began to laugh: it was a dry, high, desolate sound, that the heat-ridden air cracked and carried towards us in fragments. He shook his fist at Joseph and laughed, he shouted: 'That's the only way you'll learn that I am still the baas.'

'*Ja baas,*' Joseph said.

The matter was settled apparently, for Joseph turned and began walking briskly towards the gate. Fletcher stared after him, his fist still raised, laughing no longer. Joseph must have seen us as he passed through the gate, but he made no sign that he had, nor did he look back once he had begun walking along the track towards the village.

We turned to look at Fletcher. Fletcher was dancing. Alone in the veld, in the middle of his dusty piece of ground, Fletcher was dancing with humiliation and rage and despair. He stamped his feet into the dust, and gnawed his knuckles, and twisted his ears, and pulled at his chin, and brandished his fists. He was still lifting his knees, he was still raising the dust about his ankles when we turned our backs on him. We left him dancing there, solitary in the veld, a grotesque little figure, capering under a blazing sun.

OXFORD

MORE OXFORD PAPERBACKS

Details of a selection of other books follow. A complete list of Oxford Paperbacks, including The World's Classics, Twentieth-Century Classics, OPUS, Past Masters, Oxford Authors, Oxford Shakespeare, and Oxford Paperback Reference, is available in the UK from the General Publicity Department, Oxford University Press (JN), Walton Street, Oxford OX2 6DP.

In the USA, complete lists are available from the Paperbacks Marketing Manager, Oxford University Press, 200 Madison Avenue, New York, NY 10016.

Oxford Paperbacks are available from all good bookshops. In case of difficulty, customers in the UK can order direct from Oxford University Press Bookshop, 116 High Street, Oxford, Freepost, OX1 4BR, enclosing full payment. Please add 10 per cent of published price for postage and packing.

THE WOMAN IN THE DUNES
Kobo Abe
Introduced by Anthony Thwaite

'One day in August a man disappeared . . .' Seven years later he is declared a missing person, presumed dead. What happens in the interim is the substance of this novel.

Niki Jumpei is a rare person, a loner. When, on one of his solitary insect-hunting expeditions to a nearby beach, he finds himself stranded in the dunes, the prisoner of a mysterious woman, it is not clear whether he is properly to be considered lost or found. As he struggles to escape, 'escape' itself becomes oddly ambiguous. At the same time his captor, a mixture of enigmatic reserve and earthly sensuality, arouses both his fear and his desire.

The Woman in the Dunes won the Yomiuri Prize in 1960 and Hiroshi Teshigahare's film won the jury prize at the 1963 Cannes Film Festival.

THE SMALL BACK ROOM
Nigel Balchin
Introduced by Benny Green

Sammy Rice is one of the 'back-room boys' of the Second World War. The small back room of the title may also be Sammy's own living quarters, where he tries to control a drinking habit, and lives with a woman he loves but won't marry for fear of imprisoning her in a life he sees being slowly eroded by the unreality of war.

As an account of the war experience, the book is realistic and unsettling, and as a study of a personality under stress, it reveals perennial truths. As Benny Green says, 'to the battle which Sammy Rice wages against himself no precise date can be attached. The struggle goes on.'

'His theme is of intense and irresistible interest.' *New Statesman*

KIPPS

H. G. Wells

Introduced by Benny Green

The story of Arthur Kipps, a poor, uneducated draper's assistant who inherits not only a fortune, but all the problems that a sudden elevation in social status can bring, recalls Wells's early life in the drapery trade.

'*Kipps* is the finest of H. G. Wells's deeply personal novels using his early experience in the draper's shop, an autobiographical theme explored by Benny Green in a fine introduction.'
Sunday Times

THE CHERRY TREE

Adrian Bell

Introduced by Humphrey Phelps

This is the final novel of Adrian Bell's Suffolk trilogy, completing the story begun in *Corduroy* and continued in *Silver Ley*. It is a deeply personal account of two loves, for his wife and for the land she helped him farm, and it vividly evokes a rural life that was changing even as he wrote.

IN ANOTHER COUNTRY

John Bayley

Introduced by A. N. Wilson

John Bayley's only novel explores the effect of 'the first cold winter of peace' on a group of British servicemen stationed in a small town on the Rhine. Some, like the ruthless Duncan Holt, use army life to further their own ends; while others, like the naïve Oliver Childers, must fight against their own personal defeat in the wake of national victory.

'now that you can't get "books from Boots" any more, and country lanes and democracy seem to be going the same way as "proper drains", there is every reason to savour an intelligence as extraordinary as John Bayley's, and a novel as good as this' A. N. Wilson

MY UNCLE SILAS

H. E. Bates

Introduced by V. S. Pritchett

Illustrations by Edward Ardizzone

H. E. Bates's *Uncle Silas* stories are among his most famous and best-loved writings. Silas's roguish but lovable character is recaptured in the memory of his bewitched, yet sometimes sceptical, young nephew.

LOVE AND MR LEWISHAM

H. G. Wells

Introduced by Benny Green

Mr Lewisham regards himself as a young man poised on the brink of dazzling academic achievement. With degrees and diplomas brandished like lances, he will smash his way out of the prison of class and poverty. And yet, on the very threshold of his advancement, all his fine plans are swept aside. For Lewisham falls in love—with Ethel, stepdaughter of the shameless confidence trickster Chaffrey—and before long he is made to realize that the world is a more tormenting place then ever he had supposed. A cautionary tale, *Love and Mr Lewisham* is one of Wells's most carefully planned novels and one of his most deeply personal.

THE FOUR MEN

Hilaire Belloc

Introduced by A. N. Wilson

Written in 1911, *The Four Men* is an imaginary ramble through the Sussex of 1902 in which Hilaire Belloc immortalizes a disappearing world through the eyes of his four characters— Myself, Grizzlebeard, The Sailor, and The Poet. The book is a mixture of humour and reflection, nonsense and poignant detail, celebrating the vanishing landscape of unspoilt rural England.

'anyone who is interested in Sussex will love this book' *Punch*

THE DEATH OF VIRGIL

Hermann Broch

Translated by Jean Starr Untermeyer

Introduced by Bernard Levin

Broch's magnificent novel describes the poet Virgil's last hours as he questions the nature of art, and mourns the death of a civilization.

'One of the most representative and advanced works of our time . . . an astonishing performance.' Thomas Mann

'Broch is the greatest novelist European literature has produced since Joyce.' George Steiner

'One of our century's great novels.' *Sunday Times*

HIGH TABLE

Joanna Cannan

Introduced by Anthony Quinton

Theodore Fletcher is a bit of a misfit, but he *is* clever. So it hardly seems surprising that a boyhood devoted to study is followed by an academic career and, finally, by the Wardenship of an Oxford College. All seems secure and untroubled in his life, until a guilty secret from his past appears in the shape of a young man who might be his son. Joanna Cannan constructs her plot deftly and with considerable irony. No one writes better of academic life at Oxford.

'A plot of extraordinary delicacy, pathos, and irony.' *Observer*

THE ESSENTIAL G. K. CHESTERTON

G. K. Chesterton

Introduced by P. J. Kavanagh

The extent to which G. K. Chesterton is still quoted by modern writers testifies to his outstanding importance in twentieth-century literature. In this selection from his work, P. J. Kavanagh fully explores the many sides to Chesterton's personality and writing. Chesterton the novelist is represented by a complete work, *The Man Who was Thursday,* and his poetic gift is displayed in a fine selection of verse. But the lion's share of the volume goes to Chesterton as essayist and journalist. Here we can enjoy his lively writings on the issues and debates of his day.

'Mr Kavanagh's selection is extremely rewarding.' John Gross, *Observer*

RICEYMAN STEPS

Arnold Bennett

Introduced by Frank Kermode

Bennett's reputation as a novelist waned after the publication of his great pre-war novels, *Anna of the Five Towns, The Old Wives' Tale,* and *Clayhanger,* but it was emphatically restored by the appearance in 1923 of *Riceyman Steps,* the story of a miserly bookseller who not only starves himself to death, but infects his wife with a passion for economy that brings her also to an untimely end.

HIS MONKEY WIFE

John Collier

Introduced by Paul Theroux

The work of this British poet and novelist who lived for many years in Hollywood has always attracted a devoted following. This, his first novel, concerns a chimpanzee called Emily who falls in love with her owner—an English schoolmaster—and embarks on a process of self-education which includes the reading of Darwin's *Origin of Species*.

'John Collier welds the strongest force with the strangest subtlety . . . It is a tremendous and terrifying satire, only made possible by the suavity of its wit.' Osbert Sitwell

'Read as either a parody of thirties' fiction or just crazy comedy, it deserves its place as a 20th-century classic.' David Holloway, *Sunday Telegraph*

A FATHER AND HIS FATE

Ivy Compton-Burnett

Introduced by Penelope Lively

First published in 1957, this novel displays Ivy Compton-Burnett's style at its most bleak and unadorned. It consists almost exclusively of dialogue. The central figure, Miles Mowbray, is one of the author's most successful domestic dictators in the marriage of comedy with sheer awfulness. His three daughters are used as symbols of powerlessness, in their bondage to him and to their unmarried state. Language is their only weapon, and it is only here that they have any chance of coming out on top.

MANSERVANT AND MAIDSERVANT

Ivy Compton-Burnett

Introduced by Penelope Lively

Ivy Compton-Burnett's novels are profound studies of family life; they are both immensely funny and completely original. *Manservant and Maidservant* describes the petty tyrannies to be found in an upper middle-class Edwardian household, and shows Dame Ivy's wit at its sharpest and her characterization at its most memorable.

'there is no doubt about her originality and the uniqueness of her world, and her mastery of a sinister comic vein, of which *Manservant and Maidservant* (1947) is a characteristic product' *Scotsman*

'There is nobody in all this writing world even remotely like her.' *Guardian*

THE UNBEARABLE BASSINGTON

Saki

At the centre of the book is Cormus Bassington, 'the beautiful wayward laughing boy, with his naughtiness, his exasperating selfishness, his insurmountable folly and perverseness, his cruelty that spared not even himself', in whom Saki invested his own ambiguous feelings for youth in his fierce indignation at the ravages of time.

NOCTURNE

Frank Swinnerton

Introduced by Benny Green

Frank Swinnerton (1884–1982), critic and prolific novelist, was a familiar figure in the literary life of the first half of this century.

In *Nocturne*, a masterly portrayal of relationships and the way they work, Frank Swinnerton takes a romantic theme and casts it in a realistic mode. As a result his lyrical evocation of the night's changing moods is matched by its powerful insights into his characters' anxieties and jealousies as two sisters struggle to make sense of their feelings for their father, the men they love, and each other. One of the novel's admirers was H. G. Wells, who wrote of it: 'this fine work . . . ends a brilliant apprenticeship and ranks Swinnerton as Master. This is a book that will not die. It is perfect, authentic, and alive.'

MEMOIRS OF A MIDGET

Walter de la Mare

Introduced by Angela Carter

'This book is an authentic masterpiece. Lucid, enigmatic, and violent with a terrible violence that leaves behind no physical trace . . . It may be read with a good deal of simple enjoyment and then it sticks like a splinter in the mind.' So writes novelist Angela Carter in her introduction to Walter de la Mare's elegiac study of the estrangement and isolation suffered by the diminutive Miss M.

BELCHAMBER

Howard Sturgis

Introduced by Noel Annan

The hero of Howard Sturgis's best-known novel, *Belchamber*, published in 1904, is 'Sainty', heir to one of Britain's premier earldoms, but constitutionally unsuited to fulfil his exalted position and exploited by all around him. Both Sainty and the novel itself are, in many ways, products of their time: Victorian values are in decay as the ancient families fall before the *nouveaux riches*. Like Henry James, Sturgis maintains the outsider's perfect poise and yet writes with the insider's sense of intimacy.

'Belchamber is more than the study of a personal calamity. It is the indictment of a society.' Noel Annan

SEVEN DAYS IN NEW CRETE

Robert Graves

Introduced by Martin Seymour-Smith

A funny, disconcerting, and uncannily prophetic novel about Edward Venn-Thomas, a cynical poet, who finds himself transported to a civilisation in the far future. He discovers that his own world ended long ago, and that the inhabitants of the new civilisation have developed a neo-archaic social system. Magic rather than science forms the basis of their free and stable society; yet, despite its near perfection, Edward finds New Cretan life insipid. He realizes that what is missing is a necessary element of evil, which he feels is his duty to restore.

'Robert Graves' cynical stab at creating a Utopia is a poetic *Brave New World* filled with much more colour and dreaming than the original *Brave New World* of Aldous Huxley.' Maeve Binchy

ACADEMIC YEAR

D. J. Enright

Introduced by Anthony Thwaite

Three expatriate Englishmen teaching in Egypt towards the end of King Farouk's splendid and shabby reign live through the academic year of this novel. Apostles of an alien culture, they stand somewhere between the refined English aesthetics of Shelley and T. S. Eliot and the chaotic squalor of the Alexandrian slums, trying to balance the unattainable against the irredeemable, the demands of scholarship against the dictates of reality, while making a modest living for themselves. Their consequent adventures and misadventures are either hilarious or tragic, and sometimes both. And, we suspect, as near the truth as makes no difference.

'This first novel is funny, extremely funny; it is an Alexandrian *Lucky Jim* with much more humanity and much less smart lacquer.' *Daily Telegraph*

THE VIOLINS OF SAINT-JACQUES

Patrick Leigh Fermor

Epilogue by Simon Winchester

The Violins of Saint-Jacques, originally published in 1953, is set in the Caribbean on an island of tropical luxury, European decadence, and romantic passion, and its story captures both the delicacy of high society entanglements and the unforeseen drama of forces beyond human control. Throughout, the writing is as beautiful and haunting as the sound of the violins which rises from the water and conceals the story's mystery.

'Beautiful is the adjective which comes uppermost ... outstanding descriptive powers.' John Betjeman